THE SHOEMAKER'S

MAGICIAN

THE SHOEMAKER'S

MAGICIAN

Cynthia Pelayo

Copyright © 2023 by Cynthia Pelayo
Cover and jacket design by Mimi Bark
Occult Artwork by Todd Keisling | Dullington Design Co.

ISBN 978-1-957957-10-4
eISBN: 978-1-957957-24-1

Library of Congress Control Number: available upon request

First hardcover edition March 2023 by Agora Books
An imprint of Polis Books, LLC
62 Ottowa Road South
Marlboro, NJ 07746
www.PolisBooks.com

To B & C

Words are spells.

"Only those who invest the time and effort to learn the teachings, meditate on the symbols, practice the rituals, and awaken the energies of the tradition are in any position to pass on the tradition to others."
—Israel Regardie, *The Golden Dawn*

At the bidding of Jupiter, Prometheus set about the creation of man and the other animals. Jupiter, seeing that mankind, the only rational creatures, were far outnumbered by the irrational beasts, bade him redress the balance by turning some of the latter into men. Prometheus did as he was bidden, and this is the reason why some people have the forms of men but the souls of beasts.

—"Prometheus and the Making of Man," *Aesop's Fables*

CHAPTER 1

THURSDAY EVENING: SEBASTIAN

Another murder.

A homicide. And what is a homicide but the intended and calculated killing of another person? There are so many ways to describe the methods and madness in which a human being can kill another. Homicide. Murder. Manslaughter. And we can break down the category of manslaughter even further with voluntary, involuntary, and vehicular. How prescriptive. As if any of those terms lessens the fact that someone's life was ultimately ended by someone else.

In all cases, we still have a body, like the one splayed before me. Arms and legs stretched out like Leonardo da Vinci's Vitruvian Man, or maybe like a snow angel. Or, perhaps, given the venue we are standing in, like a star.

I'm standing on the stage looking out at tiered rows of red-cushioned seats that stretch from the base of the stage to the exit doors in the back. Above, are more empty seats.

"What's that level called?" I point my chin in the direction of the multilevel balcony.

Detective Gutierrez is looking down at his dark wool jacket, dusting off snowflakes. He reaches down and then brushes away any snow remaining on his slacks. Like me, he's still wearing his outside gloves. It's his first week on homicide and he already looks the part, nice dark pressed suit, dark jacket, dark dress shoes. We look like a couple of morticians standing next to each other.

"You're going to get snow all over our crime scene," I say.

He shoots me a narrow look. "It's Chicago in January, Ramos. There's no escaping this stuff."

This is true.

Gutierrez takes a step downstage and points with one hand while loosening his black scarf with the other. "The level right above the main floor is the mezzanine, or box level. That's the middle. Then right above that you've got the dress circle or first balcony."

When Gutierrez got promoted to homicide, I knew I'd like working with him. He seems to know a little bit about everything, no matter how obscure, and if he doesn't know it, he'll figure it out.

I glance down at the mess around us, making sure to not step in anything that's going to get bagged or tagged later. I start removing my gloves to trade them in for latex. I'm trying to process what he said. Mezzanine. Dress circle. Balcony. I can feel the muscles in my neck stiffening. "What?"

He clears his throat. "The third floor is called the mezzanine level. The fourth floor is called the dress circle or first balcony. The level right above that is called the upper balcony."

Sometimes Gutierrez overcomplicates things. "Three balconies. Got it."

The auditorium is wider than it is tall, and there's so much red everywhere. Not just the seats, but the heavy, crimson curtains draped around exit doors and archways. The ceiling is a burst of gold, with hand-painted murals, and all along the cream-colored walls are decorative ornamental designs, floral medallions, cornice moldings, arches, and columns. That much I knew because I know Chicago architecture. It's a passion. This town is a passion, and the historic Chicago Theater is a work of art.

Massive bronze crystal chandeliers hang along the space, highlighting the murals looking down on us. They remind me of blue, red, green, and gold stained glass that wraps around some churches. Pictures meant to tell a story.

I turn my back to the empty seats to face the reason we're all here tonight.

I've seen a lot of death, people frozen dead in alleys, kids stuffed in trashcans, torsos in abandoned buildings, gunshot victims still clutching their wounds where they took their last breath on a sidewalk, and more. Always so much more to look back on; a collection of people obliterated. I especially hate it when we have to pull someone out of the Chicago River. Bloated limbs. Skin slippage. Oozing.

It's a horror show.

Now, this. I cannot even begin to piece together the type of person that could and would want to do this. Perhaps the word "piece" here is insensitive. I can already feel Gutierrez's eyes on me, but I don't know what to say. This is an awful end, lying in one's own piss, shit, and blood, where just outside a bright marquee highlighted State Street. Right now, an audience should be speaking in hushed tones, above the crackle of snack bags, as the curtain is pulled back and performers hit the stage, and not me standing here staring down another body.

"Are those Reese's Pieces?" Gutierrez is shoving his winter gloves in his coat pocket now.

I nod. All of that candy makes this seem even more surreal.

We hear the doors leading to the lobby open. My gaze remains fixed on the yellow, orange, and brown discs of candy sprinkled atop and around the butchered corpse still wearing the bottom half of their theater manager uniform.

Boxes of M&Ms, Skittles, Snickers, Sour Patch Kids, and

Twizzlers were emptied on the stage, their contents soaking in the thick red liquid on the floor.

"Dammit," I say through clenched teeth.

"What?" Gutierrez asks.

"Twizzlers are my favorite, and this asshole has gone and ruined them for me."

Puddles of liquid had spilled out from soda cans that were opened and tossed across the stage, and then there's popcorn. It's everywhere like confetti.

When we arrived at the entrance of the theater, Officer Jones and his partner Officer Delgado insisted we dig out plastic coverings from our car and slip them on our shoes. I figured, okay, maybe there's a little blood. Maybe there's shell casings. What I didn't expect was that there'd be corn kernels everywhere. Every step we take there's another crunch beneath our feet as we walk carefully across the hardwood floor.

"What's that smell?" Gutierrez asks.

"Buttered popcorn and urine," I say a little too quickly, but then catch a hint of something else. Wood polish. "Smells like the floor was just polished recently."

"Detective Ramos…" one of the uniforms below the stage says. I can already tell by the dazed look on Officer Jones's face, the sheen above his upper lip, and between the heat from the lights above and the smells of chocolate and popcorn mixed with fecal matter that he's not going to be able to hold it in much longer. I can always tell a rookie by how quickly their color shifts when they see a body for the first time.

"Jones!" his partner calls behind him as she sees him sway. She grabs his shoulder, spins him around, and lets go just as Jones vomits down the front of his jacket, covering his badge.

I tilt my head to the ceiling and let out a heavy sign. This is going to be a long night. I focus on Officer Delgado. "Get your partner back to the station."

Gutierrez has got a stupid grin on his face. "The show's obviously canceled tonight, right?"

"The show never ends for us," I say. "We gotta get those people out of here," I say, referring to the crowd standing outside in the negative wind chill on State Street.

I look around, searching for my new friend. "Officer Delgado!"

"Yeah, detective?" She's by the exit doors now, holding one door open as Officer Jones exits.

I shout. "None of those people outside entered the building, right?"

"Right, detective. They were all lined up waiting for the doors to open."

From behind me, Gutierrez says, "Are you really going to have them put up yellow tape all along the outside of the theater?"

I turn around and eye him. "You got a better idea?"

He lowers his eyes back to the mess we need to deal with, and I know what he's thinking. Downtown. Tourists. Media attention. And especially after last year, the mayor is not going to be happy.

"Delgado!" I call once more. "Are you sure everything inside has been secured as well?"

She hesitates. "It's a huge space. We'll double check we got everything."

"Your team better triple check, because this is gonna be a…" I pause, looking around. Then groan. "This is gonna be a thing." We all know what that means. McCarthy, the mayor, and the media, our three favorite M's, are going to be all over this within the next few minutes.

Officers Delgado and Jones exit the theater as more uniforms enter.

I hear Gutierrez's phone start vibrating, one text after the other. I'm sure it's Commander McCarthy on his way, probably texting while speeding through red lights, trying to hurry up and get here to try to control this situation, but it's already out of control.

Gutierrez reaches for his phone and confirms my suspicion. "McCarthy's on his way," he says, and shoves his phone back in his jacket.

With each text alert's buzz, I can sense McCarthy's blood pressure increasing. Then the noise stops.

"Either he's parking, or he finally had that heart attack he said we've all been trying to give him," I say, patting my coat pockets, wondering why he hadn't messaged me, but my empty pockets give me my answer. "I think I left my phone in the car."

"And your gloves too." Gutierrez hands me a pair of latex gloves.

He's already turning out to be the best work husband I could ask for. My last partner lasted less than a year, but maybe Gutierrez will hang around a little longer, considering all the good work he did in Humboldt Park last year.

"Guess I should message Hector?" Gutierrez says.

I slip on the gloves and say, "I think you need to text Hector and tell him we're not going to be home for a while."

"Already on it," he says, tapping away at his screen.

"Can you let Polly know for me?"

"Letting her know too."

This is the feature program for our evening, and probably for the next few nights. I know by looking at the scene that this isn't the work of a disgruntled employee or an upset theatergoer. This goes far beyond what I've ever seen in my decade on the job. This is dramatic. This is deviant. This is disturbed.

I look up to the last point that the theater manager saw before she died, a collection of bright stage lights that are managed by the control booth above the balcony. This woman bled out front stage center to an empty house. Who wants to die at work, especially like this?

"You said when we parked you got engaged here," Gutierrez says.

"*Phantom of the Opera* during intermission. It was December of 1999. Days before all of that Y2K insanity."

Like a good detective he already had his small notebook out ready to record details. "Sounds like it was special."

"It was. We were kids. Eighteen and nineteen."

"And now this…" Gutierrez kneels, careful to not get in the mess. "I can't even begin to guess what did this."

The white name tag which had likely originally been pinned to the front of her black jacket read Robin Betancourt. It was now pressed into her open right palm.

Gutierrez stood. "A scalpel. There's definitely at least some surgical training."

"Maybe, or lots of YouTube videos," I say, taking in the shape and skill of the Y incision, a deep line beginning at the top of each shoulder and running down the chest to just above Robin's pubic bone. An autopsy cut. The flaps of skin were pulled back to expose the entire chest cavity, for easy display of the lungs, liver, intestines, and more. The killer pulled back the flesh from her chest and then pinned it into her armpits so that all would remain exposed.

"YouTube videos about how to do an autopsy?"

"There's something for everybody on the internet," I say.

"What do you make of that?" Gutierrez motions to what I assume are her jacket and shirt, folded neatly next to the steps leading up to the stage.

"He probably had a gun and orders her to the stage. At first maybe she thinks it's a robbery or a sexual assault, but this is neither. He demands she remove her jacket, then shirt, and then bra. The killer wants all of her exposed."

Gutierrez takes a step back, kicking an M&M that rolls off the stage. "Our killer's creative."

The medical examiner is not going to be happy with this one, especially since part of their job has been started for them. No one expects to receive a body with a post-mortem examination in progress.

"Do you think she was dead first?" Gutierrez asks, and I know he doesn't want the answer. I don't even want to begin to think of the terror Robin lived through in her final moments, experiencing her chest cavity being hacked away and pinned back onto herself.

The sprays of blood, like red glitter, stretching far across the floor suggest her heart was still beating furiously as she was being ripped open. The victim was conscious as her flesh was opened like a curtain. The pain must have been excruciating, and I can only hope that shock, that biological wave of confusion, punctuated by a rapid heartbeat, cold sweat, and dizziness carried her away before she died from the deep gash that nearly decapitated her.

"What do you think did that?" I say of the wound in her neck. I scan the stage and then add, "Never mind. Looks like they used the popcorn scoop." The device is covered in blood and hair, and is resting inside an empty tub of popcorn near her foot.

"How?" Gutierrez's mouth falls wide open.

The stainless-steel scoop is sharp enough, especially if directing the right amount of pressure against someone's flesh. Anything with a dull blade can decapitate you, if someone is determined enough to try.

"Anything is possible if you're committed."

"What do you think about that?" Gutierrez motions to the smears around the victim. A circle within a circle, symbols or letters all painted with what looks like the victim's blood. It looks like the killer used their fingers to draw the design.

"I think we're not going to be sleeping for a while."

From somewhere behind us in the seats I hear a cough. I wasn't expecting a reunion.

"Officer Jones, we've got enough vomit over here," I say, not even turning around. I'm too focused on trying to make out the characters around our victim. "I told you to get back to the station."

It's Officer Delgado. She's holding a cellphone. "Your phone, Detective Ramos. You dropped it in the lobby."

"Just leave it there," I say, pointing to one of the front seats. "I'll grab it when I'm done here."

She pauses for a moment before setting it down.

"What now?" I throw my hands up. I can feel a migraine blooming above my left eye.

She presses her lips together tightly and then says. "Do you think...? I mean..."

"Get it out, officer!"

Officer Delgado stands rigid. "Do you think *she* may know anything about this?"

"Oh hell." I feel my eyes rolling to the back of my head. I did not want to talk about her today or any day. "She is not here, and if you mention her again you can join her."

"Sorry, detective," Officer Delgado says, and rushes to the exit.

Gutierrez is standing beside me now. He raises his arm and points to what each of us are avoiding. The laminated black and white poster pinned to the dead woman's groin. "What do you think that means?"

"I don't know," I say, already dreading asking the only person I know who's an expert in this area.

"It looks like a horror movie poster."

"The Chicago Theater is only a performing arts theater. They don't show movies here, right?"

Gutierrez wrinkles his brow. "It used to show movies, a long time ago."

Not a single spot of blood appears on the poster's surface. The killer took great care here, highlighting what needed to be known and shown. They want us to know that this poster is special, that this poster is a clue.

This movie poster is the star of the show, and the body on display and everything to come is just a side character.

CHAPTER 2

FRIDAY EARLY MORNING: PALOMA

I'm sitting up in bed and jotting down notes on my tablet. It's dark and quiet except for the soft blue glow of the device and the tapping of my digital pen against the glass.

I don't mind sitting in the darkness. Most people need a light on at night to feel safe. For me, it's only ever felt safe in the dark. I should be asleep, but Bass is still not home, and as I started drifting away to sleep, I was pulled back to the memory of that old apartment and that horrible life.

Why can't I stop thinking about them?

My brother Noel once told me that death is just one of the many guarantees along this line that is life. We are born, and there is pleasure and suffering dotted along the linear path that ends only one way for us, for me, for everyone. The end. There is no pause. We all will die. There is no rewinding the cassette in the VCR.

We only play forward.

He said that when we were teenagers, desperate to leave that cramped and hot apartment where we were constantly beaten by parents who could not love us the way we begged and longed to be loved.

Now Noel rarely returns my calls.

It's funny how you can go through so much with a person,

someone who's a major part of your life for a time, but then one day something happens, and that intense bond is forever severed.

My messages to him go unread for days or weeks. I know he's busy, but what I know most of all is that he just wants to forget. I do too.

The wind picks up outside, whooshing and whistling competing against the blare of an ambulance that passes by slowly through accumulating snow. Our first snowstorm of the season.

I turn to my notes and hate that I'm planning on talking soon about something I love so much. When we talk about what we adore, that's when we open ourselves up to hurt, because we expose our cracks to everyone.

I know what most people will say, that they're dusty, dated tropes and monsters. How can something so old be relevant? But the newness of a thing does not dictate its value. These fictional creatures who emerged from their dark, dank lairs birthed from minds that lived long ago are the very reason I'm alive today.

The heater kicks on again, after turning off just a few moments ago. This house never seems to get warm enough. It always feels like the outside is begging to come in. One day I wonder if it will just enter unannounced.

We wanted this classic frame Chicago house because of its history, and because Bass believes there's something special about original Chicago architecture, and I agree. This is in part why we love this city, because one can always sense the past radiating in the present.

A shiver creeps up my neck. I remember being this cold in our old apartment as a kid. Noel would walk into my room, reach for a VHS tape, and we'd throw all of the blankets on the floor, sit down atop of them, and turn to the screen. On many nights like that he'd find me looking at his swollen cheek or I'd find him staring at my purple eyes, and he'd just say:

"Let's put on a horror movie and forget."

And that's all we could do.

We'd lean on one another, brother and sister with blankets wrapped around our shoulders, lost in the flickering images sweeping across a screen, all the while hoping the impressions of handprints across our faces or pierced flesh from our mother's nails dug into our forearms wouldn't be seen at school in the morning. And even if they were seen at school by an adult, no one would say anything. No one cared. No one ever cared.

So that's how our youth passed, in front of the television in a darkened room, fearful for when our mother would strike again. Like Hansel and Gretel, we held on to one another and we protected each other from the witch, but after we defeated her, Hansel left.

I look at the time and know I should probably get up and get some work done in my office instead of sitting here allowing my thoughts to race. I reach for a glass of water on the nightstand and take a long gulp. My mind is already spinning with all of the work I have before me, including the email I have been putting off sending for weeks.

What is the saying? Never meet your heroes or you might be disappointed. Or is it just never meet your heroes? That was my fear, that in meeting my hero, not just another fellow horror host, but *the* horror host, my reality would somehow fracture. That's how high of a pedestal I put him.

How could anyone meet those expectations for me? Even if I emailed him now requesting an interview, I doubt he'd agree. Grand no longer granted interviews. His public appearances had been relegated to the stuff of myth and legend, going viral on social media.

Grand was spotted at Calumet Fisheries ordering smoked trout to go.

I saw Grand today at Graceland Cemetery. He was standing

15

face-to-face with Eternal Silence.

Grand was seen driving down Lake Shore Drive in his black 1968 Cadillac Miller-Meteor.

In each and every sighting he was pictured in his stage makeup. What made Grand that much more mysterious is that no picture existed without him in his signature ghoul face. He was seen outside the same way he was seen on his program every Saturday night, with his face painted a dead gray, his cheekbones and jaw contoured in varying degrees of black, and harsh dark lines drawn around his eyes and nose.

Every city has their local celebrities—news reporters, baseball, basketball, and football players, local actors, and even the charismatic car salesman with the annoying commercial and accompanying jingle that gets embedded into your brain, the dreaded earworm.

Chicago has Grand.

My phone rattles on the nightstand. I reach for it and open the text message.

Gutierrez: *It's G. Bass can't find his phone. We're safe but going to be working late.*

Working late? It was already past three in the morning. For years it had gone like this, me hoping that Bass's schedule would fall into some type of routine, but there was no normality when his entire job meant unraveling why people had been murdered.

I set my tablet aside and sit up in bed.

I respond.

I'm awake. What happened?

He responds:

A call downtown.

Downtown meant high profile. Downtown meant more pressure. Downtown meant Bass would not be home for a very long time.

I grab my phone and turn on its flashlight and slip out of bed. It was useless to pretend like I was going to get any sleep tonight. In the hallway, I stop at the first door to my left. I take a deep breath, close my eyes, and place my hand against the door, listening, as if feeling for a heartbeat.

I open the door a crack and feel the ice-cold wind circling his room. I turn off the phone's light and use the illumination of his nightlight, a glowing turtle that projects green stars onto his ceiling. I push back the blue curtains and lower the window which had been raised an inch. The window closes with a thud, and I turn the latch, locking it.

"Mom?" his voice squeaks

"I'm sorry I woke you," I whisper. "It's freezing in here." I look out the glass, into the ash-gray light, and know there is no way he could have opened this heavy window on his own. The latch is out of his reach for my little boy's height. "You didn't open the window, right, baby?"

"No," he says as he pulls the covers up to his chin. His long brown hair rests against his pillow and his eyes are wide open now. In this light he still looks like a chubby-faced toddler, even though he is eight.

"I had a dream," he says with excitement.

I gasp. "You did?"

He closes his eyes tight. "I'm going to find it again."

"And you will."

He nods his head against his pillow. He isn't like the rest of the kids in his class at school. Even though he is eight, he seems younger. Bela still sets cookies out for Santa Claus on Christmas

Eve, and he puts on shows in his puppet theater, and believes that magic is as real as the air we breathe.

My phone buzzes in my hand.

"Is that Dad?" Bela moves to sit up, but I motion for him to stay down, and sit at the edge of his bed, beside him.

Bass's message reads:

Found my phone. I'll be here a while. McCarthy is on his way.

I groan.

"Mom, I have to tell you…" Bela props himself up on his elbow. "In my dream, there was a dove, a fish, a wolf, and a black bird."

I run my fingers through his hair. "That sounds like a nice group of friends, but you need to go back to sleep."

"No," he yawns. "Not all of them are friends."

"Bela, you have school in a few hours."

He lies back down. "Is Dad home?"

With McCarthy on his way I know Bass wouldn't be home for a long time. "Not yet. Did you want me to send him a message?"

He smiles. "Goodnight, Dad. I love you very much."

"That is a very nice message," I say as I tap my fingers against the screen. I did not relay Bela's message, but instead asked:

Did you leave Bela's window open?

I set my phone down on my lap and adjust the comforter around his shoulders. "You and me…"

"Forever," he finishes.

"Forever." I kiss his forehead.

"Can you sing me songs?" he asks, and, of course, I would never deny him a compilation of his favorites. He still prefers the simplicity and sweetness of classic children's songs mixed with lullabies. I start with "Twinkle, Twinkle Little Star," and then move into a rotation of others he enjoys. "Row, Row, Row Your Boat," "Jack and Jill," and "Mary Had a Little Lamb."

His breathing begins to slow, but I can tell he is not yet fully asleep. I take a deep breath, exhale, and then repeat all of the songs once more, my focus on Bass, wondering what is going on.

When Bela's chest slowly begins to rise and fall, signaling he is drifting away to that dream he wanted to catch, I finish with his favorite lullaby, "Little Boy Blue":

Little Boy Blue, come blow your horn,
The sheep's in the meadow, the cow's in the corn.
Where is that boy who looks after the sheep?
He's under a haystack, fast asleep.
Will you wake him? Oh no, not I.
For if I do, he'll surely cry.

With Bela fast asleep, I close the door behind me and enter my office across the hall. I turn on the light and take a seat at my cluttered desk. There are too many half-started notepads and notebooks, Post-It notes with names, dates, and times, and too many Sharpie pens, because those are the best to write with. I've never been an overly organized social media influencer that shows off their perfectly curated space. I learned to embrace creative chaos.

I stare at my blank computer screen, not knowing what to do next. I can't sleep. I can't check in with Bass, as McCarthy is likely there and in a rage. I should work on my show notes, but what I really need to do is send that email. Procrastination sometimes is our method of avoiding rejection in real time.

I look over to the VCR stacked on top of my bookshelf, the same one that had brought Noel and I peace. It looks down on me like some sort of guardian angel. Some people have statues of saints, crystals or herbs that fill their home for protection. I have this VCR and a collection of video cassettes and DVDs of old horror movies that watch over me.

I tap a key and the computer screen bursts to life. I'm dreading the email I need to send. Even if I email him now requesting an interview, I cannot imagine he would agree. He was the elusive midnight horror host who showcased old films in between film history and gruesome skits that were a nod to Le Théâtre du Grand-Guignol.

No matter my delay in reaching out, I knew I had to talk to him. Maybe he would think I was silly for bringing up an obscure film legend. It didn't matter. I just needed to know if it was true.

My phone vibrates on the desk. I reach for it quickly, so the rattling doesn't wake Bela.

Bass responded to my question:

No, I didn't leave his window open. Maybe he opened it?

There was no way Bela could open that old, heavy window that sticks. It must have been Bass. Maybe he'd forgotten? But why open the window leading up to a snowstorm? Before I can ask him again, he texts:

Bass: *This looks bad. Can you take Bela to school in the morning?*
Polly: *What happened exactly?*
Bass: *Homicide at Chicago Theater.*
Polly: *A homicide in the actual theater?*

Bass: *Will explain when I can get home. Question though.*
Do you know anything about Georges Méliès?

I want to laugh, but I don't. If I ever needed a sign to contact Grand, here it is, blazing and bright, practically shouting at me.

Of course, I know who Georges Méliès was. I studied film history. I was fascinated by the son of a shoemaker, turned stage magician, turned the father of genre film who created hundreds of movies in his lifetime, many of which have never been seen since they were first made.

Polly: *Yes, why?*

Bass: *Evidence.*

Polly: *Evidence?*

Bass: *I'll show you when I get home.*

Murders downtown are rare. Sometimes domestic disputes within the high-rises that dotted the lakefront exploded into violence. Often there were traffic incidents, a cracked bumper, or a car that came a little too close to a bicyclist on the Mag Mile, and sometimes those incidents spiraled into physical confrontations involving fists, blood, or broken bones. When anger was added to any situation, unpredictability could usher in death.

What stood out from this were two things, a murder at the historic Chicago Theater and a piece of crime scene evidence connected to one of the fathers of film.

I turn back to my computer screen. I need to focus, and there is nothing I can do about Bass, or Georges Méliès, at least not yet.

I started graduate studies in film because I loved school and movies. I wanted to learn everything I could about film and movie making. Then Bela came, and a few years later his diagnosis. I feared being away from him during the day, but didn't want to lose my sense of self, and so I started my channel, first as a means of having a space to create what I love, and now as a way

21

to earn a stable income.

All that remains in the way of completing that Master of Fine Arts in Cinema and Television Art is that interview. The entire project hinges on Grand agreeing to sit down and talk to me. And, yes, while I finally want to complete this degree, that's not really why I want to talk to Grand. I tell myself again, if anyone knows if the rumors are true, it would be him. I suppose in a way I want the rumor to be true, because if it was, that would give me comfort that this life, this reality, was much more complex than I thought.

If he doesn't answer or agree to be interviewed, then I would need to begin a new thesis, but that really would not be the tragedy. The tragedy would be in the not knowing, the not being able to have the simple excuse to ask Grand that single question, is *that* movie real?

I look to the folder on my desktop, the name taunting me, reminding me that there is much more to know and learn. I know that horror isn't just a genre to be cast away on the back shelves or spoken of in hushed tones when asking for a ticket at the local movie theater.

The horror genre tells us that our existence is complex, and that ghosts trapped behind movie screens, creatures banished to the woods, and that monsters locked away in castle towers are always waiting to be summoned.

I click on compose and begin typing the email I hope will lead me to the answer I so desperately need:

Dear Grand Vespertilio,
My name is Paloma Ramos…

CHAPTER 3

FRIDAY EARLY MORNING: GRAND

It's well past four in the morning and I am sitting in my brown leather chair. The lights are dim. The television on the wall is on, and creeping music begins to play. It is "Music for Strings, Percussion and Celesta" by Béla Bartók. A song wrapped in dread.

The strings play, and we enter into a slow fugue, a short melody overtaken by a wave. The interweaving parts are meant to tug on one's nerves. It is the kind of music that makes most people look around and over their shoulders, searching for movement in the dark corners of the room, when no one else is there. The music spikes, then falls, alerting to something, or someone, approaching.

On the screen, the camera rises to a short hallway. These images are black and white. This program was filmed in 1954.

The floor is obscured by a thick, swirling mist. Strips of gauzy fabric dangle from the ceiling. There appears to be a staircase to the left, but it's too difficult to tell given the corridor is bathed in shadow.

Cobwebs glisten beneath one of the lone lights in the narrow hallway. Two different violas play now, and then a twisting begins with the strings muted. The music is tension. The camera remains fixed. The mist rises and falls, and then, from the far end of the hallway, a figure appears.

First, we see white arms at their side. A silver décolleté in what appears to be a snug black V-neck dress, and then a face appears in the light. As quickly as the face comes into view it is cast completely in shadow. A timpani strikes, followed by the thunder crash of cymbals. We move into a climax, shocked by a bass drum. The strings pierce through the sounds again. The shape quickens, and then she appears in all her perfection. An icon. A legend. The mother of all horror hosts, for she birthed the format of what it is to present a terrifying film to audiences at home.

The theme music continues to play. It's a perfectly diabolical composition for a perfectly diabolical woman gracing my television screen.

Ribbons of black fabric extend from either sleeve at her elbow. She looks like a vampire who has emerged from her day of slumber. Her dress is cinched at a barely there waist, dipping into hips that support a force that will never be wiped from memory.

This creeping and loathsome space is her runway, and we who came after her are all so lucky to call her the first.

Now she is standing in front of and demanding the camera's attention. Her neck is straight, a swan. Her long black hair rests behind her shoulders, but her short bangs are razor sharp, an exclamation.

She is in full view now, filling up the screen from her waist up. She stops, her right shoulder goes back some, and she opens her mouth and her thick black eyebrows arch further up her forehead. The camera zooms in on her face as she screeches, a piercing sound that fills me with joy each time I hear it. She closes her eyes in a sort of Gothic ecstasy. Her right hand comes up to her shoulder and she smiles. She purrs.

"Oh, screaming relaxes me so." Her body exudes pleasure. What is a scream, but a release?

"She was beautiful," I say to myself in my empty room that

I've filled with antiques and artifacts I've collected throughout the years, so that I will never forget the pain that is passing time.

Just outside my door I hear Wren call: "Grand…"

I reach for the remote control and raise the volume. I do not want to be disturbed, but I know she'll be here in a moment to check in on me. That is her duty, after all. I don't want to respond to her because my attention is on the woman on my television, the dead woman who is more important to me than anyone I've ever encountered in this accursed lifetime.

There's an ache in the center of my chest, a ball of longing and despair, of knowing what is on the screen is not flesh, just a replication, a simulacrum.

A title card appears for just a flash in that ghoulish white, smokey text: *VAMPIRA.*

I hear the door squeak open, but I don't turn around.

"Grand, we need to talk…" She stops right at my shoulder. She's in her black silk pajama pants and silk buttoned shirt. She's been awake for some time. I heard her stirring in the kitchen, making coffee, always making and drinking coffee, fighting to stay awake so that she can be alert if I need her. Of course, I know what she wants to discuss. I am just not prepared to speak of it this evening.

"Oh," she says. "You're watching her again." There's a re-signed jealously in Wren's tone.

It shouldn't be said, but there's no competing with the dead.

Wren takes a seat beside me, and we both watch the scene unfold. A bubbling cocktail glass sits on a headstone etched with *Rest In Peace.* Long black fingernails enter into view. Vampira is sitting on a dark-cushioned velvet settee. Her glossy black hair is parted down the middle of her head and flows down her shoulders in sweeping waves. She raises the glass that's releasing wispy tendrils of smoke along her hand.

Vampira says, "What I need is a vampire cocktail to settle

my nerves. It will not only settle them, it will petrify them." She gives the camera a piercing look. The plumes float down around her hands. She moans, then takes a sip.

"A vampire cocktail. You like it? It hates you. I've had several letters asking whether olives or cherries should be used in making my cocktail. Well, actually, neither is necessary since they don't disintegrate upon being put into the cocktail. However, if you want to use some garnish, you can drop in an eyeball."

I laugh. "Her delivery was always perfect."

Vampira sets down her glass. She stands and lifts a cigarette to a burning black candle and takes in a drag. "Our little fairy tale tonight is called *Vampyr*. It's about a traveler who comes across a woman who has been bitten by a vampire, and he must break this curse. It's based on *In a Glass Darkly*, a short story collection from 1872 written by Sheridan Le Fanu. The collection contains five short stories, "Green Tea," "The Familiar," "Mr. Justice Hardbottle," "The Room in the Dragon Volant," and an obscure tale that perhaps you may have never heard about, "Carmilla.""

She takes another puff of her cigarette and says, "Here, let me darken the room. And we shall commence." She leans over the candle and blows out the flame.

"No one has ever been able to come close to her," I say. "I wanted to have her always."

"You're quoting movies again," Wren says, sounding annoyed.

"That I am," I admit.

"We need to talk," she says again. "It's about an email…"

"We can talk later," I say, because I just want to watch whatever short clips I have of Vampira and her program and think of all that will unfold at another time. It's all upon us. I focus on the screen. It is a crime no full episodes exist. So much of film and television history is lost because its caretakers failed to realize the importance of preserving it. I should have made a bigger push to preserve them, to preserve her. I feel like I'm always trying to wake from this feeling of being eaten alive. No matter what snippets I have of her, I'll forever be chasing a feeling I cannot relive. I thought my previous punishment was torture, but this living without the one you love is hell.

"The past does not exist."

Wren's words cut. I know she said this to hurt me, but I did not feel things as she felt.

She lowers her head, already realizing her intent was to cause me pain. "I'm sorry…"

"There can be no apologies for the natural progression of life, and for all which I cannot control."

Wren had dedicated her life completely to me, and for that I was sorry. She sacrificed her own existence to serve mine. She is the only one who can see my face in its natural state. No one has looked at me without my mask in years. Wren often behaved as if this was a privilege, or an honor of sorts. I had begged her to leave me, to live, but she refused, dedicating her life to me, or to an idea. no matter how miserable it is.

"Maila," she uttered.

Maila Elizabeth Nurmi who played the legendary role of Vampira in 1959.

"She was the very core and meaning of my life." If even for a short time. I raise the remote, but she presses.

"This is important…"

I lift my left hand to my left temple. My head aches.

"You are in a mood this evening, aren't you?" she says, and walks over to the window. Outside I can hear the chime of a bus coming to a stop. A car passes. The whine of a snowplow making its way down a side street. City noises before the city fully awakens.

"I can still sense death in the air."

Now it's Wren who quotes a film.

This one is easy. *"The Black Cat.* Nineteen thirty-four."

Wren points to the poster on my wall. The face of each star-ring actor in one of the corners, Boris Karloff, Bela Lugosi, Jacqueline Wells, and David Manners. The actors are all highlighted in reds and black. The profile of a black cat hunched between the two Hollywood stars of horror, Karloff and Lugosi. Those names forever imprinted on our genre.

"It was the first film in which Lugosi and Karloff appeared together. It upset audiences. Many went into it thinking it was an adaptation, or at least inspired by Edgar Allan Poe's short story of the same name. The movie poster even noted it," I pointed, "Edgar Allan Poe's "The Black Cat.""

"But the creators mislead audiences," Wren said. "The film had nothing to do with Poe, except, of course, the black cat that crept around the modern-looking home. Well, that and Karloff's character was named Hjalmar Poelzig. I'm sure they wanted audiences to think of Poe, but Poelzig here is really inspired by real life occultist Aleister Crowley."

And that is why we are here, in this city. The occult.

This once muddy little outpost turned bustling international city vibrated, or maybe was magnetized with an electricity so few would ever realize possible. This land lured Jean Baptiste Point du Sable from the Caribbean. Point du Sable was of African descent and was the first non-indigenous settler of what became Chicago. It doesn't escape me, the magick and power that exists in the Caribbean, and I wonder if Point du Sable brought some of that here. The city then became home to the legendary World Columbian Exposition of 1893, that spotlighted cultural, scientific, and technological marvels, including showcasing moving pictures. Later in 1893, the city hosted the Parliament of World Religions.

These two events were both deeply cultural, but also held

manifestations of the occult. The Theosophical Society then made their headquarters in Chicago. Part of what Theosophy teaches is that there's a group of people across the world called Masters, and these Masters hold great wisdom and supernatural powers. Years and years later, Anton LaVey was born here and he would go on to found The Church of Satan. Chicago both lured and created people who were seeking something more. This city, this great city, hasn't only attracted ghosts and luminary phantoms, but the ideas of great magickal systems: Theosophy, Thelema, Hermeticism, and Hoodoo.

I clasp my hands together. "You have learned a lot in such a short time."

Wren laughs. "It's been three decades."

Three decades is not even a blink in the universe. It's utterly insignificant.

Wren continues. "At the time, some people thought *The Black Cat* foolish, but that didn't matter. It was Universal's most successful film of the year. Still, it's quite different than other Universal horror offerings. This one hints at necrophilia, a satanic human sacrifice, and a scene where one of the characters is flayed. It's bizarre, and unlike the romantic sweeping horrors we often attach to this studio. This film is a nightmare."

I take a deep breath and exhale. A love for the dead. Demon worship. It all does sounds grim and familiar. "Did you know they appeared together in eight films in total?"

Wren grins, amused. "Yes, I've paid attention around here."

"Have you?" I smile, and it feels nice to do so without the layers of makeup, one of the many reasons I no longer want to be seen in public. The makeup had become necessary, and my greatest fear is that the public would soon begin to suspect. I needed to end this all on my own. "What are the names of the other films Karloff and Lugosi appeared in together? You've already named one."

Wren spent most of her days here, preparing, researching, studying. She loved movies because that's what I loved, and so my passions became hers, not because I asked her, but because that is what she chose to do. She had become an expert on everything there was to know about horror, Grand Guignol, vaudeville, horror cinema, and, of course, magick and the occult.

"The first was *The Black Cat*. *The Raven* followed in 1935. *Son of Frankenstein* in 1939, *Black Friday* in 1940, and *The Body Snatcher* in 1945. *Murders in the Rue Morgue* in 1932, and *The Invisible Ray* in 1936.

I raise a finger in the air. "You're missing one."

"Oh, well, *You'll Find Out*, from 1940, but that was a comedy."

"Very impressive, Wren. Alright," I accept my defeat. "Tell me about this email," I say, even though I already know what it says.

Wren clasps her hands in front of her, standing straight. "I know you no longer grant interviews, but a woman would like to interview you. I think you may want to consider this." She produces her cellphone from her pants pocket and hands it to me. She takes a seat, and I can feel her studying my face as I look down at the picture of a woman seated on a chair. Her hair is pulled back. She's in a dark sweatshirt, and she's smiling, a beaming bright smile.

"Her name is Paloma Ramos."

I stand from my chair and walk to the window. The snow fall has slowed. Lazy flakes cascade from the sky, settling and glimmering on sidewalks and front lawns.

There's a gleam in her eye. "She says it's for a project for her school."

"That's certainly one way to lie about what it is she really wants to know." I peer down at the image in my hand. "I do know already," I say.

"Oh." Her eyes widen. "Of course you do. My apologies. And so, you know…"

"She has a husband and a small child," I say.

"Then you of course know she has her own program on the internet. She's a horror host, like…Maila."

These things take time, but they cycle through. When we lose something that we loved so much, it's the greatest pain we can encounter. Yet the universe grants us these small and rare opportunities to align ourselves with those things once again. And when they arrive, we must recognize it as something special, as something magickal, and that is what she is.

Wren is still talking, and I am listening to all of the things I already know.

"She likes classic horror movies, but she enjoys them all really." Her voice drifts away, and then she stands. "Let me know how you would like me to respond."

"Well, we both know," I say, knowing this will be my undoing. I hold the phone out to Wren and turn my gaze back to the window. "Tell her I will grant her, and of course Bela, whatever they need."

Wren raises an eyebrow. "You know the boy's name?"

I smile. "I know everything, my beautiful Wren."

She nods. "Of course, Grand."

At the door, Wren pauses. "She does look like *her*, doesn't she?"

The universe often speaks to us in whispers, and I can hear it so clearly now. My time with Maila is forever over, but at least I can admire her doppelgänger, and provide her with the assistance she will desperately need to survive.

"She looks like an exact copy."

CHAPTER 4

FRIDAY EARLY MORNING, BREAKFAST: PALOMA

I'll never understand how a parent can hit their child. I'll never really understand how anyone can hurt any child. We are supposed to protect our children, even if it means coming into harm's way ourselves.

I'm watching Bela play his game. He's wearing a yellow hoodie and his brown hair is pulled back in a ponytail. His face is down, focused on the screen before him, and the color blocks and shapes of the virtual world he has created and continues to refine. One waffle, chopped into little pieces, with only a teaspoon of maple syrup drizzled on top, and a cup of water in a blue plastic cup with a straw sits untouched in front of him.

Romero, our little black Shih Tzu-poodle mix is seated beneath the table, hoping Bela sneaks him a bit of his food. It's the same breakfast he has had each morning for at least two years. Routine. He needs the security of routine.

I'm drinking yerba mate with steamed oat milk and a little bit of honey as I work on my show notes for what I will be recording while Bela is at school.

He doesn't notice that I'm staring, as he's absorbed in his Puzzleworld game. I look out the back window to the snowy yard and see the bare magnolia tree outlined in white, snow resting along its branches. After our first snowfall of the season the city always seems so alien. It was our city, but not, in a way. The energy shifted with the temperature drop and the layers of white resting on top of garages and cars, and covering streets and lawns made the exterior of our home almost unrecognizable. Images on the news of the lakefront this morning showed massive chunks of ice, the size of boulders, bobbing in the water. Ribbons of ice and frost accumulated along the shore. Our once crisp blue sky was exchanged for the color of a defective cloudy pearl, and would remain that way until May.

Bela glances up at me for a moment and smiles. "Love you," he says, and returns to his world.

"I love you too, forever."

I'm grateful the universe gifted me someone so sweet, and what I promised myself was no matter what, I'd always make sure Bela had a reason to smile. My memories of my own childhood are punctuated with the sensation of cheeks stained with tears, of sorrow and my chest aching from my cries. Then there was my mother, always my mother, towering over me in a frenzy as she shouted at me, lashed out at me, struck me, about anything really. There is no explaining her abuse.

It's because of her I find myself still sitting up at night in bed unable to sleep, tense and fearful that at any moment she will come barging into my room to demand why I didn't dry the dishes properly, who was that boy I was talking to outside of school, why was I on the phone, why was I so obsessed with horror movies. Always an attack on my horror movies, but they were all I had, and she would never take them away from me.

My room was always bare, because every time I fell in love with something, a comfortable black hoodie, a kind letter Bass had written me, she would rip it up and throw it away. Throwing away the things I loved was another layer to her abuse. When she threatened to throw away my television set and VCR in one of her moods, I raced to the kitchen and drew a knife. I told her I'd rather see her dead than lose the only thing that gave me comfort in that cursed apartment.

Bela reaches over to his waffle with his hand, his eyes fixed on his screen, and I remind him to use his fork. He doesn't respond, but complies, taking his fork in his hand and stabbing a small piece of the waffle.

Bela glances at me quickly. Eye contact is easier for him now, but learning to lock eyes with me, with anyone, really, at first was a struggle, as was so much else. He tilts his head. "Love you," then, again, he slips into his world. He will repeat this dozens of times throughout the day, sometimes minutes apart.

I don't mind. I am grateful that the repetitive phrase he latched on to was *love you*. I could hear it a million times a day and never tire.

"Forever," I add once again, but he doesn't acknowledge this.

And that was Bela, not there, but always there, in a sense. Just like Noel.

It was my brother Noel who tried to shield me from my mother as best he could. We both counted down the days until we could leave and be rid of their abuse. Noel's free time was spent studying or working downstairs from our apartment for Bruce. When I was old enough, I started working for Bruce too, vacuuming floors, cleaning windows, covered in a haze of Windex. Inside, there was the constant wiping down of high-touch areas, the counter, the seats, the seat rests, and then there was endless sweeping. The smell of popcorn, the texture of it between my fingers, and the sensation and crunch it makes as I step down always seemed to be there.

When I turned fifteen, Bruce finally allowed me to work the cash register. This made me feel like I was peeking into people's personal lives, for even just a few moments. I listened in on thousands of first dates as they exchanged which candy they liked and didn't, interacted with those who attended the movies alone who didn't want any small talk, just their nachos and as little human interaction as possible. I also took in the pleas of mothers who begged their children to behave. Somehow within all of that frenzy of the movie theater, the book found me.

I take a sip of my tea and then say, "Don't forget, we're going to see Bruce today."

Bela nods, stabbing the last piece of his waffle and putting it in his mouth and chewing. I was dreading telling him that Bruce was selling the movie theater and moving. Change upsets Bela, the instability and not knowing what will happen next. There would be no more frequent dinners of popcorn, pretzels, and hotdogs as we watched monster movies on our own private screen with Bruce, a family friend who was more than a family friend. Bruce was like a father to me, and the only real grandfather Bela has ever known.

It was also Bruce who bought Noel and me that VCR long ago. It was then Noel who went down to the video store and convinced the owner to give him a rental card since he wasn't eighteen yet. Everyone in the neighborhood knew our parents. Some felt bad for us. Others ignored it. No one wants to get involved in anyone else's problems, especially when they're trying to figure out their own.

So, people just pretended like they didn't see when my mom would snatch me by my hair and drag me inside. They pretended not to hear Noel's pleas for her to stop hitting him when she found him at the end of the block playing softball when he had not asked for permission. They all turned away from the slaps, the insults, the bruises. No one cared that she hurt us.

My mother never wanted us outside. She said it was because she was scared of the gangs, or she was scared that one of the neighborhood boys would get me pregnant, or that someone would kidnap me, rape me, and dismember my body in a bathtub. She told me if that happened, the hacked-up pieces of me would be wrapped in plastic, and my killer would slowly drive down alleyways, discarding me piece by piece in dumpsters.

Our mother not only tormented us with beatings and public humiliations, but also with the horrifying things that casually happened out in the world each day. She warned us that awful things would happen to us if we didn't obey her. I always hoped the opposite would happen.

Growing up, between movie screenings downstairs at work, and a VCR in my room, I consumed monsters all day long. At first, it was a means to block out my mother, and to dissolve away into a new reality. In the end, it was in that world of black and white and silver, of deep Hammer movie reds and the striking synth chords of 1980s slashers that I realized I was loved more by monsters than I ever was by my mother.

Bela drops his tablet on the table and shouts, his small fists shooting up to his temples. His eyes shut tight.

"Buddy." I am at his side.

Romero is pawing at Bela's leg.

"He's fine, Romero," I say, also trying to comfort our little dog who is so attuned to Bela.

His breath is sharp. "I messed up!"

"Bela." I gently pull his hands away from his head. He's rocking back and forth in his chair now. "It's fine. I'm sure it will be fine."

"No! I have to make it perfect, or it will not have the right meaning. It's not good!"

My phone alarm blares, indicating it is time to leave for school. I feel Bela's hands loosening under my hold. I look over to his tablet, but it is face down on the table.

"Look." I kneel and look him in his face. His large brown

eyes are now open, but looking down at the table, and like the day he was born, I'm mesmerized by his full, sweeping lashes. "Everything you do is good. YOU are good. You can keep working in the car, okay?"

He takes a deep breath and exhales through his nose. Bela's meltdowns sometimes are easy to manage, and other times it is like he is a ball of fire tearing through the house, and all I can do is hold him and catch fire with him. We cry as he flails, kicks, and screams, until finally, somehow, his breathing slows and he can speak calmly once again.

When he was four, his distress could last hours, screaming, crying, biting. One time, his occupational therapist had to teach me how to press my pointer finger and thumb against the sides of his jaw to release his bite from my forearm. Because when Bela would dig his teeth into my arms when he was upset, there was no stopping the hold, even as he broke through skin and drew blood.

"It's time to get going. Go wash your hands," I say, and thankfully, he goes to the bathroom without protesting. I take one more look through my notes, looking forward to spending my afternoon with Boris Karloff and Bela Lugosi.

When people think of Universal Monsters, they often think of *Frankenstein* and *Dracula*, two icons of literature transferred to the screen in legendary roles played by Karloff and Lugosi.

Horror movies are sometimes defined by their iconic roles and distinguished subgenres. People enjoy slashers, *Black Christmas*, *Halloween*, *Friday the 13th*, and *A Nightmare on Elm Street*, which follow the unstoppable predators lasering in on one intention—to kill the babysitter, camp counselors having sex in a cabin, or that victim from years ago that got away.

People even love Chucky, a possessed doll who is both crude and cruel. How many *Child's Play* movies are there again? Seven? Eight? Nine? Practically the same number of films starring unstoppable slasher Michael Meyers, also known as The Shape, because he is void of all emotion and humanity. And do we want our killers always to be void of emotion? Freddy Krueger, Ghost Face, and Jigsaw have some endearing qualities, able to mimic markers of humanity, but they can just as swiftly spin into monstrosity, reminding us that even if someone is funny for a moment, or nice, they still have capacity to harm us.

People love an unsympathetic killer, and we've been seeing this coldness performed by horror movie villains since the beginning of cinema. Bela Lugosi played calculated Count Dracula while Boris Karloff played The Monster who struggles with reconciling his very own existence. An existential nightmare. Two feared monsters existing via the supernatural, uncaring, or unaware, of the destruction they cause.

Bass likes to tell his coworkers I've seen every single horror movie ever made. An impossible task really. Even though it's not true that I have seen every horror movie ever made, it does make for a nice promotional claim for my channel. Tons of big budget horror movies are released each year, followed by independent films, and ones made by content creators. There is no way for me to keep up with all of them, but I do try to watch a new horror movie each day. If there's time, I'll rewatch an old favorite, and it was in rewatching my old favorites that I realized there's so much more to share with my audience than recent releases, or films from even the past few decades.

My audience enjoyed my recent series on 1980s slashers. I had over sixty thousand new subscribers because of those videos alone. The year before that I focused on science fiction horror: *Alien*, *The Thing*, *The Fly*. *The Fly*—the original with Vincent Price and the remake with Jeff Goldblum—straddles the world of body horror and science fiction, but, ultimately, I cataloged it under science fiction. There were a few comments from trolls, but if anyone wants to waste their energy on complaining about something so insignificant, then they can talk to the ether.

It was my channel, after all. My art and my mission.

The year before science fiction, I focused on body horror, and that was difficult for me to process, because watching too much Cronenberg made me question each twitch beneath my skin, every freckle that formed across my nose during the summer months, and every physical sensation that coursed through my veins. Anytime I watched a Cronenberg film, *Scanners*, *The Brood*, *Videodrome*, *Rabid*, I feared I'd wake up the next day unaware, or perhaps too aware, that my body was no longer my body.

The year before that I focused on what I call Gothic modern horror. That was the year my channel started taking off, when advertisers took notice, and when I finally hit my goal of having one of my videos viewed by one million viewers—thanks to Daphne du Maurier's 1971 adaptation of *Don't Look Now*.

For many people, when they think of the word "Gothic," they think of four-hundred-page books packed with windswept moors and betrayed brides in flowing silk gowns fleeing down dark and damp corridors within ancient moss-covered castles. But for that series I talked about recent haunted house tales, *The Changeling*, *The Sentinel*, *The Amityville Horror*, *The Haunting of Hill House*, *The Woman in Black*. I guess I just could have called it a series on haunted houses, but that didn't sound quite as exciting. You throw the word "Gothic" in any title or description and people will sign on for it.

It was my scene-by-scene analysis of *Sinister*, starring Ethan Hawke, that generated enough to pay off my student loans. People watched again and again as I dissected the box of Super 8 films Hawke's character locates in a newly purchased home. While watching the films, Hawke's character, Ellison Oswalt, a true crime writer, is horrified to discover the films depict families being murdered. One family is drowned in a pool, another set on fire, and another family has their throats slit. They are bound, re-strained, and all the while, as they plea for help, muffled by rope and duct tape, a camera zooms in on their faces, taking pleasure in their anguish. Soon, Oswalt discovers that each of the films contain a fleeting image of a disfigured demonic-looking creature who watches from the sidelines as each member of the family dies. As Oswalt investigates, he begins to wonder if that presence was really at the crime scenes, or whether it existed solely in the film, or in the mind of his victims, or even in his mind.

Was the occult involved?

Was the film cursed?

Chicago has a bit of history itself with cursed and haunted things, especially dealing with cinema. Even the theater I grew up in and worked at, the Logan Theater, had a notoriously haunt-ed theater, theater number five. People love the idea of a cursed or haunted film. Sometimes I wonder if it's us regular people who unintentionally imbue something with power because we want to be scared of it, we want to explain away the disturbing images we register as being due to some otherworldly evil.

We're afraid, and so we speak in hushed tones around it or tell others to avoid it because we once heard from one person a long time ago about a bad thing dealing with that object, or that place, or that film. Then those stories get told again and again, a tangled game of telephone, and we're the very ones twisting the cords around our neck, because we want to suffocate on the terror of the possibility of something cursed. And what is a curse, but magick? Magick placed on a person or object with the intent of causing harm and misfortune. And who can place a curse? Another person skilled in magick—a magician, or a god.

"Bela," I call. "We're going to be late."

"I'm almost finished!" he shouts from the bathroom.

Beneath Lugosi and Karloff's names, I jot down the titles of all of the films I would be discussing in the upcoming weeks.

This year I will be celebrating my fifth year of the channel and need something to stay relevant in a crowded horror entertainment market. There are thousands of other channels devoted to horror—horror books, horror comics, horror games, extreme horror films, dissecting the kills in horror movies, horror baking, horror makeup, horror fashion , the horror home aesthetic, and, of course, horror movies.

My formula is pretty traditional. I analyze a film, discussing its actors, the film's history, and its influence on the horror landscape. It was a classic horror host blueprint. Regardless, viewers today demanded new and interesting content near daily, not just weekly like old school horror hosts.

When I told my audience I would be covering the foundations of horror this year, they didn't seem that enthusiastic.

"I get it," I said into the camera as I was wearing my favorite Elvira Mistress of the Night hoodie, and unlike the Gothic queen, who looked eternally flawless, I didn't have a stitch of makeup on. I long ago reckoned with the fact that I would be happier making content if I was not held prisoner to this idea that I always had to look polished for the audience. I feel most comfortable with my long dark hair parted down the middle and brushed down over my shoulders, no makeup, yoga pants and one of my favorite horror hoodies, of which I had dozens, and a warm mug of tea in hand.

I reassured them. "Even if we don't get scared by these movies today, they're still foundational to what we think of when we think of horror. Even if it's not scary to you, that doesn't mean it's not horror. Just think of Max Schreck's gaunt vampire in *Nosferatu*. Or the mesmerizing swirls and blocks of black and white in *The Cabinet of Dr. Caligari*, the contrasts which obviously influenced Tim Burton. And of our spellcasting witches and Satan at their side in *Haxan*. Much of these themes, and much of this imagery, we still see incorporated in horror today.

The past may be gone, but it's still part of us."

This week, I thought I'd start off with something everyone knew, but hadn't necessarily seen, Universal Studios *Dracula* series. There are technically seven films in which Count Dracula appears: *Dracula* (1931) both the English and the Spanish version, *Dracula's Daughter* (1936), *Son of Dracula* (1943), *The House of Frankenstein* (1944), *House of Dracula* (1945), and *Abbott and Costello Meet Frankenstein* (1948). Yes, there are two films on that list with Frankenstein in the title, but they are important to include given *House of Frankenstein* includes an ensemble cast where Dracula appears. Then, *Abbott and Costello Meet Frankenstein* was the final time Bela Lugosi played Dracula. Some people may think that Lugosi's final appearance as Dracula was in Ed Wood's *Planet 9 From Outer Space*. That's only half true. Planet 9 was Lugosi's final film appearance, but the character he played was named Old Man/Ghoul Man in the credits.

Bela returns from washing his hands. I close my notebook and shove it in my backpack and reach for his bright red coat with two small reflective strips on the arms hanging on the stand beside the door. All of Bela's clothes are bright and bold. This makes it easier to keep track of him in crowds. Bela gets down on the floor and squeezes Romero and gives him a kiss atop his head.

We step out to the indoor back porch and put on our winter boots and gloves. Bela is oddly quiet throughout. He clutches his tablet to his chest with his mitten-covered hands as we walk down the sidewalk, the sound of snow crunching beneath our feet. The ground is covered in rock salt, those small, dull-looking crystals that help melt the walkway and prevent sheets of ice from settling. The shock of the cold wind blowing into my face stings my eyes. I reach for the garage door key and unlock the door. Bela pushes past me to the car and climbs in the backseat.

Usually, he complains the entire short walk to the garage in this weather, but he hadn't said a word.

He pulls on his seatbelt and sets his tablet on his lap.

"Why are you so quiet?" I finally ask as I turn on the car and open the garage door. I'm looking at him I the rearview mirror.

Bela leans forward in his seat. I watch him from the rearview mirror. His eyes narrow. His voice is accusatory. "Why didn't you tell me that Bruce was leaving?"

"What? Who told you that?"

His hands are fists now. He's kicking the passenger seat in front of him. I take my eyes off of him as I drive out of the garage and close the door.

"Why didn't you tell me Bruce was leaving?" he shouts.

I keep my voice low and steady. "Bela, who told you that?"

"The bird told me. The black bird."

"Bela, you're not making any sense. What black bird?"

"The black bird that visits my room at night. He said Bruce is leaving. That he's going to die, and that you're going to die too, Mom, in theater number five."

CHAPTER 5

FRIDAY MORNING, DRIVE TO SCHOOL: PALOMA

Bela slips back into his world, refusing to tell me more about theater five and the black bird. He must have overheard me talking to Bass or Bruce at one point about that space. Yes, the rumor was that theater number five was haunted, but there was so much more than that that I could never really tell anyone. I knew I saw something on that screen, but no one believed me. Now that Bela brought it up, I only hoped more so that Grand would reach out so that I could ask him. I needed someone to validate that what I saw that day was real.

Logan Theater's screen number five rests in that sacred place of neighborhood legends and lore. The dilapidated house at the end of town with weather-worn wood siding and the old woman who lives there alone, and who therefore must be a witch. The rural community cemetery and its oldest headstones that have been faded with rain and time. These and more are stitched into the fabric of neighborhood haunted legend, making them perfect places for ghost hunting and local teens to swing by to try to tempt the spirits, all for photographic evidence for social media points.

Small towns, though, are different from big cities, aren't

they? Our scares in places populated by millions tend to be like those jump scares in horror movies. Jump scares are sudden. Your heart races. Your breath catches in your throat. You're disoriented. But it's all only for an instant, and when the next scene arrives, you've forgotten the last appearance of a shadow, shock of blood, or show of an ambling monster that frightened you. Now, you are frustrated, disappointed in yourself because the scare 'got you,' and so you promise yourself, you demand your physiology to remain regulated until the next unexpected event.

This is how we feel about crime in the city.

A family is bludgeoned in their beds. A social worker attending a regularly scheduled meeting is stabbed to death by a parent as their children watch. A young teenager is shot and killed by the police, even after they stopped as instructed and raised their arms in the air. These are our jump scares in the city, a sweeping chorus of screams, gunshots, firetruck and ambulance sirens, the screech of tires racing away, or is it toward something? That sound coalescing in the night charging forth chaos and death, that sound is our lullaby. What follows are the murders, and then the mixing and melding of names, faces, and dates with the hundreds of others who have been made into memory that year.

Chicago doesn't just contain a scary house at the end of town. Chicago isn't the home to that one creepy unkempt cemetery where people claim to see spirits rise. Chicago, the entire city, itself is the heinous and menacing thing that sprung from a swamp encompassing all of those threats and more. Theater number five at Logan Theater, and what I believe I saw there long ago, is a reminder that there is so much we still don't understand.

"Bela." I glance in the rearview and then return my focus to morning traffic ahead of me. The major streets have been plowed and city trucks have scattered rock salt, but still, it's a slushy, steady, and icy crawl along the road. "What did I say?"

"If anything happens, tell Mr. Vicari," he repeats my words. When he does that, I worry he is just playing back what I said. A recording, and thus he did not absorb the actual weight of what was being said. Other times he says my words slowly, carefully, relishing in the sound each consonant and vowel makes as it tumbles out of his mouth. The world for Bela is a charged kaleidoscope, a never-ending sensory wonderland.

Bela once again repeats what I said, the tone of his voice low. "If anything happens, tell Mr. Vicari."

I tighten my grip around the steering wheel and remind myself he isn't doing this to mock me. He does this often, echolalia, the repetition of sounds, words, phrases, or full sentences. Echolalia is just one of the many characteristics that sets Bela apart from the other children. Most of his classmates are forgiving of his mannerisms, for now. They often brush aside how he speaks at length about his interests, often horror movies, the monotone pitch of his voice, or how, sometimes, his fingers flap at the ends of his hands like insects while the rest of him remains still. As he grew older, he learned to control his body's movements. But sometimes all of society's unsaid rules about how one should sit or stand still or remain silent overwhelmed his senses so much that he'd rush to gather sensory input, by jumping, singing, or any quick burst of physical motion to feel something.

Ms. Martin emailed me last week about Bela's spinning. She was fearful he would become too dizzy, lose control, and crash into a desk, a child, or a bookshelf. Bela never gets vertigo. The vestibular system in some people like Bela often demands stimulation. It's this tiny mechanism in one's ear that shoots information to one's brain about spatial orientation and motion. And it is this system that craves stimulation in Bela, and he does so through running, twirling, and very often spinning in place with his arms out at his sides and his head back and eyes closed. Ms. Martin said she and Mr. Vicari would explore safer methods to help Bela regulate—yoga, a wiggle seat, or a wide rubber band that could be stretched across the two front legs of his chair that he could kick with his feet beneath his desk without disrupting the class.

Bela's focus remains on his electronic device and inside the world he created, one of bright colors, shapes, and various pieces he had constructed to make buildings, houses, and towns.

At the red light I ask, "If Daniel comes up to you in gym class, what are you supposed to do?"

The fingers of his right hand pull away from the screen. I can see the question broke his concentration. His nose scrunches up and I see his baby cheeks are still red from the cold.

"Well…"

He doesn't answer, and so I repeat the question.

His lips pull into a pout, and he shouts, "Okay, Mom! Okay! Okay!"

"I just don't want you getting hurt," I say as he continues saying "Okay" until I tell him to please stop.

The light turns green, and I remove my foot from the brake and inch along the slick road.

Yesterday, Daniel threw a book at Sam. Bela saw what happened and rushed to Sam's side to ask him if he was alright. Daniel then called Bela a traitor and punched him in his stomach. It wasn't until bedtime that Bela told me what happened.

"Daniel's mean," I say. "Stay away from Daniel."

He frowns, looking at his screen, and then says, "Why did Daniel throw a book at Sam? That wasn't very nice."

"I don't know," I say, feeling helpless in that moment. Even as an adult I still don't understand why people do mean things to one another.

There are a lot of things Bela doesn't fully comprehend. He became so upset when I'd watch the evening news that he begged me to no longer turn it on because he didn't like hearing stories about people hurting one another or dying. When we'd watch horror movies together, Bela would watch intently, very often talking aloud to himself, trying to rationalize what it was the monster wanted and why.

"Why does Beetlejuice want to trick his friends?" he asked me the very first time we watched Michael Keaton play the infamous ghost, whose black and white vertically striped suit now regularly makes appearances as a Halloween costume.

Then when we learned that gremlins should never be fed after midnight, Bela asked, "Why are the gremlins mean to Gizmo?"

When we first watched *Coraline*, he cried and demanded to know, "Why does the Other Mother want to keep Coraline away from her real mother?"

In all of these instances he wanted to know why the monster was evil.

Bela wanted to understand evil as much as I did, and when he'd ask me to explain why some people were wicked, I knew no matter how hard I tried, I could never give him a just response.

"Some people are just bad," I'd say, and he'd nod, turn back to our movie unfolding before us, the corners of his mouth dipping downward, and sadness settling in because sometimes no answer could justify why the bad thing was occurring.

"Bela...can you tell me about the black bird?"

"Did you know the Northern Cardinal is our state bird?"

"I feel like I should know that, but now I know that, so thank you. Can you tell me about the black bird?"

"Is Bruce leaving?"

He is avoiding my question, but I reason he must have heard Bass and me talking the other night. "Yes, Bela. Bruce is selling the theater, but he's not moving right away."

Please don't cry. Please don't cry. Please don't cry.

I don't want to lose him in a pit of sadness, especially not moments before he starts school. I brace myself and steal a glance in the rearview, but he isn't crying.

His eyes meet mine. "Can we talk about the Northern Cardinal now?"

This wasn't completely strange. He processed things differently, and given Bruce wasn't leaving yet, maybe we'd be fine for a while. "Okay...where'd you learn about the Northern Cardinal?"

"I watched a video," he says.

"Remember when we used to get visits from that cardinal last summer? It would hang out in our tree in the backyard."

"We're still going to see Bruce tonight, right?"

"Yes," I say. "But Dad's going to be at work. It'll just be you and me." Which I actually preferred. Bass wasn't the greatest person to see a movie with. He's impatient. If he's not shaking his leg, he's checking his phone, or stepping outside the theater to make a call. Most homicide detectives in the city manage five to six cases. Most recently, Bass was managing eleven.

We're approaching Bela's school. Some parents drop their kids off at the kiss and fly, right in front of the building. Cars would line up, and once you'd reach the school entryway, a school administrator or parent volunteer would open your back door and your child would get out, say goodbye, and then run off into the schoolyard.

The process seemed simple enough, but not for Bela.

He could not be trusted to get out of the car and walk the few yards down and stand in line with his class. In those few moments without me or Bass escorting him, Bela could easily get confused, or distracted, by the splash of color from a bright backpack, a fluffy dog some parent had brought along with them for morning drop off, which they were not supposed to do, the blast of music from a passing car, anything really.

Bela often lost focus in an instant, becoming disoriented

and confused as to what he was doing just moments before and where he was supposed to go. It is times like those I most fear he could wander off and become lost.

"We're going to have to move fast," I say as I park way too close to a fire hydrant. "Buddy. Unbuckle." I turn around, but he is once again engrossed in his game. "Give me that." I reach for his tablet and slide it beneath the passenger seat.

"Mom…" he whines.

"Bela, the last thing I need is for someone to break my car window to take your tablet."

"People would do that?"

"It's Chicago. People'll do anything."

He looks out his window and raises a finger, tapping the glass. "There's a woman on that bench," he points.

"Good thing we put your tablet away, then," I say, and then open my car door. I move around to the rear passenger door and open it. "Buddy, I asked you to unbuckle. Please. We're late."

Bela reaches down and presses the red button, releasing his seatbelt. "No one ever sits on that bench."

"Well, someone is sitting on that bench now." I take his hand and help him out of the car and then reach in and grab his backpack. "Maybe she's looking for cardinals."

He whispers. "No. She's looking for a dove. A magical dove."

"Lucky her, then, there are lots around here."

"No, only one," he says.

I scan the school grounds and spot the woman Bela is talking about. From this distance I cannot see her face, but I can see she is wearing all black.

And just then, the first bell rings. "Uh-oh! Let's move," I say, and slam the car door shut.

Bela's eyes widen. "We're going to be late!"

"I'm going to race you," I say, and then take his hand, because even in a simple game of race I cannot let him go.

We run down to the end of the block to the playground entrance. The swings and slides have already been cleared out by Principal Rutkowski, who is speaking into a walkie talkie inches from his face, likely telling Mr. Aguilar, the school security guard, inside that the lot has been cleared of children.

Mr. Rutkowski raises a hand and waves. "Morning Bela." Nearly all of the administrators and teachers in the building know Bela, having run into him during one of the many times he's wandered out of class.

Our run slows to a walk as we turn right. A small, snow-covered field stretches out before us.

"Mom." A white puff of water vapor from the cold floats above his head. "The lady is not at the bench anymore."

There's the steady sound of salt crunching beneath our winter boots as we rush up the sidewalk.

It is so cold it hurts to talk, to move, to breathe. "Because the bell rang and her kid is probably in school already, and my kid is still not in school. Guess who's the better parent right now?"

"You're the best, Mom," Bela says, his mittens squeezing my gloved hand. "But the lady, she's not a mom."

"Maybe she's someone's aunt, sister, grandmother?"

"I don't know the name for it. I think she's a bird like you, Mom. A beautiful bird."

"Wait, am I the black bird?"

Bela shakes his head, his knit cap gently lowering down over his eyebrows.

Sometimes I long to live in his imagination. Everything in Bela's world is sweet and bright and whimsical, where animals tell stories and epic adventures unfold. Not just "the floor is lava," and we hop up onto the sofa. In Bela's world, there are wonderous tales of dragons emerging from between sidewalk cracks, of werewolves howling outside our window, and of timeless magicians who use Bela's closet as a time machine, traveling across dimensions to relay messages. Although often it is as if his world seeps out here into reality and I cannot tell if he really believes in the tales he tells. I try to reason sometimes that it is just childhood fantasy combined with the old horror movies we enjoy watching, but is it really?

"The lady on the bench, then? Is she the black bird?"

Parents of children with disabilities live in this constant elevated state of anxiety, sometimes even teetering between despair and dread. We know our children have this beaming innocence within them, but because of that they sometimes misinterpret human intention. Even something as simple as a smile. Bela cannot distinguish between a sinister and a friendly smile because he cannot read facial reactions like most people do. Our children are lambs in the barn, oblivious when a wolf dons one of their skins.

Bela shrugs. "No."

"Teacher's assistant?"

Bela bites his lower lip. "Uh huh. Yes, an assistant. That's the word for it."

Mr. Vicari is standing in front of the school doors, waiting for us. Bela's class has already entered the building, but Mr. Vicari, his special education classroom assistant who is there for him in the morning, throughout the school day, and who hands Bela off to me at the end of the day, is waiting for us.

"Good morning, Bela, you ready?"

I let go of Bela's hand. "Thanks, Sam. I'll see you all later."

I kneel and wrap my arms once more around my little boy. "You and me," I say.

"Forever."

Bela pulls away. His eyes wide. "Mom, this is important. If you see the lady—"

"The assistant lady?"

"Yes, if you see the assistant lady, tell her the book hasn't gotten to our house yet."

The second bell rings, alerting class is now in session. Bela is trying to shout something above the noise, but I cannot catch it.

"Come on, bud," Mr. Vicari says as the sound fades, and both of them enter the building.

Bela turns around and shouts, "Don't forget what I said, Mom."

I walk back to my car, crossing the empty schoolyard, my thoughts turning to the hours ahead of me. There is enough time to record an episode, and perhaps start the research on the following. If I am lucky, maybe I'll have time to watch a movie before picking Bela up from school before heading over to visit Bruce at the theater.

And, of course, there will be time to stare at my email, fixating on hitting refresh, actively listening for the alert when a new message lands in my inbox and being disappointed when it isn't from Grand. If he doesn't respond, then I will take that as my sign to finally let it go. How much time should one devote themselves to an obsession before accepting that some questions will never be answered?

If he doesn't respond, then at least I still have enough material to discuss the history of the horror host. He has done this longer than Vampira, who was only on the air for nine months, Ghoulardi, Dr. Shock, Joe Bob Briggs, Count Gore de Vol and more. Grand seems to know everything about every horror movie ever created no matter how obscure. I had delayed this project so long because I wanted to talk to him, to ask him what it is he knows, and I was too scared to ask. I hope he'll answer me and give me the reassurance I need, and confirm that real magick, the kind spelled with a letter K exists.

It's taken me this long to build up the courage to even email him. And even after all of this time, I fear I'll be left with nothing. Just theories and suspicions.

In one famous interview, when asked how he knew so much about the genre, he said, "We are all tapped into the darkness and are moved to want to know what stirs in there. Some of us turn away, I walk toward it."

Walk toward it, I did, and I just need to know if Georges Méliès had done the same, leaving behind not only genius work, but something that defied what we believed were the laws of reality. And given Bass' question—if I knew who Méliès was—I worried if someone else was searching for the answer to the question that had been hovering in my mind for so long.

Heading down the sidewalk toward my car, I notice a woman a half block away in a black pencil skirt, black pumps, and a form-fitting black tweed coat. Not only is she the only other person outside at this time, but the shifting of her form-hugging skirt just below her knees, the way her heels clack against the sidewalk—I'm impressed she braves heels in this icy, slippery weather—the way she moves, all of it makes her stand out.

Even from this distance I can see the sheen of her fully fashioned nylons with the black line running up the center of her pale calves. Her hair is styled in a smooth bob with curled tips, and it's glossy black, almost reflecting the sun that's decided to peek out for the first time in days. The woman from the bench just moments before, and I am mesmerized because she seems so out of place, as if plucked from a memory.

I open my car door, pull on my seatbelt, and look in the rearview mirror before turning the key.

The woman in black is gone.

A soft tune startles me, and I remember Bela's tablet is beneath the passenger seat. I reach down and look at the screen. The device slips out of my hand, falling between my feet. I pick it up and stare at the screen, trying to make sense of what it was he was drawing, and why.

Lines in a storm of circles and shapes. Symbols with infinite possibilities, meant to open doors, summon, control, and divine.

How did Bela know how to construct this? Who had taught him how to create a sigil using the Rose Cross?

CHAPTER 6

FRIDAY MORNING, SCHOOL: BELA

Look people in the eye when you are talking to them, I think as I hold the pencil tightly in my hand.

It's too loud in the classroom. Kids talking. Chairs moving. People in the hallway laughing. The lights feel too bright, and the sweater Mom asked me to wear today is scratchy on my neck.

I look at the page. I had to write a sentence of what I was going to do this weekend, but I keep thinking about what Ms. Martin told me, that I should practice today looking people in the eye when they are talking because people like that. That's strange. Why do I have to look people in the eye if they are talking? I can just listen with my ears at what is being said. That seems more important.

Other things Ms. Martin tells me to do is to try to ignore everything else around me, even if those things seem very important. Like right now, I see Daniel get up and walk over to the computers. He is done with his assignment, he tells Mr. Vicari.

Michaela is tapping her pencil against the desk next to me. She is still not done with her assignment. Neither am I. I like Michaela, but I do not like that she is tapping her pencil against the desk.

More kids start getting up from their seats. Some walk to the bookshelves, others to the computers to join Daniel. Mom said to stay away from Daniel because he threw a book at Sam, so today I will stay away from Daniel.

Other kids gather at each other's tables, and they are talking about what they are going to do this weekend. My head hurts because I hear everything, and everyone is so loud. All of their voices blend together into one whirring-buzzing sort of sound, like the microwave at home. I want to get up and go for a walk, but I can't get up yet, because I am not yet done with my assignment.

"Do you need help, buddy?" Mr. Vicari sits down next to me. He keeps his voice low when he talks to me because he knows I do not like loud noise. I just need to finish this last sentence, and I know I can do it, so I tell him I can finish it on my own.

There are many rules, and sometimes it feels impossible to remember all of these rules, just like you can't get up from your seat for break until you finish your assignment. I repeat other rules in my head sometimes, and sometimes I place them in a cabinet in my mind.

Mom and Ms. Martin and Mr. Vicari say that what I call the cabinet in my head is my memory, but I still like to think about it like a cabinet. There are many cabinets in my head. When I need something, I just go to the cabinet with the thing I am looking for. Sometimes I look for rules or the right words to use, but there are so many things that I am told to remember. Sometimes it takes me a long time to find the right thing to do or say. Everyone has so many rules, rules about what to say, how to say it, how to act, how to move.

It is very hard to remember so many things.

Michaela is smiling at me. I will look her in the eye because maybe she has something she wants to say.

Michaela is tall and has long light brown hair and today she is wearing earrings. They are green stars.

"Did you finish?" she asks me.

"Not yet," I say, and look down to the pencil in my hand. Then I remember I should be looking in her eyes.

Michaela is smiling. "My dad's taking me to get pizza after school. What are you doing today after school?"

I am still looking in her eyes. "My mom and I are going to Logan Theater to watch a movie. My dad can't come because someone was murdered yesterday. So, my dad is busy on an investigation."

Investigation is a big word. I like the way it sounds, and I want to say it again, but I don't. My mom and I watch a lot of movies about monsters and ghosts, but we also watch a lot of movies about investigators, detectives, and private detectives. Mom said that when Dad was little, he would watch a lot of these movies because he wanted to be a detective. We watched *Maltese Falcon* with Sam Spade, *Murder My Sweet*, *The Big Sleep*, and *The Long Goodbye* with Philip Marlowe, *Young Sherlock Holmes*, and then last week we watched *Angel Heart*. *Angel Heart* is like a horror movie and investigator movie smooshed into one. As we watched *Angel Heart*, Mom kept fast forwarding and apologizing, saying, "I'm so sorry, I didn't remember this being so graphic."

"What's graphic?" I ask Mr. Vicari, who's standing beside us now. He has a look on his face I don't understand. Sometimes people stand around and are unable to say anything right away. People can be very confusing.

Mom watches a lot of scary movies, but I think they are all the same. Mom says there are different types of movies and different types of stories because there are different types of plots. She told me the different types of plots, but I forgot them all, even though I tried to put them away in my cabinet. She said them too fast. Still, I think there is really only one type of plot:

things happen.

I think my mom likes to watch a lot of scary movies because she is sad, not because Bruce is selling the theater and not because Dad works a lot, but because when Mom was a little girl, her mom and her dad were mean to her. What makes her happy are her monster movies, and so she goes to them again and again so as not to feel so sad.

At night, sometimes I hear Mom cry, but if I walk into her office after I hear her crying, she wipes her face quickly with her sleeves and says she just has allergies.

When I told Mom maybe she should not watch any more monster movies because I am scared they are making her sad, she said, "The monsters have been good to me. They gave me everything I have."

I hug my mom a lot, and right now, I miss her. I know she wants me to be happy. She is always doing nice things for me, like making me my waffles for breakfast. Yesterday, when I asked her if we could have ice cream for breakfast, she said yes, and she scooped chocolate and vanilla ice cream into waffle cones. We then sat at the breakfast table and watched the snow fall outside the window.

"Bela said someone was murdered!" Michaela shouts.

I don't know why she is crying. I was looking in her eyes. I thought I was doing a good thing. I am rocking back and forth in my seat now. My hands are over my ears, but everything is still so loud. Michaela is covering her eyes with her arm. Her cries sound like the car alarms that go off outside at night and ring and ring and ring until someone turns them off.

My insides feel squishy. I remember now, I am not supposed to talk about dad's investigations because sometimes people get upset.

"I'm sorry!" I say, but I'm not sure if the words come out wrong and so I say it again, but this time I think it's louder than I should have said.

Maybe I shouted the words accidentally.

"Thanks for apologizing, Bela," Mr. Vicari says. He's kneeling now in front of Michaela, telling her that everything is alright, but I don't think she believes him because she's still crying.

My mom tells me not to worry sometimes, so that is what I am trying to do right now, not worry, but Michaela is crying louder and my ears are ringing. It's so loud it sounds like thunder is right here in this room with us. It's like the blender on high when Dad is making his smoothies. Everyone is looking at us, Daniel and Sam, Anna, Ms. Martin and the rest of the class.

I'm standing up now and I don't know what to do with my body. My arms feel like noodles at my sides. What do I do with them? My legs feel like they are not standing in the right spot, like one foot should be closer to the other. I shift my weight from foot to foot, but that makes my head hurt more. My stomach feels twisty. It feels like the floor is moving beneath me. It reminds me of that one time Mom and Dad took me on a Chicago River boat tour downtown.

There are too many noises now. Mr. Vicari and Ms. Martin. Michaela. Daniel. Sam. More. So many voices that I don't know where they stop or where they start. Sometimes when I feel like this, my words don't work the way I want them to, but for now they do.

"Can I go for a walk?"

Just as Mr. Vicari says, "Yes," my feet move and I'm already in the hallway. I hear Mr. Vicari say, "Hold on." Mr. Vicari says that a lot. So does Ms. Martin. But that makes no sense. Hold on to what? There is nothing to hold on to except the wall. "Wait!" Mr. Vicari shouts instead, and I guess that's what "Hold on" means.

Sometimes what people say is confusing.

Mr. Vicari is supposed to come with me on my walks. When I was little and in kindergarten, I would leave the classroom and go on walks by myself, and the security guard would find me in the hallway and take me to the principal's office. Principal Rutkowski would then walk me back to my classroom. Principal Rutkowski told me it is not safe to go exploring on my own. I was not exploring. I was just going on a walk, but they did not understand. Not too long after is when Mr. Vicari started being my helper.

"I have to go to the restroom first!" I shout back and start jogging toward the restroom.

I hear Mr. Vicari's sneakers squeak behind me. "Okay," he says. "I'll wait for you out here in the hallway."

There is no one in the restroom. I rush into the stall at the very end and close the door and just stand there. It is small in the stall, and it is cold here, but it feels safe and quiet. I look down and see the white and back tiled floor and then look up and see the ceiling. The fluorescent light above me is flickering on and off. It makes a *zzzzing* sound like a fly buzzing over my ears. There's a small pop and the light above me blinks out. It's dim now, but not dark. I am still safe.

I hear tapping on the tile right outside the stall.

I call out. "Hello?"

There is more tapping. It is a like when Michaela taps the tip of her pencil against the table.

Tiny gray bird feet appear beneath the stall door.

"It's me, Bela," I say. "You can come in." I do not open the door because the bird is so tiny it can walk right beneath the space of the door into the stall. It is small and black. A little poof of black feathers.

The bird's head turns upward a bit and looks to me. It coos.

"I told my mom about the book that's coming, but I don't think she believes me. I know about her books, but I have not told her. I did what you told me. I found the Rose Cross in Mom's book, and I followed your instruction. I copied the circle. I drew the symbols. It's on my tablet. I'm happy the sigil will keep me safe."

The black bird ruffles its feathers and a sharp tune escapes its black beak.

I lower my head. "I did tell her about theater five."

Its tiny feet go *tip tap tip tap* and then it stops.

"I promise I won't do it again."

The baby bird whistles softly.

"That's nice."

The bird turns around and moves back under the door from where it came, out of view.

I try to open the door to see where it is going, but the latch will not budge. "Wait, where are you going?"

The bird returns with a red ADMIT ONE movie theater ticket, the same kind Bruce uses at the theater.

The bird whistles a beautiful song that feels like every birthday morning I've ever had.

"If I tell her the story, she's going to be upset. She'll worry about my dad."

Mr. Vicari calls from outside the restroom. "Bela, are you almost done?" His voice sounds like an echo, like he's calling me from far, far away.

The black bird opens its beak and screeches. It's shrill and hurts my head and teeth.

"That hurts!"

The screeching stops and the black bird blinks and lowers its head.

I move my hands away from my ears. "That wasn't very nice."

There's a soft cooing now, and I hear Mr. Vicari again.

"I'm almost finished," I shout. I push the ticket in my back pocket so I will remember to tell Mom the story I have been told, the one that I really do not want to tell. I don't like knowing that bad things are going to happen, but sometimes we do not have control over them.

It's like all of our lives are a story. There is a beginning. A middle. An end.

Everything will end. Sometimes people have short stories and sometimes people have very long stories.

Or maybe our lives are more like movies, a few scenes pasted together.

I'm sad that I know so much about all that will happen.

I reach out and pet the top of the black bird's head.

"Fine, I will tell her, but I don't like knowing that so many people have to die."

CHAPTER 7

FRIDAY AFTERNOON: PALOMA

"We are always where we are meant to be," I say into the camera. "This is difficult to comprehend, especially if we find ourselves in a moment of tragedy or experiencing pain. We wonder, how can something valuable come from suffering? What's meant for us will always find us, and this is true for our monsters. Many of us came to horror movies for a similar reason, a longing to feel understood, identifying with the persecuted, or simply because we just love the gore. Whatever brought you to horror still matters in some ways, but this is your home. Horror."

I display an image of a pink star outlined in gold. The profile of an old movie camera in the center and above it the name LON CHANEY. The next image that appears is that of a man from the waist up, wearing a vest, white shirt, and tie. The background is black, a bright light shines on the right side of his face. His eyes look distant, but he is smiling, a smile that appears to now be fading.

"Leonidas Frank 'Lon' Chaney was born in 1883 to two deaf parents. He attended what was later renamed Colorado's School for the Deaf and Blind. In an attempt to best communicate with his parents, he became of master of pantomime, think black and white monochromatic clowns pressing their hands in the air around them, as if trapped in an imaginary box. He expressed himself through big physical gestures using his arms and legs and exaggerated facial reactions to communicate, and this skill is what led him to the stage. He started acting around 1902 and traveling with vaudeville acts. He even landed in Chicago, but was broke by the time he got here."

I pause the recording and turn to my notes. I write down the word "vaudeville" and circle it because I know no one is going to know what it is I am talking about.

The spirit of vaudeville exists today in the microbursts of online social media sites where people upload short clips of themselves dancing, cooking, or showing their cute dog with a background audio narrating their pet's supposed thoughts. Vaudeville artists were just that, a diverse range of performers given a specified amount of time, not much, who would hit the stage, perform and entertain, then be applauded or booed. These performances included singers, dancers, burlesque, comedians, and magicians.

Some vaudeville groups traveled the country and others were designated to their geographic location. The early American variety act was vaudeville. Chicago was a major stop along this entertainment circuit, until Balaban and Katz opened the Chicago Theater, which offered movies and live acts for the same price as a vaudeville performance.

By the 1930s, vaudeville was dead, crushed by a large screen and moving images.

Many Hollywood legends of silent film and beyond started their acting career in vaudeville: Julie Andrews, our original Mary Poppins, the powerful Mae West, Sammy Davis Jr., before he was a member of the rat pack, our eternal Dorothy from *The Wonderful Wizard of Oz*, Judy Garland, and Charlie Chaplin.

I check my email, because that's what I do, constantly refreshing to see if there are any updates from my sponsors, viewers, and now hoping there's something from Grand.

Nothing.

How long does it take someone to respond to a message? It seemed like silence was the only answer I would get. Ignored, and so, rejected.

I needed to finish my project, and if that meant he wouldn't be included, then so be it. I would have to accept that I may never really know what I saw in theater number five, if anything.

All we really know about Grand is that he once worked for radio before moving on to his successful long-running television program, becoming cemented as a master of horror. In a day where everything and everyone's history can unfold in the palm of our hand, we still only know Grand was once a radio reporter for WBBM covering local news.

I turn back to the black and white image of Lon Chaney frozen on my computer and hit record again.

"He was dubbed "The Man of 1,000 Faces," because unlike other silver screen leading men of the time who carefully curated their image to that of handsome and alluring, Chaney challenged conventionality. He embraced movie makeup magic, often completely changing his appearance from film to film. This wasn't through special effects or CGI. He would sit in a makeup chair for hours as creams and prosthetics were pressed and set against his skin. His preference skewed toward the absurd, bizarre, and grotesque, often portraying criminals, clowns, pirates, ghouls, and vampires."

I recall once how Grand said that *The Hunchback of Notre Dame* starring Lon Chaney as Quasimodo was one of the most terrifying depictions he had ever seen. He said it wasn't the film's grainy, shaky footage that unsettled him. He even commented that most modern horror audiences seeking a volt of adrenaline would likely find the film timid. Grand said it wasn't the hunchback himself that was scary. It was quite the opposite.

What was scary was how Quasimodo was gawked upon, mistreated and tortured by society. That is what sickened him. The way we often treat those who do not look like us or act like us is truly diabolical.

"Monstrosity does not a monster make," Grand once said during one of his show's introductions. "Beautiful, normal people are often what we should really fear. They are quick to lurk and descend upon that which looks different in order to mock it, abuse it, and ultimately destroy it. Think of some of the most vicious monsters in cinematic history. Anthony Perkins in *Psycho* or Christian Bale in *American Psycho*, for example. Often, it's the one who charms you who wants you destroyed."

I take a deep breath and continue recording. "Most audiences do not know that the role of Dracula in Universal's iconic film was written with Lon Chaney in mind, but Chaney died of throat cancer before filming could begin. I'll talk to you more later about how a relatively unknown Hungarian actor was cast for one of the most famous horror films in history, and in turn himself became a legend."

Once again, I pause the recording and look over my show notes in between sips of my matcha latte. Bass drinks coffee all day long. It is his primary beverage, beating out water. I can't consume that much caffeine, but I suppose he turns to it as a dependence, a device to remind him that he has to work in urgency, because if he doesn't, then another body will appear and another, all accumulating with unfortunate ends as stories he needs to piece together. There is no slowing down. There is only living in the exhaustion that each day he has killers to catch, and the only way to do that often means he needs to slip into their psychology, no matter how deviant. It means swallowing fire.

I check the time. Bass has reached twenty-four hours away from the house at work. He had promised me that he wouldn't become this, that he wouldn't let this consume him. We had all

seen last year what happens when one allows the anger and hatred that lives in this city to slowly peel away at your humanity.
You soon moved in all sorts of directions, no longer knowing if
you were doing good or contributing to the chaos. I didn't want
him to become like her, so trapped in protecting something that
was amorphous, an idea of what Chicagoans and Chicago should
be.

I turn back to my computer, going to Grand's website to once
again find his events and appearance schedule empty.

He had shaken hands and taken photos with thousands of
people throughout his career. He was once a beloved cornerstone
of local and national horror convention circuits. Old pictures of
him with smiling fans often crossed my social media feeds as
people reminisced about seeing him at events, taking their children and grandchildren to meet him. His influence has spanned
generations. Yet, as I studied those last few photos of him in public, he seemed distracted, jittery, often appearing blurry or out of
focus, as if avoiding the camera's flash.

Forty years was a long time to host a television program.
Forty years was also a long time to never be seen in public without one's stage makeup, but audiences didn't mind. A bit of mystery was appreciated today, especially in an environment where
anything could be known instantly, dissected, and reassembled.
With Grand, though, it had always been different. People accepted him as he was, ghoulish, but soft spoken, a connoisseur of the
gruesome, but always so kind and gentle. In so many ways, he
was the character he played, and he embraced that.

After all of these years, I doubted he was gearing up to retire.
Just last week, as he was concluding his introduction to the
evening's movie, his assistant Wren appeared. She walked right
up to him and thrust a dagger into his neck, blood spurting from
the hole like a fire hydrant wrenched opened on a city street on a
summer's afternoon.

This was the *Grand Vespertilio Show*, with a nod to the terrifying legacy of Paris's Le Théâter du Grand-Guignol, while remaining grounded in the formula laid out before him by earlier American horror hosts, that of casual humor, a bit of cinematic history, and the lingering challenge to be fined by the television censors if he stepped out of bounds.

My phone rings, buzzing and alerting a video call from Bass. Finally.

I answer. Part of Bass's face is missing in the frame. In the background, voices mix and meld into one another, a steady, low hum.

He turns his head, out of focus now. "Sorry about that. Let me find a quiet spot."

He often does this, calls me in progress of finding a suitable place to talk, but I don't mind.

"I was just thinking about you."

He yawns. His eyes are watery and pink.

"You look tired. Where are you now? Hospital?"

He raises his eyebrows and shakes his head no.

Morgue, then.

He nods. "Sorry, I'm going to have to miss tonight."

"I talked to Bruce earlier. He knows you've been busy with work."

"Polly." Bass lowers his voice. "This isn't good. They're taking me off of all of my other cases to work this. It's going to be all over the news. It's bad." He turns around, likely checking who is within earshot. The volume of his voice returns to normal. "Please tell Bruce I am so sorry. I'll swing by to see him tomorrow, if only just for a few minutes."

"Bela's going to be sad to miss you another night."

"I know." He looks pained. "I feel awful about it."

Bass had taken over bedtime duties, making sure Bela got into his pajamas and brushed his teeth. It was Bass who would read books and sing lullabies until our little boy, the one so many medical professionals told us we would never have, drifted away to beautiful sleep. But the past few months, that had changed. We barely saw Bass. It was just Bela and me, and sometimes I wondered, what was the point of Bass's career if it kept him from us?

"You seem worried," he says.

"I'm always worried about Bela."

Sebastian smiles. "You shouldn't be so worried. He's doing great."

"How did his window get opened last night?

"Maybe he was hot and opened it?"

"When weird things like this happen, I worry he doesn't realize what he's doing."

"Yes, worry about him. It's because we worried about him so much that he's doing fine today."

That wasn't an answer. I am scared, scared that there is something unfolding outside of my control. The window. The stories. Whispering to imaginary animals. Then, Bass's question as to Georges Méliès. Theater number five. Then, the sigil today.

"Everything is going to be fine," Bass said, as if he had just read my spiraling thoughts.

That's Bass, always positive, even as he is sitting in the morgue. His nature was to protect me, often keeping things from me about his job so that I would not worry.

He changes the topic. "Have you heard from Grand?"

"No," I say, and reach over and click on my inbox. "And I've only refreshed my emails a hundred times this morning."

Gutierrez pops up behind Bass and waves. "Hey, Polly."

"Hey, G. Bass was telling me you're both going to be a bit."

"I'll make sure he gets some food. Tell Bela I say hi." Gutierrez turns to Bass. "I'm going to grab some coffee. You want?"

"Please." Bass runs his fingers through his dark, greasy hair. He needs to get home, shower, and sleep, but I know that isn't going to happen any time soon.

I look down to my notes and realize what it is I am missing for this program.

"What are you writing?" Bass asks.

"Vincent Price never played a vampire."

Bass laughs. "Thank you, human encyclopedia of all things horror movies."

I turn back to my screen and smile at him. "I was recording part of my Universal vampire series before you called."

Bass rubs his forehead with his free hand and yawns. "Doesn't Grand technically play a vampire?"

That is a mystery as well.

I think of Grand's makeup, the grays and blacks, the shadowy depths of his cheekbones. "He's never really said, but he emerges from a coffin at the beginning of his show and returns to it at the end."

He raises a finger in the air. "Wait, I know this one. He could be a ghoul."

I'm impressed that Sebastian has even picked up some of my horror terminology, knowing there's a difference between ghoul and vampire. "Maybe. He's definitely playing some undead something."

I had certainly picked up on more than enough detective terminology. For instance, there are certain basics around a crime scene and how they are spoken about and managed. From there, the investigation really begins, gathering the victim's name, sex, race, date of birth, address, noting the nature of the injury, obtaining suspect information, documenting if a firearm was used, and if so, the make, model, serial number, and caliber, gathering eyewitness information, establishing the medical personnel on the scene, and, of course, marking the time of death.

Mysteries start and stop with the body.

The initial squad sets up a command post and gives safe

entry to responding units while assuming incident command, and when the sergeant arrives, they take over and inform the dispatcher that they have taken control of the scene.

The fact that Bass is practically tethered to this case and is relieved of all his others screams that there's something different about this one. The department, and the city, really, do not want a repeat of last year.

I hear a familiar south side Chicago accent booming from out of view that it's time to head back to the station.

"McCarthy's there?"

Bass raises his eyebrows and stares into the camera. "Oh yeah."

I know now that whatever happened downtown isn't something that's going to go away any time soon.

"Ramos," McCarthy shouts, shoving his phone into his coat pocket. He's in view behind Bass now, looking around. "Where the hell is Gutierrez?"

"Right there." Bass points out of view.

McCarthy places a hand on Bass's shoulder.

McCarthy takes Bass's phone. "Yeah. Yeah. Yeah. We love you, Polly. We gotta get your husband back to work. Don't worry. We'll keep him safe." He hands the phone back to Bass.

"He seems in a good mood," I say.

"He's probably going to have a heart attack by the end of the day, but yeah, we're all doing as best we can." The sarcasm is very real.

I don't want to ask, but I have to. It's lingering there between us. "Is it worse than Humboldt Park?"

Bass takes a deep breath. "I don't know yet. It could be. We're worried it's connected somehow."

How could that even be possible? "Has anyone reached out to her to ask?"

"No." He shakes his head. "I just don't see how she could

even be involved in this. I heard from the security detail sta-tioned outside her house that she hasn't left in weeks."

"Ramos!"

"I've gotta go." Bass is standing up now. "I'll try to swing by to shower and sleep for a few hours."

"Be careful," I say, and it feels like a weak reminder.

"Polly…" he hesitates.

"Yeah?"

"Just…let me know if anything weird happens. You know, this is kinda horror movie related and all."

"Bass," I look directly in his eyes. "Nothing weird is going to happen to me. You don't have to worry. I'll be fine."

"I love you," he says.

"Forever."

And we end the call.

I'll be with you forever. It was what Bass whispered in my ear as he cradled me on the kitchen floor that night my parents were murdered. He promised he'd never leave me. He promised he'd take care of me, because I didn't even know how to take care of myself. I didn't even know how to simply love myself. Maybe I was a project of his, like his crime cases now, some-thing to work on. Maybe he felt sorry for me, a battered kid who no one really loved. I suppose it doesn't matter. I have someone who takes care of me now, and I guess we don't need any label beyond family to explain what we are, because he is more than my husband. He's my family. I really only hope that no matter what happens, nothing will shake my belief in our forever.

CHAPTER 8

DECEMBER 1999: LUIS

Signs are everywhere. You just have to be receptive to them.

For a long time, I didn't believe in signs—numerology, astrology, tarot cards, none of it—but that changed. Today, the signs are impossible to ignore.

I wake up to my mother vacuuming just outside my bedroom.

"Luis!" she calls. "You're going to be late for your test."

What she really wanted was to yell for me to get out of bed and go look for a job that I would work at and hate until the day I died, only to be replaced days later before my corpse could be buried. My father took great pride in his thirty-one years working at Streets and Sanitation. He suffered a heart attack outside the doors of city hall as he was shoveling snow. I saw his job posted that very next day.

"I'm up," I say. I wasn't going to be late for my test. I was already awake in bed, looking up at my ceiling, thinking about the wonderful building I was going to buy my mother as soon as I could. The money would come. The opportunity would come. Of that, I am certain.

"Hurry up and come eat," she says, this time knocking on my door.

There is this expectation that if you don't leap out of bed, stumble through your bedroom, stub your toe on the edge of your dresser, jump into a cold shower, dress quickly, down your coffee, and burst outside to catch a bus then train downtown to a job you hate and that hates you, that your life does not have meaning. My parent's life's philosophy, and people like them, is completely skewed.

Rush to serve.

Rush to make more money for other people

Move quickly, so as to do a good job. Move silently, so as not to offend with your presence. And in the end, you will have no concept of yourself, with no space for ever truly fulfilling your own wants and needs.

This thought process is all in error. It's a design planted by them, the people who have benefited from controlling us for generations. Because if we are rushing, then we are not thinking. If we are not sitting in silence and reflection, then we are not evolving and expanding into our full potential. Being forced to move. Being forced to be silent. This allows them to control us, and I will never be controlled.

When I wake up in the morning now, the very first thing I do is thank the universe for giving me another day. I imagine all of the good things I want for myself. I play out the day before me in my head, imagining all of the scenarios working out in my favor. When I get out of bed, I sit at my desk, reach for my Lenormand cards, and see what they have to tell me.

I am not my parents, and I am not going to follow the programming they have designed for me, that was designed for them, because it was also how they were taught. I am breaking out of that limited blueprint.

After my father died, my mother Julia's existence was defined by a constant state of worry. How were we going to pay the utilities, rent, food? And then, as her worries intensified, our apartment building was purchased by a developer. We were priced out and pushed out.

Gentrification works fast sometimes.

I'm not saying that her obsession with things getting worse created her reality, but I'm sure it helped to turn the dial. Thoughts become things, I told my mother. If she wants to think the worst, then let her, but I am creating my reality, and suffering is not part of that life.

We waited it out as long as we could, until the pounding came at our door. Eviction. When I turned the doorknob, a sheriff handed me a paper, spoke some words my brain couldn't absorb in the moment as a group of people stepped past me. Our belongings were gathered and tossed outside onto the sidewalk on Wrightwood Avenue, and the locks of our apartment were changed. It was a December evening. A sheet of ice covered the walkway. Snow-slush piles, dotted by long decayed brown autumn leaves, covered the front lawn of the apartment building. People walked past from the Logan Square train station. They gave our discarded items a look of shock and concern, but immediately moved their gaze to the sidewalk in front of them, because in the city, no one wants to help a stranger being kicked out of their home, especially after working all day downtown in a corporate slog of a job.

My mother died a little bit on the sidewalk that day, crying in shame as she looked over her wooden dresser. The dresser drawers holding her slacks, blouses, beige-colored underwear, and bras were all stacked on top of each other, like crooked teeth. Her clothing getting wet from the light iced rain that began to fall. Her leather-bound family photo albums were open, and their plastic coverings were dotted with raindrops. As dirt-stained slush seeped into what little we owned, I promised her I would buy her that entire building one day.

I didn't believe in God, heaven, hell, angels, or demons, but if any of them existed, I promised myself I'd call on all of them to help me to never feel helpless again. This neighborhood, this place, was our home, and I would do everything in my power and beyond to make sure no one ever took anything away from me again.

Today, the numbers on my alarm clock signal things are already going my way. Seven eleven isn't just the name of some convenience store. Those numbers combined mark a sacred numeric series, and if you spot it along your day, especially at the beginning, it means you are spiritually evolving. That is more than enough of a signal for me to wake up and get on with my day.

Later that morning, I was instructed to sit at computer nine for my GMAT. Nine is a powerful number, meaning completeness and perfection. Nearly four hours later when I emerged out of the test onto Jackson Boulevard downtown, it was three degrees outside at 3:33 p.m. I was surrounded by tall buildings full of people who wanted to be anywhere but there. That would not be me. I was already consciously creating my future. When the number three appears in that sequence of numbers it represents a life change. It was then that I was confident my score on the Graduate Management Admission Test would get me into a top-tier MBA program.

You see, the trick isn't affirmations. You can sit there and tell yourself, "I am abundant. I am rich. I am successful," until your mouth goes dry. Saying it does not make it so. You have to believe it, really feel it in your being that you are worthy of all of the greatness the universe has to offer, and I did.

When I descended into the Jackson Blue Line Station, a blast of warm air hit me that smelled like metal and mold. I found the train idling there, almost as if it were waiting for me.

Wait, it *was* waiting for me, I told myself.

I often had to remind myself that I was in control of my thoughts, and in turn I was the creator of my reality. I didn't have to believe. I had to know with full certainty that good things were happening to me and for me. I could feel it, like the bite of wind chill rolling off Lake Michigan. It was the subtle shift I needed to realize that the universe was slowly rearranging itself for me.

When I emerged from the Logan Square Blue Line station, the sun had set, and so much snow had fallen that the city salt trucks had yet to make it to this part of town. They were likely all occupied plowing the Gold Coast up through Lincoln Park, and then once those expensive zip codes were all cleaned up, west of Western could finally dig itself out. People out this way didn't wait for the city to do anything for them.

A man comes walking down the sidewalk, his winter boots crunching in the snow. He wears a heavy coat and knit hat atop his head pulled down over his ears. He carries a bright yellow shovel that is pressed against his left shoulder, holding it steadily there with his workman gloves.

I step out of his way, and then he turns over his shoulder and says above the wind and city noises, "You're always where you're supposed to be."

Residents on the West Side did what they could, keeping their sidewalks, gangways, and alleys cleared so they could make it out to their jobs the next day. Because, even in a snowstorm, most bosses for the people around here expected them to be clocked in and ready to go in the morning.

But not me.

I was already securing my future working for myself in real estate, and if I had to, I'd buy up this entire neighborhood to guarantee I'd never work for anyone else.

The entire morning, test, and first half of my commute had gone smoothly. Now, fighting against the wind and flurries snapping across my face, I could see that there were no visible tire tracks from the bus. It had likely been a good while since it had left the station here, and it would probably still be a good while before another number 56 Milwaukee bus would arrive and take me up to Diversey, where I lived for now with my mom in our aunt's house.

I walked out toward Milwaukee Avenue, searching through the speckled haze of white dots for two large bright headlights signaling the bus's approach, but all I see are the headlights of cars crawling down the street.

The snow digs into the sides of my boots when I step down off the curb and cross the street. I walk past Intelligentsia Coffee, which recently opened, serving expensive coffee to people who have moved into the neighborhood from surrounding states, like Indiana, Wisconsin, Iowa, and Michigan, and who look at me like an outsider when I enter.

That's how urban renewal works. It's insidious. People move in and treat those who have lived in the community before them like they are the foreigner, like they are the strange thing that doesn't belong. What I also know is that this is my home, this neighborhood and this city, and I'm not going to get pushed out to the suburbs or to another state to make room for people who pretend they like the concept of diversity. This is where I belong.

The barista is wiping the counter with a white cloth when I enter. He sets it aside when I step up to the register and order an espresso for here.

He adjusts the glasses on his face. "Would you like Black Cat or Diablo?" Both seem ominous, but Diablo seems appropriate given the weather.

I pay, and shortly after I hear the grinding of the coffee beans, followed by the clinking of the espresso glass being set on its accompanying white porcelain plate. I down my drink and set it on the bar, a little too hard. Two white women seated at the end of the counter stop their conversation and stare in my direction, as if it's some exotic activity watching a Mexican kid drink a single shot of caffeine. I shoot them a smile and then leave. I am always where I am supposed to be, even though my presence is uncomfortable to some.

The wind pushes against me, and I stumble back for a moment before regaining my balance. Then, I see it. In front of me, the faded lights of Logan Theater glow brilliant and gold, beckoning people to enter with the promise of stale popcorn, soda slick floors, and worn fabric seats whose fibers are embedded with the smell of cigarette smoke. It's surprising this place is still in operation. Other old movie theaters have closed on the Northwest Side—the Congress, the Patio, and more.

Logan Theater was one of a few old movie theaters offering cheap tickets priced about the same as I could pay to rent a film at Blockbuster Video. People have moved on to theaters with re-clining leather seats, multi screens, and sound systems that seep into your insides. Basic concession stand fare wasn't enough to draw people in. People wanted more. People always wanted more, even though they often didn't know exactly what it was they wanted.

The pro of the Logan Theater was watching a film on a large screen for very cheap. The con was the smell of urine that wafted out of the men's rooms into the hallway and the strange characters who would pay a few dollars to watch a film, but in turn would stay the entire day, shuffling from screen to screen. It wasn't dangerous at Logan. It was just…sad because you knew as soon as you walked in that it was a place that was once spec-tacular, a palace, but today that glory was long stained, faded, and cracked.

It had been years since I'd come here. The last time was when I was in high school, when I should have been in class, and I ducked inside when I saw a patrol car approach. The police didn't come inside to look for me, and so I stayed and watched *The Exorcist III*. I'd heard rumors that the place was getting cleaned up, and by cleaned up I assumed I wouldn't be kicking around leftover empty Mad Dog blue raspberry wine and forty-ounce beer bottles on the floor. Perhaps it'd get sold and turned into one of those fancy movie theaters. In that moment, I imagined this place belonging to me, and what I could do with it—a bar, a lounge area in back that could be used for small events, and updated bathrooms honoring its glamorous 1920s roots.

I didn't believe in things like purpose or destiny before, but I knew I was meant to pause in front of the Logan Theater tonight, to read those letters on the marquee, and to walk up to the ticket booth and to ask for a single ticket to see *The Exorcist III* once again after all of these years. The same movie played when I needed a safe place to hide, like tonight. It wasn't just a sign, the universe was screaming at me to take notice of everything around me.

The box office was manned by a gentleman who didn't even look up from his *Chicago Sun-Times* as he took my two dollars and fifty cents and handed out a red ticket stub that said ADMIT ONE.

Inside, the sun faded red carpeted floor was sticky; yes, a carpeted floor was sticky. The entryway led to a single dimly lit hallway and on the left-hand side was a series of short hallways leading to one of the five screens, but before I went and found my seat, I knew I should speak to her.

I see her standing behind the concession stand on the right, a book open on top of the glass case. When I pulled my two Lenormand cards this morning, I selected the book and the woman. Two cards with one combined meaning, and that meaning was standing right in front of me.

I hesitate before moving forward.

At the counter she doesn't even look up from her book as I approach. "What do you want?" She turns a page and I try to focus on the title, but she tells it to me instead. She places her index finger in between the pages, closes the cover, and says, "*Legion*."

"The sequel," I say, referring to *The Exorcist*.

"I heard." She reaches in front of the register and grabs a straw from the dispenser, which then takes the place of her index finger as a bookmark.

"Have you seen the movie?" I point a thumb behind me, and she raises an eyebrow.

"Part of the perks of working here. I saw the movie first and figured I'd read the book."

"Which do you like more?"

"From what I've read, I like them both." She pushes the book aside. "What do you want?"

I want whatever she can give me, and since I don't really know what that is yet, I settle for a small popcorn.

She sets the small popcorn down for me, which I won't eat, but that gives me a few more minutes to talk to her. I reach for my wallet and hand her a few bills. I want to tell her everything I know about the operations and the sigils as she hands me my change, but I know she will never believe me.

She opens the book, sets aside the bookmark straw, and resumes reading.

"I'm Luis," I say.

Without looking up, she points to the nametag on the left side of her chest. "Be careful in theater five."

"Why's that?"

She turns a page. "It's haunted."

That's it, the other sign I've been waiting for.

"Thanks for the warning. I'll see you around, Polly," I say, knowing it's not just a saying or a wish, because the universe has already told me she is my future.

CHAPTER 9

FRIDAY AFTERNOONG: PALOMA

My eyes move to the bottom bookshelf across the room, to the large black book I could not part with, no matter how many times I said I would. I knew all it would take would just be one simple operation, some lines or movements, words spoken, and it could be done. Some people called it ritual, but in this book, they were known as operations. I knew I could make Grand contact me using a simple operation from the book, even though I promised myself I wouldn't turn to that route anymore.

Ritual. Operation. Magick.

I did carry some fear in knowing I could make whatever I desired manifest. All I needed to do was to believe, to know, to choose the appropriate operation and execute it to its completion, and I did that, for a long time. I hid my practice of magick from Bass, because as I learned, a true high magician never allows their efforts to be known by non-magicians. I stopped practicing magick that day in Logan Theater, the very day I had summoned them all. I wanted to conjure them someplace powerful and so I chose theater number five, but when I saw those images streak across the screen I panicked and left.

I lay my head back against the computer chair. How could manipulating what should be allowed to play out naturally be bad? What was good? What was evil? Did either really matter?

We have forgotten about duality, that both can and should exist, just like angels and demons, who are really two sides of the same coin, as neither can exist without the other.

Maybe that's what is wrong with this, all of this. Life. We are allowing life to happen to us and we are not taking charge and commanding things to be as we want them to be. We have more power than we know.

Thoughts. Words. Breath.

That's all it takes to change one's reality.

Sometimes, even less.

This is in part why films are magick themselves, because they manipulate what we believe to be real and not. Bela Lugosi knew this, Boris Karloff, Lon Chaney, the man of a thousand faces, knew this as well, as did the very man who started to experiment with perception on screen, Georges Méliès. And, of course, Grand knows this, as did all horror hosts before him. Films distort our reality, if just for a few hours, and we are active participants, embracing the deceit, the manipulation, and accepting the reality that is spread before us, for that short amount of time.

The founders of filmmaking knew the power they had discovered. Not just those early filmmakers, but those early movie palace designers, the movie palace owners and workers, because they knew film deserved a cathedral, a holy sanctuary, where the masses could come and worship black and white magick on a silver screen.

Those words, lines, and characters flickering in and out of the light, many of them came with messages that can't be ignored. Chicago didn't ignore it. Balaban and Katz, who owned a chain of over fifty movie palaces in the Chicagoland area didn't ignore it. Nor did architectural firm Rapp and Rapp, who designed the ornate buildings, with marble statues, grand murals, soaring ceilings, and entryways.

Film is an alchemical process, a process of change.

And my brother and I were alchemists, magicians. Noel promised me that all we needed to do was utter a few words to make the change we needed, and I remember those words now: "The process is simple. The reward is great. You just need to speak the words to finish it all."

And so, like the desperate children we were—we did.

Just like a collection of images gathered together on film. It's all more than just an image. It's all magick. On that night so long ago, we concentrated on a series of symbols, in that very book that sits on my shelf now, as the red fluorescent lights of the Logan Theater sign pulsated just outside my bedroom window.

My brother wished for life, and I wished for death.

Words on a page meant and intended to reshape and shift. And isn't that what language is? What art is? What film is meant to do? Reshape and shift? Abracadabra. I speak, therefore it is. My brother redesigned our lives that night. Was it moral? What was morality when I feared that each night in that apartment would be my last as the beatings escalated? What did right and wrong matter when I needed to save my life? There was no lesson in this other than I needed to do what I could to survive.

My computer pings, indicating an email message has come through, followed by the notification at the upper righthand of my screen. The name of the sender, Quasimodo. The subject line: The film.

I turn to my email and open the message. There is only a single question:

"Where is the film?"

I sit there for a moment, rereading the question, trying to piece together what it is they are exactly inquiring about, and then settle with the most logical answer: it is just another strange person in a long line of people who find it acceptable to harass me through the digital veil. People email me to complain about anything and everything, what I wore, what I didn't wear, my makeup or lack thereof, my movie selection, the historical analysis I provided was too much, not enough, that it was inaccurate, how I spoke, and any other perceived missteps along the way. So many people find sport in tearing down someone that exists to them only digitally.

I've always believed one creates their own reality, each moment and each day. So what I always found so strange about people who harass strangers online is that they are willingly enveloping themselves in negativity when they could just do something else, something better with their life.

At first the criticism hurt. How could talking about horror movies, my absolute love, turn into a negative experience? People, I later learned, will try to strip you of any of your joy because there are those threatened by the happiness of others. And so, what happened? I spiraled back to that little girl crying into her pillow at night. Bass told me I couldn't allow people to abuse me, that other people's perceptions of me were not me, and that there were individuals out there who scoured the world searching for something to be offended by, and for someone to hurt.

I spent so much of my life trying to avoid upsetting people. It was all internalized conditioning from fear of upsetting my parents, my mother in particular. Because if I upset my mother, that would quickly make me a victim of one of her violent episodes. I had to learn that I cannot be everything to everyone, and if someone left an offensive comment on my page, or made fun of the way I looked, or how I managed my program, their perception of me was not me.

I accepted that, in many ways, I existed under a microscope, even though I worked from home for myself. As a horror influencer, every aspect of my online life is open to critique, given some viewers feel they have ownership over every aspect of my life, including this individual disrupting my privacy now.

This is all part of being online and exposed. Bass had gotten recommendations and tips from his cybersecurity team on how I could best protect myself and my privacy, but the nature of a troll is ultimately disruption. People savor the idea of knowing their message will be seen by you and that you will be injured by their words. It is elementary school bullying made adult and dangerous. What I learned was this: never address their harm in public and never respond to their attacks because their egos are fed by attention.

I move my curser over and click on delete. There is a whoosh sound as the email disappears, but then there is another ping. A new notification appears on my screen. It is from the same sender, with the same subject line as before, the body still reading: "Where is the film?"

For a moment I think it's a mistake. Maybe the original message didn't delete. I click on the icon to discard the message. The electronic alert indicates the email is now gone. Immediately, another a chime notifies me a new message is waiting.

Same sender. Same subject line. Same question.

I turn to my channel, scrolling through my recent posts to try to understand what film they could possibly be referencing. There were no controversial films in my recent history. It's not like I'd discussed *Nekromantik* or *A Serbian Film*, which I know are too intense for my wide-ranging audience. My show was definitely not the place for hardcore horror reviews. I kept things, for the most part, PG-13 and R, given I wanted to be sure I had material I could watch with Bela.

I stayed away from heated debates with my audience and tried to mediate any tense discussions among my viewers. Still, some people were sensitive about their art and did not like the things they enjoyed being analyzed. Because of this, I had always made sure when talking about a film to never use words or phrases such as, "I liked it," "I hated it," "This was good," or, "This was bad." Reducing a horror movie, any work of art, really, to these degrees felt simplistic. Art is subjective and everyone should be allowed to like the creations they enjoy, while not having to feel pressured by another's preferences.

I search again through my show notes. The titles had been clearly stated. I had even prepared my audience for weeks that we would be discussing Universal Monsters this year, and that this week we would be focusing on the seven Universal Studio films in which Dracula appears.

I delete another email, but a new one appears, only this time the subject line is different. "READ ME"

The body says:

Vassago tells me you have seen the film. You will show it to me. If not, there will be another stage performance. Their blood will spread across floorboards, shining like constellations, and their screams will reverberate down corridors and I will delight in their suffering, and you shall suffer in knowing more will come until you tell me where the film is.

The movies, how powerful they are.

Lumière knew it, as did Méliès, and, Paloma, you have always known this as well too. You are like them. I suppose this explains your lifelong interests. "As above, so below, as within, so without, as the universe, so the soul," as Hermes said.

Is this why you are so afraid to leave your house? Crippled by the possibility that so much is attainable with just a few words? It's frightening, isn't it? This power. I suppose you're afraid to explore more, given your protectiveness over Bela.

Chicago seemed a fitting place for the movie to be stored, don't you think? It's cold here, and that deep chill sinks within, leaving so many numb to the dark and wicked truth that this life can all be manipulated so easily.

I will see you soon. I know this because it's always been a part of our great design.

Bela. The sender mentioned Bela, and Vassago. How could they know? How could anyone know what one does in the privacy of their own home, and what lives in their very minds? I've never told anyone, including Noel. For years I tried to ignore what was done, refusing even to open the book for future petitions.

I look to the bottom bookcase, and all of those books that line that shelf, the ones Bass asked me about only once, to which I responded, "I just keep them around for movie research." It was like they existed behind an imaginary barrier. In case of emergency break glass.

Vassago. I know the name. After my parents died, I spent time memorizing the names and keys, because there was so much time to finally sit and think without the fear of my mother's anger pressing so closely. In an instant of violence both she and my father were gone, and I was left in that apartment, alone.

I reach for the large dictionary and wipe away the thin layer of dust that accumulated along its spine. The table of contents instructs me to turn to page 396.

Vassago is depicted like a hideous sea witch. The image is made from a medieval woodcut. Its face is of a dragon, with curved horns atop its head and its body is that of a monstrous mermaid.

Vassago: The third demon named in the Ars Goetia is said to be the finder of lost things and can speak to matters of the past and future.

The sender of the email knew what they were talking about because they were communicating something the demon had told them, which meant they brought the demon into full existence. Theirs is not a quick request. This isn't a novice working for their first time using the principles of low magick—herbs, oils, incense, and candles—which could be used easily by anyone and everyone. Low magick appeals to the masses because it is fool-proof in many ways, because the magick resides within the oil and the herbs themselves, your tools. All you need to do is come to the working with the right intention before you proceed with acting out your spell. Then from there you anoint your candle and light the wick.

High magick is different. You become the magickal thing. You become the tool, and the only way to do this is through intense meditation, purification, and ritual. You speak the words. You believe in the result.

It can take months, years, really, to become proficient in visualization, directing energy, the middle pillar, lesser banish-ing ritual of the pentagram, the rose cross ritual, the ritual of the hexagram, celestial lotus, shem operation, and calling on the angels, or demons.

High magick is ultimately a series of rituals used to promote enlightenment, in this life and beyond. There's a point between this world and our death, an abyss, and to cross that abyss we must let go of all of our attachments to the ego, to things in this world, including the material.

Magick is not a belief or religion. Magick is a system of ritu-al, meditation, and prayer that works to shape our reality.

Bass cannot know any of this, or else he'll be at risk. And so, just like with high magick, I'll have to keep this from him.

"Vassago." I say the name without intending to do so. It merely slipped off my tongue. The evocation keys then activat-ed on their own. My thoughts drift to a shiny black surface like that of melted glass, with the rough texture of charcoal. I smell the sharp scent of burnt leaves. My stomach turns when I taste stagnant water in my mouth. The evocation keys are the specific images, sensations, and tastes associated with a demon to stir it so that it can become aware of the one calling it.

Each of the seventy-two demons have their own series of evocation keys, and I memorized all of them.

"I didn't mean to call you," I say. I close my eyes and take a deep breath because I know whoever sent that email is an established occultist, and it seems like they also know I am one too.

My email pings again, and again.

CHAPTER 10

FRIDAY AFTERNOON: SEBASTIAN

It seems like all of homicide is here at the precinct waiting on Commander McCarthy. I'm tacking up the official photographs taken by the evidence tech whose eyes were wide as he handed them over to me.

"You alright?" I asked.

Their voice is low. "Never seen anyone do that with a popcorn scoop."

"Maybe you should stick to nachos the next time you catch a movie," I said, but they didn't seem amused and headed out the door.

Most of the seats in the room are taken and we can all hear McCarthy shouting from his office. He's on the phone with the mayor, who's demanding the Chicago Theater reopen. The city doesn't like it when crime spills over to its tourist destinations. It's bad for business.

I personally think we should start thinking about patrolling more movie theaters, but that's a fight I'll have with McCarthy later.

Gutierrez is sitting in the front row, scrolling through his phone. We've been ordered by the department not to talk to media. So far no one's talked, not about what happened last night or what happened last year.

The official word about what happened in Humboldt Park last year was Detective Van was killed by a young man. Detective Medina continues to dispute that story, which is why she's working desk duty from home. The last time she was in the station and someone said Detective Van was murdered by Detective Medina's mentee, Medina jumped over a desk and put that person in a chokehold until they passed out on the floor.

Rutkowski enters, another newly minted detective of the dead. She put in a lot of time on the street, in vice then robbery, before being tapped for homicide while on patrol. Rutkowski said she'd never thought of homicide as a career. She said she liked working in the community, getting to know neighbors. After seeing how poorly things were handled last year, though, she stepped into homicide saying the dead deserved better.

McCarthy bursts through the doors. He's scratching his chin and murmuring to himself as he walks down the aisle, the room on either side staring at him.

He takes an aisle seat in the front row across from Gutierrez, crosses his legs, and says, "This is your show, Ramos." He waves a large hand at me when I don't move fast enough. "Why aren't you at the board? Get over there." He interlocks his fingers and leans forward.

I run my hand down the ledge of the whiteboard. "Does anyone have a marker?"

McCarthy takes a deep breath, closes his eyes, and runs his hand down his face. "Gutierrez, can you please get your partner together?"

"I got it, detective," Officer Jones in the back says as he stands up, goes to the desk in the corner, retrieves a dry erase marker, and brings it over to me.

"Look at that." McCarthy gives a slow clap. "Working together. Taxpayers would be thrilled to know it only took three people to make that work."

Officer Jones moves to head back to his seat when McCarthy tells him to stay right where he is. "Actually, you go first. Tell us what's in the report. If you missed anything, just fill us in and start at the beginning."

Officer Jones looks from McCarthy to me, but I can't save the rookie. His hands are clasped together in front of his bullet proof vest.

His voice shakes and then he shoves his hands in his black pant pockets.

"Saturday around ten thirty p.m. we get a call—"

"Who's 'we'? Who's your partner?"

"Delgado." He nods to the back of the room.

Heads turn and Delgado raises a hand from a seat beside the door.

"You shy or something, Delgado? Why're you hiding over there?" McCarthy waves her down.

"I, um…" Delgado stands up.

"Get up here."

Delgado walks along the side of the room, her hands in tight fists, and she stands beside her partner.

"Was this the shooting outside Walgreens over on Randolph and Michigan?"

I uncap the marker and write down: *Walgreens. 10:30 p.m. Fight.*

"What does any of this matter?" I ask.

"Ramos," McCarthy says. "That's your problem. You don't have any patience. You gotta connect everything together, but you need some damn patience to do that. Just listen."

Officer Jones continues. "No, no shooting. Just hands."

McCarthy points. "Delgado, what happens next?"

She stands erect. "We get a call that someone's been hurt at the Chicago Theater. It's about six forty-three p.m. at this point."

"This is you, Ramos." McCarthy is nodding. "Get it on the board."

I write down: *Chicago Theater. 6:43 p.m.*

I'm thinking of the distance between the Walgreens on Michigan Avenue and the Chicago Theater on State Street. "It takes you how long to get there?"

"We get in the car. Drive. And we're there in less than five minutes." Delgado turns her back to the room, facing the white board.

"What did you see?" I press the tip of the marker to the board.

"There was a small crowd of people outside waiting. It looked like the doors hadn't opened yet."

I write *small crowd* on the white board.

"Who opens the door for you?"

"One of the ushers. He was really shaken up. He didn't want to go back inside. He told us, 'On the stage. On the stage.' And he stood there by the door until we came back."

I write *usher* and ask for the name.

McCarthy is leaning back in his chair right now, looking from Delgado to me and back.

"So, you enter the theater and what do you see?" I ask.

"It's completely dark except for the center stage light. The victim was not moving at all. We could tell right away they were not in good shape."

Officer Jones interrupts. "I called for medical help right away, then for backup."

"Good job using your personal phone," McCarthy says.

"A lot of people got police scanner apps," Gutierrez says from his seat in front of me. "They could've been listening in, waiting for when we arrived."

I turn from the board and face McCarthy. "You're saying you're going to pay for my personal phone too?"

There are spots of laughter throughout the room.

McCarthy raises his eyebrows. "No," he says pointedly, and the laughter subsides. "Alright." He's craning his neck, trying to look around me to get a view of the board. "Where are we at with all of this, Ramos?"

I cap the marker and step out of the way, scanning what I've written down so far. "There's going to be another victim. I can almost guarantee it. William Heirens didn't stop after he kidnapped, cut up, and scattered six-year-old Suzanne Degnan's body throughout Evanston's sewers…"

"Who?" Gutierrez asks.

McCarthy answers. "The Lipstick Killer. Look it up."

"Not just Heirens. Joseph Miller killed two women, was locked up, released, and then killed four more people in the seventies and eighties. Andre Crawford killed over eleven women in Englewood in the nineties. Robin Gecht, Edward Spreitzer, and brothers Andrew and Thomas Kokoraleis raped, mutilated, and killed eighteen women. John Wayne Gacy killed thirty-three, that we know of, hiding the bodies of most under his house and dumping others in the waterways."

"Ramos," McCarthy interrupts. "I appreciate this history lesson. I really do, but what the hell does this have to do with anything?"

"We're dealing with the mind of a serial killer."

"Whoa!" McCarthy throws his hands up. "Ramos, you have nothing to go by that we're dealing with a serial killer, and if you start spreading the S word around here, people are going to either get real scared real fast or think you ain't right."

"By their very nature, a serial killer is a manipulative narcissist. They're egocentric. There's often some fantasy in place." I return to the board. "Some belief that's fueling this desire, and this one has something to do with movies. I think he specifically chose this victim. He knew she was going to be there, nearly alone at this time. He was familiar with the theater enough to know that a side door would be unlocked for staff. He is also comfortable with the layout of the interior. He's been there multiple times, and I bet he's been there again, if not inside, then certainly outside since the murder. This killer, though, he's not a nobody. He's successful. I guess in a way all serial killers are, because they've successfully killed several people undetected until suspicion of their activity arose. We have to be ahead of them."

"I disagree on all counts," Detective Boyd says. His face is always severe, and it sounds like everything that comes out of his mouth is a personal attack. "This is some pissed off ex-partner, stalker something. Look into her recent associates and relationships. Check her socials."

"We've started. No social media history. No recent relationships. All immediate family is deceased. We're looking into everyone she's had contact with recently." I want to conclude my response to him with, "You asshole," but McCarthy's face is already covered in red splotches.

McCarthy leans forward in his seat. He clears his throat. "Ramos…"

"I'm not wrong," I say. "I need everyone I can get on this. I especially need our occult expert—"

"Wait, we have one of those?" Detective Rutkowsi says. "I thought Richter retired."

"He did, and it's probably what you need right now, an expert, because Ramos has this all wrong," Detective Boyd answers, with that smug look on his face I just want to rip off.

"Let me guess. Florida, where he's living comfortably off a blue state's pension." I feel my phone vibrate in my back pocket. It is probably Polly. I haven't had an extended moment of privacy to speak to her about all of this. A death with a horror movie figuring prominently. It was strange. It was worrisome. Polly loved all things horror movies, and while my mind didn't want to drift there, that she could somehow be at risk, I couldn't help thinking it. I needed to answer as much as I could as quickly as I could, and then make sure she was okay.

McCarthy scanned the room. "Guess that's you now, Ramos."

I wanted to laugh. "How? I don't have any experience in the occult."

"I had three detectives resign last month." He holds up three fingers on one hand and four fingers on the other. "Four retired earlier this month, and let's not forget the two we lost last year." He lowers his hands.

"I wasn't suggesting it was the occult," I say, although, I'm not denying that either. We had yet to understand the markings drawn on the stage in blood and their meaning.

"Is it occult? Or is it a distraction to make it look like the occult because of everything that happened in Humboldt Park?" Detective Rutkowski asks. "It could just as easily have been a thrill killing. Just look at the pictures. There's utter chaos there. Rage. Concession items are ripped open and thrown everywhere. There's liquid pooling across the stage, except for around the victim. But this doesn't look like it was carefully planned. At least that's not how I'm interpreting these images."

I look at the pinned image of the symbol. "This took time."

Detective Boyd crosses his arms across his chest and clears his throat. "If this is a serial killer, and I'm not saying this is a serial killer because we have no evidence suggesting such… well, if it is…we're all going to be in a bad spot, especially after Detective Medina."

This is true. Most people didn't know exactly what went down in Humboldt Park last year with Detective Medina. It was impossible to keep everything out of the media, but what was public was enough to make the city erupt. Protests were organized in front of the mayor's house for weeks, quieting only recently because of the cold. A growing number of aldermen were calling to defund the police. The national news blasted Chicago as corrupt and violent, and both sides of the political aisle took glee in pointing out our city's faults.

On one side, we had a homicide detective engaged in roughing up suspects and criminals to garner confessions and prosecutions. On the other side, we had a community outraged that a dead teenager was accused of killing Detective Medina's partner. The community believed it was all a department cover up to continue protecting one of their own, Medina. And all of this happening the same year our homicide count hit over one thousand in the county.

"Oh good, looks like you have an assistant occult expert, Ramos." McCarthy stood up. "If you need any help, ask Detective Rutkowski."

They tapped me right out of the academy, straight to undercover. I've worked vice, narco, and now homicide. I knew how to break up an illegal gambling ring, detect the unlawful production and distribution of pornography, and while I respected sex workers, I did not respect the pimps who trafficked, used, and abused them—I loved getting those guys of the streets. Working narco taught me about the specialized distribution system that ran across the city, a multilayered spiderweb stretching into the suburbs. We know Chicago as a city of neighborhoods, seventy-seven neighborhoods, in fact, with names like Archer Heights, Edison Park, Lincoln Square, Old Town, Streeterville, and West Pullman. But there's another map, the Chicago Gang Map, that segregates neighborhoods based on which gangs run it. Spanish Cobras, who covered parts of Logan Square, Gangster Disciples, who covered parts of Garfield Park, and the list goes on.

Because of my time in narco, I had confidential informants from the North Shore down through Indiana, and west heading into St. Louis. What's the saying? I know a guy who knows a guy. Well, I knew all the guys from my time on narco, from the OGs to the shorties to the shooters, including the hit squads.

I knew Chicago's streets.

I knew who ran the neighborhoods.

What I did not know was anything at all having to do with the occult.

"Wait, I don't have any experience in this."

McCarthy smiles. "But you ask good questions."

I hold back a laugh. "Am I going to get paid more?"

"Of course not."

"This is bullshit."

"Welcome to homicide, detective," he says, taking his phone out of his pocket and tapping away at the screen. "Get your plan together and we'll get you what you need."

Detective Boyd stands up and scans the pinned photographs. "Wait, no juju bees?"

"Are you serious right now, Boyd?"

He smirks. "Thought I'd ask."

Officer Delgado comes closer to look over the photographs. She nods at one of the images. "There are juju bees. Right there, look."

McCarthy closes his eyes and rubs his temples. "You all are the reason I'm retiring at the end of the year."

I look over my notes on the white board that include:

- *Motivation*
- *Similar murders*
- *Interview friends and family*
- *Symbols, what do they mean?*
- *Poster, where is it from?*

Gutierrez leans forward in his seat. "So, what *do* we got? We got movies. Candy. The occult."

I turn to Officer Jones, who has been quiet. "Was there anything else you noticed on the scene?"

There's a trace of a frown on his face, and then he says, "The poster...and the way her body was...cut."

"I'm having a movie expert look at the poster," I say. "And we're seeing the ME after this."

"When do we get the results back from the medical examiner?" Gutierrez asks, checking his phone.

"Full autopsy? We're looking at a week to ten days."

McCarthy's phone rings once and it's nearly instantly pressed to his ear. "Yeah, mayor. We're finishing our meeting with the rest of the department. We've got our best on this." His voice fades as he exits the room. Others follow.

I'm staring at the pictures now, trying to weave together a tale. "What's the motivation?" I whisper to myself, but Gutierrez is at my side and he answers.

"Not everyone is going to be driven by a motivation. Some things just are. We think of the world as too black and white, good and bad, a moral to every story.

The meaning is in front of us, I know it, but we don't yet have a full grasp on the story. I start removing the pictures from the board, plucking out one thumbtack at a time. "That's because there is a moral to every story, even if that moral is just madness," I say.

"Now I know you've been watching a lot of horror movies with Polly. You're starting to sound all dark and philosophical like her."

That was Polly, always searching for meaning, for any sign of life stirring in death.

"We'll need to know everything about the victim, and fast, because someone who kills like this isn't looking for just attention. They're looking to send a message, and if that message isn't answered we're going to be seeing a lot more bodies like this across the city."

CHAPTER 10

FRIDAY AFTERNOON, BEFORE SCHOOL PICK UP: SEBASTIAN

After a short virtual meeting with one of my local coffee sponsors, I get back to recording my program for tonight.

Bass always thought it was funny that many of my sponsors were coffee related, even though I couldn't drink it myself. It made me too jittery, and I already lived in a heightened sense of awareness each day. I didn't need the additional jolt of anxiety caffeine promised. I already had enough to worry about during my day to day. At least he benefited from all of the extra coffee we had in the house all of the time.

I check my email once more, just in case, but the harassing messages ceased after I marked the sender as spam. Still, there were reasons to worry—the sigil on Bela's tablet, and the name of one of the goetic demons mentioned in a strange email all in one day. Was it coincidence? Synchronicity? Something more?

So much of our fears about the demonic are drawn from Judeo-Christian demonology, sourced from the New Testament. What many don't realize is that demons are much, much older, informed not just by the ancient Babylonians, but thousands of years further back to the Sumerians.

Those ancients knew that the name of the demon could do more than draw that being's attention. That very demonic name could also compel and control the entity, giving the summoner power.

Demons are much more complex than people think, or than horror novels and movies would have us believe.

Some think they're just ghastly energies that infiltrate a human's body, putrefying flesh and spirit, driving the possessed to cannibalize their spouses and drown their children in scalding hot bathtubs, but that's not so. People in modern society still say, "The devil made me do it," when accused of crimes they verily wanted to commit.

Don't blame demons for your own heart.

Demons are complex, unlike their portrayal in *The Evil Dead*, *Night of the Demons*, *The Exorcism of Emily Rose*, *Insidious*, *Noroi: The Curse*, and *The Possession*. Demons have structure, titles and ranks, a royal hierarchy, an order reflective of feudal European society. There are demons devoted to the cardinal directions, planetary associations, every planetary hour, day of the week, and so much more. These timeless, earthly entities are present in every aspect of our physical world, you just need to utter their name and they will come.

Yes, there are demons associated with destruction and illness, but there are also demons associated with love, lust, abundance, healing, wealth, and power. You don't need to sell your soul, but you do have to make an offering, and it all starts with simply uttering a name.

The Sumerians knew this.

The Babylonians knew this too.

Much of what these early people knew we've relegated to childish myth or legend, to fairy tales, but so much of these old beliefs are true. We're just too clouded by our worldly distractions, too distracted by the screens and socio-political media scandals to realize we're all capable of tapping into magick. We're all capable of directing the outcomes of our lives.

Demons will forever allure us, in movies, in crime, and when bad dreams stir us awake, or when we're alone in our houses and see jagged shadows stretch across our walls.

My email pings, and I'm reminded I don't have much time to wrap up this episode. I check my inbox and it's a payment confirmation from one of my sponsors. Coffee doesn't pay too bad. There will be more than enough time later to talk to Bela about demons and to think through those harassing emails.

I sit cross-legged on my chair and shove my hands in my *Carnival of Souls* hoodie, with an image of the Man, or the main ghoul, reaching out to Mary Henry. I scan my notes once more, in the event the teleprompter app fails on me again like it did before when I was discussing *Dead Man's Eyes*. In that film, Lon Chaney Jr. plays artist David Stuart. Stuart is blinded, but he's told by his soon to be father-in-law that as soon as a benefactor dies, Stuart can have their eyes implanted. When the donor dies mysteriously, Stuart becomes suspected of murder.

That's the key to horror, and all mysteries, really, the killer is very often presented to us early on, otherwise we feel betrayed as a viewer or reader.

I check my chair's positioning in the camera frame. I stand and reach in front of me and adjust the ring light just an inch to my right. Back in the chair, I hit record.

"Before we go into today's movie, I first want to talk about its star. You'll notice that their last name is familiar. Much like his father, Lon Chaney Jr. is known as a Hollywood legend. He's most famously known for his role in Universal's 1941 *The Wolf Man* as Larry Talbot. One evening, Talbot is attacked and bitten by a werewolf. A fortuneteller confesses that her son Bela transforms into a werewolf, and it was he who bit Talbot, and is thus the cause of his lycanthropy.

"Lon Chaney Jr. also reprised his role as the Wolf Man two years later in *Frankenstein Meets the Wolf Man*. What a lot of people don't realize is that Lon Chaney Jr. stands out from other Hollywood horror legends like Boris Karloff, Bela Lugosi, and later key figures we'll discuss in coming weeks.

"Right after *The Wolf Man*, in 1942, Universal offered Lon Chaney Jr. the role of Frankenstein's Monster in *The Ghost of Frankenstein* after Boris Karloff declined to reappear as Mary Shelley's legendary figure.

"If you're following me," I say jotting down on my notepad a quick reminder to place a graphic in this section, "in 1941, Lon Chaney Jr. appeared as the Wolf Man. Then the next year, in 1942, he played Frankenstein's Monster. Now, 1942 was a pretty busy year for Universal Studios and our actor, because that same year he appeared in *The Mummy's Tomb* as, you probably have guessed it already, the Mummy.

"Now, what are we missing?"

I pause the recording and reach for the glow in the dark vampire teeth sitting on my desk that seem to never really glow that well. But they'd do for a silly effect for now.

"You are correct," I say, my voice muffled with the plastic covering my teeth. I pause the recording again and remove the vampire teeth and toss them in my garbage can.

"In 1943, Lon Chaney Jr. played the role of Count Dracula in *Calling Dr. Death*. This makes Lon Chaney Jr. not only an icon of Universal monsters for his role as the Wolf Man but the only actor to have ever played all four of the major Universal Monsters, the Wolf Man, Frankenstein's Monster, the Mummy, and Dracula."

I pause the recording and look at the names written on the next page: Lon Chaney Jr., Boris Karloff, and Bela Lugosi. I remembered when Bass asked what I wanted the baby's name to be. There was never any doubt it would be Bela. When I told him, he smiled.

"That's perfect, and a middle name?" he asked the day we moved into our house. All that we owned was stacked in the living room in cardboard boxes. We sat on our wooden floor, a blanket laid out beneath us as a temporary dining table, and ate pizza off paper plates.

The middle name was a little more difficult to decide than the first. The obvious choices seemed to be Boris or Lon, but after I re-watched *Theater of Blood*, the decision was clear.

I wiped my face with a napkin and said, "Vincent, after Vincent Price," waiting for his reaction.

Beside him on the floor, his phone vibrated. He paused to read the message before it disappeared from the screen. I wondered if he didn't rush out to respond to that message now, then when? Would he miss our baby's first steps, first words, birthdays? How much of his family's life was he willing to sacrifice for a career I didn't really feel comfortable with?

"Bass…you're off today."

"Right." He looked up and met my eyes. "Creepy British guy, right? On *Sesame Street*?"

Bass knew very little about horror movies then, and he knows very little about horror movies now, but he did know more than enough about human tragedy. In just a few years he had seen more death than most will experience in a lifetime.

A few months after moving into our house, Bela Vincent came, and while Bass was at work, I was alone to wake up every few hours to feed and change Bela. Our new baby never went back to sleep quickly after waking, and so, it was downstairs to the sofa. In my delirious post-partum state, lacking sleep, covered in breast milk, and wondering if and when my husband would come home from work alive, I did what always brought me comfort—I watched horror movies. But now, I had someone else to watch them with me, my little Bela.

One particularly grueling night last year, sirens blared outside our windows, speeding down Fullerton Avenue, heading east. It sounded like every single squad car in the city was summoned—a chorus of despair. Bela was no longer an infant, but a little boy with a sizzling fever. When I went to give him Tylenol, he slapped the spoon out of my hand, splashing the sticky red liquid all over the hardwood kitchen floor. He screamed for me to get away from him, and I could not do anything but collapse on the floor in exhaustion, leaning my head back against the kitchen cabinet and cry. The call would come later from Bass that Detective Van, Bela's godfather, had been killed. When Bela approached me as I cried in the kitchen, he thought I was mad at him. I wasn't. I was just too torn to tell him about how death is our only guarantee in life.

We later found ourselves on the sofa, turning to *Edward Scissorhands*, because there was nowhere else to turn to in the media madness that followed. Edward, played by Johnny Depp, listened as his father, The Inventor, played by Vincent Price, read him a humorous poem. At the poem's conclusion, Edward was unsure how he should react. Should he laugh? Should he smile? What is poetry supposed to make us feel?

The Inventor, like a proud father, encourages him: "Go ahead and smile. It's funny," The Inventor said with a comforting smile. The camera focused on Edward, whose lips drew upward into an awkward smile, insinuating it was one of his firsts.

When I looked down at Bela that night, I found some comfort that he had finally fallen asleep, watching a horror movie icon he had been named after, even as sirens continued to blare in the distance.

Even in my tragedies of adulthood, horror continued to be there.

I turn back to my computer, ready to hit record, when I hear

Romero whine and scratch at the living room door. I brush it off as perhaps someone walking past our gate, or maybe there is a package being delivered given that Bass is always ordering something online. The house security system beeps, indicating it is being disarmed.

The sounds of keys in the door are greeted by Romero's barking.

"It's me!' Bass shouts from downstairs. I hear him walking up the steps now.

"Why didn't you call me to tell me you were on your way?"

Bass kneels, rubbing Romero's black fur. "Figured I'd surprise you."

"I was starting to wonder if McCarthy was going to start charging you rent for sleeping on the sofa at the station."

He stands. "Nothing surprises me anymore."

Bass throws his arms around me and lays his head on my shoulder. He smells like sour coffee, and he desperately needs to get out of the clothes he's been wearing for over a day. "It's that bad?" I run my fingers through his hair.

He nods.

"Don't worry about picking up Bela," I say, pulling him away. "If you pick him up, he'll just worry." Which was true. Bela was better without a disruption in his routine.

Bass collapses on the sofa and rubs his eyes and yawns. "How's your day going?"

"I hate everything," I say, motioning around the room.

"A normal day, then?"

I point to the screen. "It's stupid. Nobody's going to watch this."

"I'll watch whatever this is, and Bela will too. He loves everything you create."

"You have to. You're my family. You have to care. It's just…" I look at the image of Lon Chaney Jr., a man who had

109

played each of the beloved Universal horror monsters, and I wonder aloud, "Will anyone even care?"

"Does it matter if anyone cares? Doesn't it only matter that you care about what you create?"

I turn my chair to face him. "I spend so much time with this, and it's not just monsters. They're not just actors and these aren't just movies. They're more than that to me."

"What is this all, then, to you? Maybe that's what you need to focus on."

"They're more than characters. They're symbols with meaning, Lugosi, Karloff, and Chaney. They all became greater than themselves." I pause, knowing I'm losing him.

"I know this is important to you," Bass says. Even in his utter state of exhaustion he is reassuring me, like he always does.

"I'm sorry. I know you're literally dealing with life and death and you're listening to me complain about movies."

"It's fine. This is your life. It's what you love, and you want people to love this too. Do you want another hug?"

I meet him at the sofa. He wraps his arms around me and all I want to do is tell him to quit. Bela and I never see him. We don't need the money and it's too dangerous. He's not a patrolman or a street cop, but I know my husband. I know he's the first one crawling into abandoned buildings because there was a tip, or interviewing a key suspect who may or may not be a killer and armed themselves. This job does not end. It either ushers you into retirement with a long case file of guilt in the form of unsolved missing and murdered cases, or this job ends you.

"You still won't be able to meet Bruce with us tonight?"

"No, I need to head back soon," he says, sitting up and rubbing his face with both hands. "I have enough time for a shower, nap, and some food before McCarthy sends a squad out to hunt me down. I'll make it up to you both with two movies."

"We'll take it."

"Now, I need that favor from you," he says, reaching for his phone. He pulls up an image. "The body at the Chicago Theater last night had this pinned to their shirt. It's a printout, but I thought you might know something about this."

"Does McCarthy know you're sharing this with me? Isn't he all sensitive after everything with Medina and Van?"

Bass draws in a deep breath, and I can feel my eyes widening.

"What? Tell me."

"We're going to go to talk to Medina."

I take his phone in my hand, studying the picture. "You think this is all connected to the killings from Humboldt Park?"

The image is that of a faded watercolor. It was surely a copy, because so much from that time was not preserved. Why would it be? It was a moment in time where experimentation and exploration were all that mattered, not documentation and archiving. A fiery drive existed among the inventors to push the boundaries of technology. Much was lost in an effort to develop and create more.

A red ribbon drawn across the top of the poster reads, *Theater Robert Houdini*. A man dressed in a white sheet looks down at another man in a tuxedo. The lower left-hand corner looks like the entrance of a cathedral, with columns stretching above. A ghost and a man kneel before a woman whose detached head floats above her body. To the right of them, another scene, a man in a tuxedo beside a small table. Atop the table is an open box, and hovering over it is a skull. Standing beside the table is the headless skeleton, its posture in a position to attack our tuxedoed man. Then to the very right of this scene stands a man dressed in red ceremonial robes. He holds a hand above the floating skull, as if commanding it with his energy to remain suspended in air.

Even in this chaotic multi-paneled poster, realism is intertwined with the supernatural, with the occult. With magick. The name across the bottom of the poster reads:

LE SPECTRES ET LE MANOIR DU DIABLE.

Bass looks over my shoulder. "Do you know what it is?

Of course, I know what it is. I had spent years obsessing over this film and all of the work developed by its creator. I was as fascinated with the filmmaker as I was the film. Georges Méliès had created hundreds of movies throughout his lifetime and had developed many of the techniques used in film today. This particular film however was a film grounded in superstition, horror, and magick, that maintained a mystical quality over a hundred years later.

"It's a replica movie poster for *The House of the Devil*," I say, not taking my eyes off the poster.

"I'm assuming you've seen that one, right?"

I've seen the film hundreds, if not thousands, of times. It was easy to do with a movie that was so short, just three minutes. I remember once I set the film on repeat on my computer, committing myself to watching it for the entirety of the day, or for at least how long I was able to stay awake. I studied each movement, each stitch of setting, the mannerisms of each actor, the shifting and movement of their costumes. I watched and I waited, hoping that what was rumored to have been embedded within that film could make itself known to me, but I realized it would not work this way, not with a replica and not on command. Only the original was magick.

"Yes, I know this movie. It's Georges Méliès's *The House of the Devil* from 1896. It's the first horror movie ever made."

CHAPTER 12

FRIDAY AFTERNOON, SCHOOL PICK UP: PALOMA

"He had a good day." Mr. Vicari smiles and looks down at Bela, who is in front of him.

I met them outside, beside the exit where the rest of Bela's class is standing behind his teacher, lined up against the red brick wall, bundled in coats, hats, and gloves. His school's teachers tended to hold the younger grades back until they recognized a familiar parent or guardian for pick up and then would dismiss the child. I could at least be reassured that Mr. Vicari was always with Bela and would hand him off to me at the end of the day, an extra layer of protection.

Another class spills out from the front doors, and older children come rushing past in a blur.

"Mom!" Bela waves to me. His face is a beam of joy.

School dismissal is the time of day that reminds me of Bela's vulnerabilities. For now, Bela's peers didn't comment on him having an aide. He would probably need one for the rest of his academic career, and I wondered what his classmates would say or do the older he got. And when Bela got older, into adulthood, then what? What types of services could he have access to in order to make sure he lived a fulfilled life?

It wasn't like I could trust Bela to leave the school grounds and walk to where I usually parked my car for school pick up. At all times Bela needed to be accompanied by Mr. Vicari for his own safety.

Like each day, I noticed students exiting the building, locking eyes with parents, grandparents, and other caretakers. Other students independently walked to parked cars where their ride was waiting.

Some students even started walking, heading home on their own. Bela couldn't do this. I wondered if one day I would be the lone parent standing outside of his high school as teenagers looked me up and down, the old woman who had to pick up her son. I then feared, if he had experienced bullying now in just the third grade, what would it be like in high school when he didn't understand how to read people's facial expressions or discern deceit in their voices.

Autism spectrum disorder is exactly that, it's a spectrum, wide ranging. If you've met one person on the spectrum you've only met one person on the spectrum. No two people on the spectrum present with identical social, emotional, and behavioral restrictions. Some children on the spectrum could become independent, graduate from college, maintain their own apartment, career, and beyond. I hoped this for Bela every day, but still I worried because he was too kind, and most people were not.

"Mom! I have to tell you my story!" Bela shouts above the schoolyard noise of children's laughter, teachers pulling parents aside to have a quick meeting, and others being asked, "Did you have a good day today?"

Mr. Vicari nods. "Oh, he's got a great story to tell you."

I reach for Bela's hand, but he rejects it.

"The story, Mom!"

"You can tell me the story in the car." I grab his hand and pull him away.

Mr. Vicari gives me a smile and waves. "See you tomorrow. Great work today, Bela!"

"You're not listening..." I feel him squirming in my hold.

I walk fast, not wanting to make eye contact with any of the other parents.

I don't really have any parent friends. I don't really have any friends. When Bela was in a behavioral based pre-school, all of the parents shunned us after he was diagnosed. Most of those parents had taken to medicating their three- and four-year-olds to stabilize their moods or put them through a series of holistic treatments, including neurofeedback, paying thousands of dollars to send electric impulses to their child's brain rather than accept that their child was neurodiverse.

But we were the ones who were ostracized when we decided to go to Rush University Hospital to meet with their child psychiatry department. When I shared Bela's diagnosis in the mom group chat, the responses were brief, that he was a great kid and we were great parents. Soon after at pick up and drop off, those same moms hurried their children past mine, giving a quick excuse that they were running late somewhere. Soon, I realized they were keeping their children away, as if their kid would somehow catch Bela's autism if they got too close. The invitations to birthday parties ceased. I was taken off the mommy group text altogether, and we were shut out.

I didn't want to go through that again, so when we started kindergarten here, I made it a point to not get close to anyone, because there was no separating autism from Bela. Bela has autism. It's woven into the brilliant fabric of who he is, and if someone cannot accept that, then they cannot accept him and do not need to be in our lives.

Bela pulls, trying to break free from my hold. I pull back.

"You're hurting me," he says too loudly as we cross the parking lot, attracting the attention of two overly put together schoolyard moms. Fresh black leggings, compared to mine that are faded and pilled. Their perfectly blown out hair, compared to mine that is pulled back in a ponytail, and their spotless Canada Goose coats, compared to my worn black Grand Vespertilio hoodie I am freezing in.

"Come on, Bela. I'm cold." I look down to him, still walking. "You can tell me your story in the car."

He purses his lips together and grunts.

"There's no reason to be upset."

"It's important!" Bela says as I unlock the rear passenger door.

"I'm sure it is," I say as I buckle him in.

In the driver seat, I adjust the rearview mirror where I can see he is still mad. "I'm ready for your story."

"Forget it," he grumbles under his breath, and brushes a loose strand of hair away from his eye.

"Bela, can you please just be nice? I want to listen to your story. Standing outside in front of the school, freezing, is not the right place to tell me a story. There were people everywhere. It's snowing. It's cold—"

"Okay!" He raises a hand and I wonder how an eight-year-old can have that much attitude.

"You're overreacting," I say, trying not to laugh as I turn onto Irving Park Road.

"You're laughing at me!"

"With you! There's a difference."

"You don't want to listen to my story."

I shake my head. "I never said that."

I take a deep breath, a centering breath, because I know my son. I know when he is hurt it can shoot straight into his core, like it did for me when my mother would laugh at me. When she'd laugh, it was in delight of my suffering. When I laughed at Bela, it was always because he brought me immense joy. I never wanted any cruelty to slip through my lips, because children know when you're being unkind. Even Bela, who struggles with understanding people's emotions and motivations, still knows pain.

Children become teenagers with memories of those who shouted and bullied them when they were younger. Those teenagers then become adults searching and wondering, looking back and reflecting on an upbringing dotted by empty efforts to please everyone just so they could be loved and accepted. And now, in my thirties, I look to the past only with sorrow, because all I see are decades of neglect and loneliness, taunted and abused by the very people who were supposed to love and protect me. A child shouldn't be afraid to utter a word in their own house, for fear it would be met with mocking, resistance, a belt, a hand yanking hair, followed by a closed fist across the face.

I give so much of myself to Bela because I had never been given anything, and I know what it's like to beg for care and affection and receive nothing but bitter abuse.

No one ever asked about the bruises as I walked the hallways in elementary school or middle school, so instead they just added to them. My classmates poured milk down my hair, threw my books down the stairs, and when that wasn't enough, they began to hit me too. That feeling of being detested, of being the awful thing in the room doesn't go away, because everyone always made it known how I was the terrible thing. I was the monster for just existing. And I could do nothing other than embrace being the other, embrace being the hated thing. But after I had Bela, I promised I would never allow him to be hated and hurt like I was. Everything I had done since Bela was born, before even, and now and for the rest of my life would be to protect him and to ensure he did not walk with this emptiness I knew.

When I started high school, Bass was the first person I met that first day in English class. He told me after first period that when I read the "Song of the Witches" in Shakespeare's *Macbeth*, it was like I was transporting them all, and I told him I was, because words are spells and Shakespeare knew that the way to make that part effective was to consult with real witches.

"You put a spell on us?" he had asked.

"Is that a bad thing?" I remember saying.

Since then, he's never really left my side, and I don't know why. I've told him to leave. I've begged him to leave, because why should anyone love me when I can't love myself? When he'd ask why, all I could say was, "I'm not used to someone taking care of me." But he promised me he would care for me, and even now, after years together, I still hold apprehension that this isn't real, that he's not real, that he really doesn't care. But every moment he can, he proves otherwise. He leaves me alone to work and read and to escape in my horror movies, and when he sees that maybe I've gone too quiet, that maybe I've slipped back to that dark place, he pulls me out. Maybe it's love. Or maybe this is part of his nature to serve, caring for me, this forever broken thing, even though I can't do the same for him.

I look at Bela in the rearview mirror. He's looking out the window. "You know I love your stories, right?"

He remains silent, refusing to respond.

"Bela," I say, starting to brake as the stoplight shifts from yellow to red. "I never said I did not want to listen to your story. Can you please just tell me your story now?"

"There are two stories," he says, his voice sounding so small. "The one I don't want to tell, and the one I have to tell."

At the red light, I watch as people cross the street, a young man holding the hand of a little girl, both of their backpacks bouncing against their shoulders as they move across the street.

Then, he appears.

The old man is holding the leash of a large German Shepherd whose brown and black coat is dusted with a light covering of snow. Both of them make it to the middle of the cross walk where our car is stopped. The man and his dog pause in front of my car and turn and face me.

"This is the story I don't want to tell," Bela says. "It's a story with a lesson, Mom."

"What?" I don't understand what he means. The pedestrian light changes to a blinking red hand, warning that the traffic light is about to change.

Bela continues. "Some stories are told to teach us something, like this story."

The man and the dog stand perfectly still in the busy city intersection of Irving Park Road and Addison Avenue, where no one seems to hold my growing discomfort that those two just feet from my car are standing too still.

The light turns green.

A car beeps behind us, and then another and another, an escalation of angry horns.

The man and his dog remain still, standing just feet from my car, unblinking.

"There's someone in the street. What am I supposed to do?" I yell at the reflection of the car behind me in the rearview mirror, hoping that the driver can see my path forward is blocked.

The light blinks yellow.

"The old man and death," Bela says from the backseat, his voice barely a whisper.

"What? What are you talking about?"

"The moral of the story is you have to be careful what you wish for because it can come true," he says.

"Buddy, I have no idea what you're talking about," I say as I finally lower my window, snowflakes drifting in. "Get out of the street! We're going to get hit here!"

"Polly!" The man calls out to me. "I've seen the movie and it's glorious." He removes his dark sunglasses, exposing deep, dark pits where his eyes should be. The edges of skin all around the holes in his head are black and crusted over.

The dog comes to life. It bares its teeth and lunges forward, its claws brushing against my bumper before the man pulls the dog back on his leash. Before I can close my window, the man is at my side, his fingers curled over the glass.

"What's the moral of your story, Polly? To suffer brings suffering? No," he looks in the backseat and begins to laugh when he spots Bela. "The moral of your story is that you will do anything to save your son. But know this, you will fail just like before, because you're too scared, Polly. You're too afraid to follow through and complete the ritual you started. And with time things get stronger. He's always known about the film, but he was just waiting, until the energies tethered to your son grew stronger and brighter. Bela reminds us that demons not only bring death, but life, and Bela's life blinks so bright, a light shining on a movie screen. All these years. Bela shines so bright, so so bright, and Bela's brilliance has alerted the man that it is time now to see the film. Can you show us the film, Polly? Or, is it you, Bela who must show us the film?"

"Mom! Go!" Bela yells. "Go, Mom!"

I hit the gas, but the car does not move. My hands shake on the steering wheel.

The car is stalled. I hit the gas over and over.

Horns continue to blare. People are shouting out their windows. Cars are cutting behind me and pulling into the opposite lane to escape.

"Polly." The man's voice is multitudinous, a wave of voices, folding in and out, like an old scratchy recording. His fingers dance along the door's edge.

"Get the hell away from me!" I try the window, but it will not close.

My chest tightens as the man sneers, taking pleasure in our

fear and discomfort. "When you watch the film, you and your boy, all of us, we'll all be together, frame by frame. A strip. A loop that will never end. You'll never end, just like we will never end. Maybe that's the moral of your story. Yes, maybe it is."

"Go away!" Bela shrieks, and the man laughs, slips on his dark sunglasses, and finally crosses the street.

The light is yellow, but I slam on the gas. The car launches forward. "Bela, are you okay?" I look in the rearview.

"He's not in the story," Bela says, leaning forward in his seat, "but he knows how the story ends. They all do."

"What?" My head is spinning. "What are you talking about?"

Bela places his hands on the passenger headrest in front of him. "The man and the dog. They know."

"They know what?" My mind is racing for answers. "You don't know them, do you?"

Bela lowers his hands to his lap and looks down to his fingers.

"Bela, you're not answering my question. Do you know that man? Have you seen him before? At the playground at school?"

Bela shrugs, his eyes fixed out the window. "No, I don't know him, but he knows the story. Some people know the story."

"Honey, you're worrying me," I say, trying to concentrate on the road in front of me, but wanting only to read Bela's body language. "I don't know what you're talking about."

"Once upon a time…" Bela starts.

"Bela…you're telling me a fairy tale when I've been asking you to explain what you meant about that man and his dog."

"Mom, you're interrupting the story," he says. "It's a not a fairy tale. It's a fable. It's an Aesop's fable. A story with a lesson. Like this story. Like all stories. Books and movies. Everything has a lesson."

I feel my hands tighten around the wheel. I want to ask him

about the sigil I found on his tablet earlier, but that would have to wait until later.

"Okay," I say. "what's the difference between a fairy tale and a fable?"

"You'll see."

CHAPTER 13

FRIDAY AFTERNOON: PALOMA

I don't know what else to call it other than Bela's Fable.

He dug his hand in his pocket, produced a red ADMIT ONE ticket, and told me the ticket was meant as a reminder to tell me the story, and he did.

I did a quick search through fables online and this seems to be entirely his story. Not made up at all. There's "The Lion and the Mouse," "The Cat and the Birds," or even the famous "The Goose that Laid the Golden Egg," and none of them, from what I've read, are the story Bela told me earlier today.

Well, I did find "The Old Man and Death." That is certainly a fable.

Bela was also right, there's no way he or I could tell Bass this story. Bass slept a few hours and then had to leave to search a break-in, and a break-in usually had nothing to do with homicide, except this break-in was at the Riviera Theater.

I'm going to write down this fable. What's the difference between a fairy tale and a fable anyway? I still don't really understand.

I need tea. My brain feels like it's on fire. That's what I'll do. I'll make some yerba mate with honey and oat milk and then

I'll sit down and maybe I'll just write the story, not the way Bela told it to me with stops and starts, but the entire way through.

I'll write it like a fable, like an Aesop's Fable, and then I'll just set it aside and promise myself I will not look at it again until morning. We'll go visit Bruce and watch a movie, and then I'll just read it when I wake, or maybe in the middle of the night when I can't sleep, because of course that is when all of the strange things happen, when darkness falls and memory and regret loom.

It could be nothing, just a strange and gruesome story told to me by my little boy. But I know, given the possibilities of that sigil, it could be something more.

I have to stay focused on tonight. Tonight will be good. Tonight is something to look forward to. We will see Bruce and we will watch *Abbott and Costello Meet Frankenstein*, and I will ask Bruce what he needs help with around the theater. I will make sure to be there for him for whatever he needs. He was there when Noel and I needed him the most. I would have called Noel to meet us, but it's almost impossible to get a hold of him. He's so busy and I'm so happy for him, but it's like I no longer have my brother, because he, like Bass, has sacrificed his life for his work. Maybe I've done the same and just don't realize it.

Where is the line between our personal and professional lives, especially when we love what we do for work? Especially when our work is the only thing that keeps us from slipping into despair?

Should our work define us?

I go downstairs. Make tea and return to my office. I blow over the top of my porcelain mug and I hear the musical beeps and boops from Bela's Puzzleworld game. I set the mug down next to my keyboard and then move the mouse, bringing the computer screen to life. When I click on my email, I gasp. My hand jolts and hot liquid splashes across my fingers. I wipe my hand on my hoodie, the pain from the hot water not enough to make me look away from the words in front of me.

I scan the text again, being sure I am not imagining it.

In my inbox there is a reply from Grand Vespertilio.

I click on the message.

Dearest Paloma,

I was delighted to find your message.

I would be honored to host you tomorrow evening before we record. We will provide all of the technical equipment necessary for the interview.

Therefore, you are only required to bring yourself.

See you tomorrow at 6 p.m.

Forever yours,

Grand

I respond immediately, thanking him and confirming I will see him tomorrow night. I call Bass, but it goes straight to voice-mail. I send him a text letting him know Grand finally responded and wants me to meet him at his studio. I notice the house has gone quiet. I walk across the hall to Bela's room. I stand right outside his door and hear him whispering.

"Why do you have to protect it?" I hear Bela whisper. "Oh. That's very sad. That's a long time."

"Bela." I open the door and scan the room. He's standing in front of the window. "Who are you talking to?"

"No one."

"Then why are you at the window?"

He points. "The snow stopped."

"Yes, it looks like that," I say as I walk over and check that the window is still locked. "Why don't you finish up your game, I'm going to get some more writing done and then we'll head over to see Bruce."

When I walk out of his room, I make sure to leave the door open a crack, in case I hear anything.

There's so much to think about and do—the sigil, Grand, Bruce—but what I need to get down right now is this story before I forget any detail.

This is the tale my little boy told me. This is a story that worries me.

Bela's Fable

A Dove lived happily with a Fish in a beautiful forest, but one day the Fish was called away, and so he ventured out to a great, but dangerous adventure.

The Dove was sad, but then one day a Baby Bat appeared in the treetop and said it needed a mother. The Dove was very happy and agreed to be its mother.

One day, when the Dove and the Baby Bat went into the forest, they were visited by a Wolf and the Wolf said, "Don't be afraid of me, for I am a good and kind Wolf."

The Dove did not trust the Wolf, and so ventured down another path, but here they met a Great Bat. The Great Bat said to not trust the Wolf for the Wolf was a great liar that had killed the Fish.

The Dove was very scared, because how could the Great Bat have known that the Fish had been killed?

The Dove was not sure who to trust, the Great Bat or the Wolf, for both of them were predators.

The Baby Bat then turned to the Dove and said, "The Great Bat will not hurt us."

"How do you know that?" The Dove asked.

"Because a Great Bat will never hurt a Baby Bat or the ones like the bat."

"But I am not a bat," the Dove said.

"No, but you are a Mourning Dove, and because of that you

know the night like the bats, where you sing your song of sorrow. A Bat will never harm one that has known great pain."

And the Great Bat agreed, "That's quite right."

Just at that moment, the Wolf leaped onto the Great Bat, but the Great Bat was strong and defeated the Wolf.

The Great Bat then led the Baby Bat and the Dove back to their garden and told them he would be nearby always, watching them and protecting them from afar as the Fish was no longer with them.

While the Baby Bat and the Dove were very sad, they knew that they could continue on, if even in great sorrow, because they had each other.

That's it, that's the story Bela told me as we sat on our sofa while I watched the snow continue to cascade down our window as the winter sun set. When I asked Bela gently where he had heard that story, he said it was told to him by the black bird that visits him.

Bela was creative, and his imagination was vibrant, but he insisted that this story was told to him.

Now that I had time to gather my thoughts, it was time to talk to Bela about his story. I call him into the living room and we sit down on the sofa cross-legged, facing each other.

"Bela," I try to be gentle with my words, "you said a black bird told you that story, but I think you made it up yourself, and if you did, that's okay."

"No, Mom. No. No. No. No."

Before he shuts down on me completely, I need him to answer a few more questions. I take his hands in mine. "Please, Bela, can you tell me, then, am I the Dove?"

He nods. "Your name is Paloma. A Paloma is a bird. A dove."

So, I was the bird in the story. I could feel my stomach twisting.

I take a deep breath. "And Dad's Sebastian, and I call him Bass and a Bass is a—"

"Fish."

The fish that dies in the story.

"I'm assuming, then, you are the Baby Bat?"

"Yeah." He lowers his head, his long hair now dangling across his eyes like a curtain. I brush his hair out of his face and hold his chin in my hand.

"I love you," I say.

"You're not mad, right? I know the fish, Dad, dies in my story…but I didn't do it. Don't be mad. It was the Wolf."

"No, never." I wrap an arm around him. "Now this is very important, who is the Great Bat and the Wolf?"

He looks at his striped black and white socks. "They're people."

"Do you know who they are?"

He opens his mouth to say something, but then stops and presses his lips together.

"Bela."

"I don't know," he says, reaching for a loose string on his sock and tugging it.

"And the Wolf is a bad person?

"Yeah," he says, pulling the string until it snaps.

"I need to ask you one more thing. There was a symbol that you created in Puzzleworld." I reach for a sheet of paper in my hoodie pocket, the tracing of his sigil I had made. "Where did you learn to draw this?"

"The black bird. He taught me how to make symbols that can protect me."

"Protect you? From who? What?"

"The Wolf."

A soft thump comes from outside on the porch. Romero

barks. Another delivery.

I open the door and find the package on our front mat. I bring it inside and place it on the dining room table. I read the label, the swirling black script.

It is addressed to Mr. Bela Vincent Ramos.

The sender was Grand Vespertilio.

"Bela..."

He's already at my side, and I can feel my entire body shaking. How had Grand known any of this? Where I lived? That I had a son? My son's name?

"That's my name!"

Bela pulls the package out of my hand.

"Bela, please don't open that..."

Before I can stop him, the box is opened, and black, red, and gold sparkling giftwrapping is spilling onto the floor around Bela's feet. He reaches into the box and takes hold of a book. The cover is facing me.

"Mom! Look! I told you a book was coming today!"

And that he did, right before he entered school this morning.

I read the book's title: *Aesop's Fables*.

I think it's now time to reach out to Noel.

CHAPTER 14

FRIDAY EVENING: SEBASTIAN

Robin Betancourt lived alone.

She had no children, no partners, and her parents died when the engine on their American Airlines flight leaving O'Hare International Airport detached on the morning of May 25, 1979. The crew lost control of the McDonnell Douglas DC-10-10 and all 273 passengers, crew members, and several people on the ground were killed in the deadliest aviation accident in U.S. history. She was raised in Avondale by an aunt who died last year.

I found that she studied at Lane Technical High School and started working part time at the Chicago Theater when she was a junior. She went on to study art history at Northeastern University in the city, and after graduating she went full time.

Robin's landlord agreed to let us in. He asked who would be picking up her stuff.

"She just died," I said. "Can't you wait a few days before you rent the place out?"

He scoffed at me, actually *scoffed* at me, like I was the ghoul wanting to toss out a dead woman's things just to make sure the place was generating income.

"Sick bastard," I muttered after he handed me the key to her apartment on the first floor.

Robin's home is a one-bedroom apartment. It is small and clean. The front door opens into a large living room. The landlord told us to the left there was a bedroom, to the right there was a small kitchen and a bathroom.

We start in the living room, where there is a wooden table in the center. Two large windows on the wall opposite the front entrance fill the room with natural sunlight. On either side of a window are large white bookcases.

Two movie posters hang on the white wall in front of the dining room table. *Charlie Chaplin in "THE KID,"* reads the first poster. In it, silent film star Charlie Chaplin is dressed as his famous tramp character, oversized pants that hang over his shoes, large coat, and a bowler hat. He's holding the hand of a little boy in coveralls, and both are looking over their left shoulder. In the upper right hand of the poster: *This is the great picture upon which the famous comedian has worked a whole year. 6 reels of joy.* Beneath the title: *Written and directed by Charles Chaplin.*

"Charlie Chaplin, right?" Gutierrez says. His hands are on his hips. "He always played a hobo."

"Tramp," I correct.

"Well, that's not very nice," he says.

"Not that kinda tramp," I sigh. "Someone who travels around by foot, sometimes they ask for money where they go, to get by. At least that's the name they used to go by." Polly had taught me a lot about horror movies, but she also taught me a lot just about old movies. She loved silent films and would spend hours watching them, including those starring Charlie Chaplin.

I walk over to the next poster. The top half of this one is taken up by a large gray circle with craters and ridges. The sphere has a left eye that is looking over to its side. It has a nose and a mouth. A large canister of some sort is lodged into its right eye.

The background is black, with white points dotted throughout. The nighttime sky. The poster reads:

A film by Georges Méliès
A TRIP TO THE MOON
"Le Voyage Dans La Lune"

It's right there in front of us. *"The House of the Devil,"* I say
to Gutierrez, "was made by the same person, Georges Méliès."
"Coincidence?"
"Doubt it." I take a step back, reach for my phone, and snap
a picture of both of the posters. "We're getting close."
We see more movie posters throughout the small apartment
as we make our way from room to room. In the short hallway
leading to the kitchen, and in the bathroom.
The space feels cold. Empty, but not…minimalist. It feels
almost like one of those art galleries Polly would drag me off to
before Bela was born—white walls, strange art meant to make
you feel things or offer some social commentary about the political or capitalist injustice of the hour, and then her art school
friends who would stand too close to her as they talked and
laughed about some movie or director I'd never heard of. They'd
sweep their eyes over me once or twice, never uttering a word
to me because I didn't belong there, with her, or anywhere, they
believed, because of my job.
The other posters throughout the apartment are large and
imposing. There's *The Cabinet of Dr. Caligari*, *Dr. Jekyll and
Mr. Hyde*, *The Haunted House* starring someone named Buster
Keaton, *The Bat*, and *Destiny*.
"Lots of black and white movies," Gutierrez says, signaling
the obvious.
"You got a good eye," I say, inspecting Robin's bookshelves,
which seem to all have to do with film and film history.
Gutierrez is beside me now, taking pictures of the titles. "Is

that sarcasm?"

"It's something alright."

I start at the top row, reading some of the titles aloud. "*A History of Narrative Film, The Speed of Sound: Hollywood and the Talkie Revolution 1926-1930, Silent Movies: The Birth of Film and the Triumph of Movie Culture, Early Cinema: Space, Frame, Narrative, Hollywood on Lake Michigan.*" There are many, many books on Georges Méliès, as well as a stack of notebooks.

"Alright, so she liked old movies, silent movies, this Georges Méliès person, and fairy tales and Greek mythology," I say, scanning across a few fiction titles, *Dracula* and *Frankenstein*, and then moving into some myths, *The Complete Fables, The Complete World of Greek Mythology, Mythology Timeless Tales of Gods and Heroes, Ancient Greek Philosophers* and *Aesop's Fables.*

"Fables," Gutierrez says, pointing to one of the titles.

"What?"

"Fables aren't fairy tales."

"Okay," I say, not really knowing or caring about the difference until Gutierrez corrects me.

"A fairy tale is just a story, for entertainment you could say," he says, stepping to the window and looking down. "Fairy tales usually include humans and animals." Gutierrez turns around, crosses his arms across his chest and leans against the bookshelf. "A fable, though, is different. Fables include only animals, but they have human characteristics. Still, that's not what sets fables apart from fairy tales. A fable is meant to teach you a moral lesson."

I don't know if it's the lack of sleep, too much coffee, or just too much of Gutierrez right now, but a migraine is starting to thread through my skull. "I have absolutely no idea what your point is."

Now my migraine is a fork carving into my right eye socket. I step away from the window. Maybe it's the light streaming in that's making my head hurt, or the thought of Robin, dead on that floor, her body torn open and exposed under blazing stage lights, and for what? For shock? Attention? Rage? Something else? I'm looking around her apartment, thinking of a motive for why someone would kill her, and all I can think about is this film, and that worries me. Polly knows about films, especially Georges Méliès's films, but Polly insists I'm not to worry about her, even though I always will.

"My point is they are different. Fairy tales and fables are not the same. Fairy tales include people, and sometimes animals. Fables will always include animals, but a fable will always end with a moral lesson, like the story about the tortoise and the hare."

"Who?"

Gutierrez raises his eyebrows, and his eyelashes are a flutter of blinking back in astonishment. "You don't know *The Tortoise and the Hare*? The turtle wins the race against the rabbit? Slow and steady wins the race was that story's moral?"

None of this is familiar, and I'm sure my blank expression is enough of an answer.

He frowns. "Who raised you?"

I motion toward the books about fables on Robin's bookshelf. "How'd you learn about all that? The difference between fairy tales and fables?"

Gutierrez's mouth drops open in a gape of astonishment. "Fairy tales were kinda all over the news last year, remember? And I figured that was a good time to read up on them and their meaning."

"Yeah, I guess," I say. "I was a little too busy burying my mentor and son's godfather to get caught up in all of that Detective Medina fairytale nonsense."

Gutierrez opens his mouth to say something but stops himself.

"What? Don't tell me you believe her?"

"I believe something happened. The graffiti. Those kids. She didn't do that. Something happened. She believed something was happening and—"

"I'm not talking about this anymore," I say, because I like Gutierrez, I do, and if he continues defending Detective Medina, I'm not going to like him anymore.

I reach for one of the notebooks and start flipping through it as Gutierrez snaps more pictures of the books on the shelves.

"What's in those notebooks?"

"Notes," I say. Robin liked her research. The notebooks are filled with what appears to be titles of films, dates and times, the names of actors, filming locations.

We move to the kitchen, where I find the refrigerator has cheese, milk, eggs, strawberries, and not much else. I look over to the counter and find a breadbasket. "She wasn't eating much at home," I say as Gutierrez is opening and closing cabinets.

The sink is empty. The cupboards are clean and organized, with just the bare essential kitchen items, a couple of cups, white porcelain salad and dinner plates and bowls.

This was the simple existence of a woman who lived alone, and who had done so for a long time. Her co-workers described her as quiet and nice, and not much else. When pressed, they all said she loved movies, and when she did talk, that's all she talked about. There was never mention of family, a partner, just movies.

"Let's keep going," I say, motioning toward the bedroom.

Gutierrez moves there first. I stay back, standing in the living room, looking at those two movie posters, hanging there prominently in the light. These two people are the focal point for this home. Why?

Charlie Chaplin.

Georges Méliès.

The killer pinned a poster of Georges Méliès's film *The House of the Devil* to Robin's chest. Why? What were they trying to tell us?

"I think you need to see this," Gutierrez calls from the bedroom.

There's no need to run. The bedroom is steps from the living room, but it's an entirely different world from the rest of the house.

"What the hell is this?" I say, taking in all of the walls, each and every portion of which seems to be taken up by articles, printouts, sketches, photographs, corkboards with various pinned notes and white boards full of blue, red, and black handwriting.

Post-It notes written in pen accompany some of the articles.

The bed is made, with a clean white comforter and pillows. On the light wood-colored nightstand there is a single book. Across from the bed is a matching desk with a laptop.

"Looks like a planner." I nod over to it, and Gutierrez opens the cover and confirms.

He starts flipping through it and stops. "She had tonight blocked off. Chicago Silent Film Society. Portage Theater. Eight o'clock. *Nosferatu*," he says.

"Alright." I focus on the living notebook of her bedroom walls. "Didn't know we had a silent film society." The writing taped to the wall is full of further dates, titles, and times. All along the room the largest prints are in black and white, the façades of movie theaters, their pictures taken long ago. A name is tacked above each one: Albany Park. Belmont. Berwyn. Biltmore. Central Park. Chicago. Congress. Covent Garden. Crystal. Gateway. Granada. Harding. LaGrange. Manor. Marbro. Maryland. McVickers. Norshore. Norton. Oriental. Pantheon. Paradise. Regal. Riviera. Roosevelt. Senate. Southtown. State. State

Lake. Tower. Tivoli. United Artists. Varsity.

"Looks like Chicago neighborhood names."

I shake my head. "Some of these are neighborhood names, but not all of them. Tivoli's not a neighborhood, or Biltmore. Look, the Congress Theater is on here." Handwritten beneath the picture is the address, 2135 N. Milwaukee, of the long-abandoned Congress Theater, a massive building that hasn't put on a performance of any kind in decades. "These are just old movie theaters, most of which no longer exist."

"I've lived here my whole life and I've never read of the Tivoli," Gutierrez says. He moves over to her laptop. "Let's hope this isn't password protected."

I laugh to myself.

"You think this is funny?"

"A little funny. I feel like we stepped into one of Polly's movies. Potential serial killer. A victim with very bizarre interests. This is all above my pay grade."

I return to scanning the walls. This reminds me of something Bela says. He says his memory is like a cabinet, and whenever he needs to recall something, he just needs to go over to his cabinet to retrieve it. This entire room is that, it's Robin's cabinet. She had a system here, of whatever it was she was trying to reach or uncover.

Her entire bedroom is devoted to this mystery, of silent films, city neighborhoods and movie theaters, and I wonder if she knew she'd be swept up in this story.

Movie theaters. Silent films. Names. Dates. Rushed notes on strips of paper pinned to the walls. I get closer to one section, a patchwork of research. One sheet reads, *Desire. Obsession. Power. And it doesn't matter who does, what's destroyed, all that matters is achieving this state of magickal grace, of holding everything, of accessing and tapping into everything.*

This was followed by a list of events and a note underneath:
- *H.H. Holmes, 1896*
- *The Iroquois Theater Fire, 1903*
- *U.S.S. Eastland Disaster, 1915*
- *Leopold and Loeb, 1924*
- *The Saint Valentine's Day Massacre, 1929*
- *John Dillinger, The Biograph Theater, 1934*
- *The Lipstick Killer, 1946*
- *The Murders of the Grimes Sisters, 1956*
- *Richard Speck, 1966*
- *John Wayne Gacy, 1972*
- *The Ripper Crew, 1982*

All of these events, and more, can be connected somehow to suspected viewings of that film.

Another note reads: *This town has history with hiding powerful and destructive devices. The atom was first split here in 1942 under Stagg Field at the University of Chicago. The Manhattan Project. The atomic bomb. The technology that has killed thousands, that can destroy us all, was built in this very city. And like the atomic bomb, someone will come and try to hone this film's power and it will go wrong. That is what this city is, an incubator, a vessel for bad things, and bad things must be contained here before they pollute everything good.*

I walk around the room, reading a collection of writings pinned to the walls, trying to make sense of Robin's thoughts.

I still don't know where it could be. Why did they have to tear so many of them down.

I've searched all of the active theaters. None of the urban explorers I've worked with have been able to pinpoint anywhere a nitrate film canister could be safely kept in any of these build-ings.

I think I found someone who can help.

"Gutierrez…"

"Yeah," he says. He's sitting at Robin's computer desk, and it looks like he's finally made it into her laptop. He's dragging his fingers along the mousepad, reading something.

"What's an urban explorer?"

He pauses scrolling. "People who break into abandoned buildings. They're mostly an underground group. There's really no way to get access to them unless you know someone. But they're harmless. They explore old buildings, taking pictures or videos of structures. They're all over social media, recording and posting their explorations for social currency."

"You sure do know something about everything, don't you?"

"I try."

I start moving toward Gutierrez, to see what he's brought up on the laptop, but I'm pulled back in again by Robin's writing. I stop and read another document.

04/01/2018

I've been able to get in some of the abandoned theaters that are still standing. I've made some urban explorer friends. They taught me how to break in to abandoned buildings and navigate the darkness safely. I found a man sleeping in the Uptown. When he awoke, I thought he was going to kill me. He asked what I was doing there, and I said exploring. He laughed and said, "You're looking for the movie. Everyone who comes here is looking for that movie, but you don't find that movie. That movie finds you. It's not here."

06/12/2018

I don't know what to think about the theaters that have been torn down. I can only assume the building holding the movie acts like a holy temple, in a way. Every Catholic church contains a relic, a piece of a saint embedded within the altar. When that church closes, and many have in Chicago in recent years, the relic is removed and returned, I can only guess to the Vatican. This film acts like a relic in a way, and it must be contained in the holiest of places, a building with a screen. A movie theater. It's been embedded in one of these theaters. It can be within the walls or floors, behind the screen, but it's in a theater. I know that for certain now. I just don't know which one.

06/18/2018

I believe now that the film has a guardian. Someone who is watching and waiting, trying to prevent more viewings from happening. But when do the viewings occur? Who coordinates the viewings?

08/12/2018

I'm reading The Golden Dawn by Israel Regardie, a former student of Aleister Crowley. Regardie had gathered the documents of what would become The Golden Dawn, a nearly thousand-page handbook and reference guide of magickal theory and practice for students of the occult. After he gathered all of his documents in 1935, no one would publish it, except occult publisher Aries Press in Chicago. The Golden Dawn was published across four volumes from 1937 to 1940.

8/15/2018

"Magical work involves change and creation. And the subject of the magician's work is the self. The magician is the focus of his or her own alchemical processes. By adapting one's per-

sonal vision to reflect the macrocosm, we can change ourselves to better reflect those divine ideas." – Israel Regardie

9/1/2018
"The Order of the Golden Dawn is a Hermetic society whose members are taught the principles of occult science and the magic of Hermes." – Israel Regardie

9/5/2018
One does not need to be a member of a lodge to become initiated. Meditation on the symbols, the practice of the teachings has the same effect as initiation.

9/7/2018
Why do this? What is the point of this magick? What does it bring?

9/8/2018
"...this is to be understood as an infinite ocean of brilliance wherein all things are held as within a matrix, from which all things were evolved, and it is that divine goal to which all life and all beings eventually must return." – Israel Regardie

What is the difference between a "life" here and a "being"? Is there something else beyond a human being?

09/09/2018
People have been viewing the film.
Not everyone knows they are a magician. Everything is pointing to Georges Méliès being a practitioner of high magick. A magician. He knew he could manipulate reality.

10/26/2018
Power corrupts quickly. I guess that's why this city has been the perfect place to store the movie.

11/09/2018
The beings. Angels and demons and beyond. There's more.
The demons exist all on their own and can be summoned all individually, but whatever Méliès did, he made this film a direct line to all 72 demons of the Goetia via ritual. They're stored there. Waiting for someone to come to them, to make a petition, and all petitions are heard and delivered, but there's something about calling that much power, that intensity that vibrates throughout space and time, that makes men and women mad and draws them to violence and makes them want to kill.
Only a powerful magician summoning those entities can contain them from causing chaos. But there's no real magicians in Chicago? Are there?

11/21/2018
Human catastrophe seems to be a byproduct of coming face to face with all of these intelligences at once. We are too weak to manage this power. But a powerful magician can control this power.

12/28/2018
Why Charlie brought the film here I'll never understand, but it's here, and for whatever reason it cannot be moved.

1/1/2019
I found it.

I shove my hands in my pockets, to prevent the urge of pulling it all down, the notes and the pictures, and carrying them off with me to pour over.

"Can you get any of these social media urban explorers to talk to us? Anyone local?"

Gutierrez laughs. "Sure, let me get right on that."

"Was that sarcasm? I'm proud."

"A real urban explorer will never talk to anyone outside of their circle, especially not to cops."

"You're insulting me. We're not street cops. We're detectives."

Gutierrez looks me up and down and gives me a smug smile. "Sorry. You're a cop. I'm a cop. Accept that we're hated because many of us are criminals ourselves and the handful of us trying to keep this together aren't enough. So, no. No urban explorer will speak with us."

He returns to scrolling and then waves me over.

"What's the recent search history look like?"

"Movies mostly. Looks like she watched a lot of them on her laptop."

"Which ones?"

He moves the cursor to her recently viewed films. He starts reading off the titles. "*His New Job*, *A Night Out*, *The Champion*, *In the Park*, *A Jitney Elopement*, *The Tramp*…"

"Okay, so, what do we got? Old movie posters. Chicago Silent Film Society date. Silent films. Let's reach out to a film historian or something and figure out if there's anything these films have in common."

"We don't need a film historian," Gutierrez says, spinning around in Robin's chair and facing me. "I can tell you that right now. They all star Charlie Chaplin."

Why would a young woman in the city of Chicago care so much about silent films? Why would she spend her time watching movies made over a hundred years ago?

"What time's that show again over at the Portage Theater?"

Gutierrez stands and looks at his phone. "Starts in thirty minutes."

"We'll get there in time for popcorn."

CHAPTER 15

FRIDAY EVENING: PALOMA

"Where are my kids?" Bruce stands from his desk in his small, cramped office off to the side of the concession stand. There are boxes toppling over with papers and old rolled up movie posters are leaning against the wall.

"Papa Bruce!" Bela shouts, and runs to him.

Bruce's arms are open and his face is beaming. Bela and I go in for a hug.

Bruce is in his faded Chicago Cubs baseball cap, jeans, and a dark polo. He moves slower these days, but that doesn't stop him from working. He'll work until the day the theater changes hands to the new owner, and then move.

Bruce leans against his desk and crosses his arms over his chest. "What are we watching today, kids?"

Bela looks to me and his eyes are dancing.

"I know what our kid wants. *Monster Squad*!"

Bela cheers.

I get close to Bruce's ear since I don't want Bela to hear, and Bruce is already reading concern on my face. "My Polly, what's wrong?" He takes one of my hands in his.

"Noel is coming."

Bruce's eyes widen and he bites his lip. "Oh, my boy. I've missed him. What's going on, Polly?"

"I just need to talk to him, but can you do me a favor? Can you and Bela start the movie? I need to talk to him alone for a bit."

He pats my hand. "Of course, Polly. Whatever you need." Bruce's eyes begin to water, and I understand the weight of time he feels. It's been a long time since we've seen Noel. "I'm looking forward to seeing my boy. It's been too, too long."

We met where we spent most of our time growing up, in the lobby of Logan Theater. We took a seat beside the window, like we used to as kids so we could people watch along Milwaukee Avenue.

Noel clasps his hands together and takes in the space. "It's been a long time."

"I know."

"Where's Bela?"

"In theater five with Bruce watching *Monster Squad*."

He blinks rapidly. "Theater five? You're okay with him being in there? You were always so scared going in there." He laughs.

"It's strange, but Bela loves it in there."

"Do you remember that horror movie you forced me to watch in there? The one about the kids putting on that B-horror movie marathon. I've never been so scared."

It was a trick of the light, I told him. The light and dark deceiving his perception. Tired eyes fixed too long on a white screen. He was just seeing things, I told him then. Even though I know now he wasn't imagining what it was he saw—images that should not have been billowing into existence.

"*Popcorn*?" I was impressed he even remembered that movie. It was a strange slasher, a group of university film students

146

who put on an all-night horror movie marathon to raise money for their university's film department. There are three main B-horror movies shown, but in preparing for the screenings, a short cult film is discovered, which the lead of *Popcorn*, Jill Schoelen, who plays Maggie Butler, becomes obsessed with. One by one the group hosting the movie marathon are stalked and murdered by one of their own, in a reveal that is a nod to *The Phantom of the Opera*. Horror is not only constantly holding a mirror up to us, but also reflecting back on itself what has come before.

While the entire film stands out in my mind, what I remember most was being impressed by the abandoned theater being outfitted with gimmicks reminiscent of William Castle's treatment of a night at the movies.

Castle, the famed B-horror movie director, producer, writer, and actor would pass out special glasses to moviegoers as they entered the theater. Attendants claimed these would aid the viewer in spotting unseen ghosts in the film. He would also set out plastic skeletons on tracks along the ceiling that would glide across the room while people were engrossed in the moving images before them. He'd outfit seats with buzzers that would ring throughout the show, shocking audiences. Castle combined novelty and horror movies, creating a haunted house-type environment for his viewings, while capitalizing on people's fears in hopes of garnering publicity, and it worked.

Castle was also the producer of *Rosemary's Baby*, one of those films many liked to claim was cursed.

"You said it was an emergency. What's up?" He unzips his coat and removes his gray knit scarf and sets it beside him.

"I didn't do the license to depart."

He shakes his head. "What are you talking about?" He opens his mouth to say something and I see the realization strike. "Ohhhhh…" he says, rolling his eyes upward to the ceiling.

"Yes, you did. I was there. You repeated my words."

"Not with Mom and Dad. With Bela."

He leans his head to the side. "What?"

"The geneticist said we couldn't have kids." I look down to my hands on my lap. "That I couldn't have kids…"

"I don't understand what you're trying to say."

I thought of them all, every single occultist and magician I had studied over the years. There were many, from dedicated practitioners, who all they did was teach ritual, to artists and innovators. All of them had turned to high magick in order to shift and design their reality, and so did I. "You petitioned to go to medical school and be a doctor and that happened. I petitioned for Mom and Dad to never hurt us again, and that happened. And so, I petitioned for Bela to happen."

Noel lowers his head, meeting my eyes. "It's a coincidence, Polly. You didn't cause Mom and Dad to get carjacked and killed. That was not your fault. No amount of magick can make a baby just happen."

"It didn't just happen," I snap. "Nine months of pregnancy and a baby is not *just* happening."

He closes his eyes and touches his brow. "I know. That's not what I meant."

The brother and sister reunion is so far not going very well.

A ribbon of tightness threads through my chest. "You seemed to believe it so much back then that you couldn't even live in the apartment with me anymore and left after the funeral."

"That's not fair. Everyone deals with trauma differently. I was eighteen."

"I was seventeen and had no one," I shot back, remembering how he packed his bags in front of me, telling me petitioning Forcalor was corrupt, that was not what we were supposed to have done.

Yet when I read the description in the book, I knew that's all

I wanted to do.

Forcalor: To bring death that appears sudden or accidental.

"Bass." Noel inhales deeply. "You had and still have Bass. You've always had Bass."

"Yes, but I wished I had my older brother with me then too."

I lost my brother when he left that apartment. Even now sitting with him, our connection felt distant. I was supposed to love him, but I didn't, not anymore. But still, I needed his help. He owed me that for abandoning me.

He lowers his head and runs his hands down his face. "I'm sorry," he says, reaching over and taking my hand in his. "I'm sorry I wasn't there, but I still don't want you to believe that Mom and Dad were your fault."

"But what if I want it to be my fault? What if it feels good knowing I took control of my life, of our lives, making sure she'd never hurt us again?"

"Magick isn't real, Polly. Life isn't the movies. You can't just move some piece of plastic across a board with some letters, burn some paper in a cast iron bowl, chant some names and expect reality to shift in your favor."

"Didn't reality shift in your favor? What was even the likelihood that you would have been accepted to UIC with your GPA and test scores the way they were? It's almost like it was a miracle."

"I busted my ass in medical school," he says.

"I know you did, but I also know what books you kept on your shelves besides your anatomy texts. You still petitioned them throughout. Don't pretend. We've gotten everything we've asked for. It's not a coincidence."

Noel and I both sat through that trial. Dad drove to pick up Mom from church, a late-night Stations of the Cross. And at a red light, a man approached the driver side with a gun and demanded they get out. Dad didn't move fast enough, or he refused or who knows what, but the next thing to happen was their killer shooting into their car eight times, striking them each in the neck and head. They died at the scene. And when the police knocked on our door that night, the streets ablaze in red and blue beating lights, and told us what had happened, I cried not because my parents had been shot and killed, but because I knew I wouldn't be hit anymore or called stupid or told by my mother that she always wanted a daughter, just not the one she got. I cried with the utter and complete relief in knowing she could never hurt me again.

Sometimes it takes years to deprogram yourself from the abuse inflicted by your tormentors. Even with them dead, it's hard to shake off years of physical, mental, and emotional abuse. It becomes part of your battered identity, a part of your story, that you aren't good enough, that you are an awful thing, that you deserved that beating.

Growing up, my fears, my anxiety were crippling all because I was taught that I deserved to be hit and spit on, thrown to the ground and punched, that I deserved to cry myself to sleep, that I deserved to wake up in the morning still choking back tears. My story became so twisted, so skewed, that I started to hate myself as much as my mother hated me, and when Luis brought me that book, I begged whatever was out there listening to me in the folds of reality to help me, because I could no longer continue with the hatred I had for myself. Either she would kill me or I would kill myself. My imaginary monsters on the screen could no longer help. I needed real monsters to help me end her.

"Explain Bela. I wasn't able to have kids. We had six miscarriages, and I was so tired of my body working against me that I reached for the book, and I made the call."

"What did you do?"

"I summoned them. I didn't just do the petition for results.

Or the connective evocation. I did the full evocation."

He spoke slowly. "What do you mean you summoned 'them'? Wasn't it only one per request? The full evocation? Polly? What did you do?"

"I did the evocation for all seventy-two demons of the Ars Goetia."

Noel lets my hand go and lowers his head. "I love you, Polly, but you and Bass made Bela. No supernatural influence had any part in him."

"Maybe I just manifested it," I whisper.

The manifestation of murder. The conjuring of a life. What was the consequence for manipulating the fates? I hoped they'd be forgiving and sympathetic given the abuse my mother inflicted. Then later in life, it wasn't the abuse by my mother, but the deception of my own body and how it refused to create life. I wondered sometimes if this was still a ripple from the beatings, my body thinking it wasn't good enough to create love.

Maybe those beings I charged with my destiny sought pity on me, because how many times can a woman cry in her own blood on the bathroom floor, begging to be a mother? I knew I'd be a better mother than my mother ever was. My desperation to create life stretched beyond the madness of Dr. Frankenstein. I wanted a child, and maybe there was something in me that knew that child would be Bela, who loved me, and who was utterly perfect in every way.

My leg was shaking so much now I could feel the bench moving beneath us. I wanted to tell him about Grand, about the book, but I didn't know how he would react.

"I can tell this is all bothering you. So, let's say that even if the supernatural had something to do with making Bela, then what? I still don't understand what the emergency is."

It all sounded impossible, and I couldn't imagine what it would sound like uttering it out loud now. What was I supposed to say?

"There's this rumor that the filmmaker Georges Méliès's wasn't just a magician in the traditional sense, but that he was a master occultist. Another rumor says that his first horror movie, *The House of the Devil*, wasn't just made with his class of special effects, but was made with the help of all of the Goetic Demons, which he conjured by embedding their essence into the film. Oh, and to make things better, it's believed that Charlie Chaplin came across the film while he was in Paris and brought it here to Chicago while he was filming at Essanay Studio. Essanay Studio also happens to be the home of the Grand Vespertilio show. Charlie Chaplin knew the film was dangerous and believed Chicago the perfect place to store it, for whatever reason. By the way, Grand refuses to talk about the film publicly."

Noel opens his mouth to say something, but his attention has moved out the window and across the street.

He stands. "I think I'm getting a ticket."

He pats his coat pocket. "Dammit, I left my phone in the car. I could have sworn I paid after I parked. I'll be back."

The sidewalk is covered in a light sheet of snow, even though Bruce had just shoveled before Bela and I arrived. The parking attendant has moved on to the other side of the street. A bright orange envelope is tucked beneath Noel's passenger windshield wiper. Great, one of the few times he rushes out to meet me he gets a parking ticket. I feel bad and will offer to pay for it. I watch as Noel removes the ticket and opens the passenger side door. He reaches in and then appears holding his phone in his hand. He pushes the door closed and looks down as he steps into the street. I can see his eyebrows knit together in worry, reading whatever message was waiting for him in his phone.

Then, for whatever reason, Noel walks to the middle of the street and stands there, unmoving, just staring at me.

I want to think that the driver of the SUV didn't see him, but that doesn't matter. My feet are already moving me toward the door, sliding across the slick sidewalk. I slip and fall. The pain is so sharp everything goes white for a moment. All around me I hear people shouting, a car horn warning, and then metal crash.

I stand and scramble into the street, pushing past people until I see red mixed with white mixed with the dirty gray of street snow.

I step over broken glass and bent metal. The car horn continues to roar, a mechanical animal in pain.

I fall at my brother's side on the street.

He is on his back. His legs askew, a shattered puppet. His right arm frozen, reaching up, twitching.

I take hold of it.

His jaw is torn off his face.

A gaping hole in the bottom of his head exposes his tongue, darting in out of his mouth, searching for somewhere to rest.

His upper teeth are chipped and shattered, and others are scattered around him, broken little blood-stained pearls.

His body convulses at my touch.

His eyes roll around, unable to stay fixed on any single point.

I squeeze his hand. "Noel, I'm right here." I turn to the crowd. "Don't just stare! Someone call a fucking ambulance!"

His other hand shoots up, a strip of mangled flesh from his wrist to his elbow flapping in the cold wind like a flag.

Noel's grip tightens, crushing my fingers, and then he pulls me into his face. I can hear him gurgling, trying to form words with breath. Blood splashes onto my face.

"The evocation," he hisses. "You have to finish it."

CHAPTER 16

FRIDAY EVENING, THE SILENT FILM SOCIETY: SEBASTIAN

It smells like right after a renovation has taken place, but not in a good way. No one is at the ticket booth, so we walk right in. It looks like it had not been used continually at least since the 1980s. It is dim inside, not because the lights have been lowered, but because many of the fluorescent lights above behind plastic paneling seem to be burned out.

We are right down the block from Six Corners. We call a lot places in Chicago "Six Corners." There's one in Wicker Park, the intersections of Milwaukee, Damen, and North Avenues, an area with a little more development and a lot more nightlife. Most of the folks in Wicker Park are newer arrivals to the city and think that the only Six Corners is in their neighborhood, with over-priced cocktails, condos, and coffee. Then there's where we find ourselves now, in Portage Park, at the intersection of Milwaukee, Cicero, and Irving Park. It's a little more working class here. A little more quiet. And yes, a little less fancy, and a lot more rough around the edges.

But this is Chicago, and if there's anything we pride ourselves on, it's being rough around the edges.

The hulking box of the original Sears department store looms over us. Growing up, we went there for everything. School clothes? We went to Sears. Appliances? You better believe we went to Sears and picked up a gleaming white Frigidaire. Dad needed a new hammer or drill? It was off to the Sears hardware department in the lower level to pick up a Craftsman. My mother always made sure we dressed nice when we went to Sears, no matter what we were buying. We never stayed there too long. We went in directly for what we needed, paid, and then left.

I later realized that the reason we rushed in and out so much was to avoid any unnecessary interaction with the White staff who worked there. My parents were self-conscious of their accents, the color of their skin, the texture of their hair, where we lived. They did what they could to prevent any situation from turning uncomfortable, and they should not have lived their life that way, constantly functioning on a level of heightened anxiety, fearful they would be mocked, belittled, or attacked just for existing. My parents did what they could with what they had, and I hope that wherever they are, if there is even some place we go to after we die, that they are proud of me.

"Do you think anyone's here?" Gutierrez asks.

It doesn't look like it. The lights to the concession stand are off. There are no contents in the display, and I was sure if you looked in the popcorn machine, you'd find cobwebs.

"Are you sure we're at the right place? Right time? What'd her planner say?"

Gutierrez reaches for his coat pocket and produces his cell phone. "I took a picture of it. It says Portage Theater for a showing of *Nosferatu*. At this time."

A door opens. A woman appears with a wool coat two sizes too large for her, wearing an equally large cable knit scarf. Her hair is wrapped in a paisley yellow and blue silk scarf, and curls peek out along the edges.

"I'm sorry if you didn't get the notice, but we've canceled the movie for tonight."

"No, we didn't get the message. Why is that?"

"We've lost one of our members…" The woman clasps her hands in front of her, now eyeing us suspiciously. Two men in dark suits, dark wool coats. Asking too many questions.

"That's why we're here, actually," I say, producing my badge. "We just have a few questions about Robin."

The woman's face shifts from somber to rigid. "Are you now?" she asks, accusatory. "I don't have to talk to you, and, quite frankly, no one should be talking to anyone in the Chicago Police Department after everything you all have done."

I turn to Gutierrez. *Everything you all have done?* And it's like he is reading my mind.

"Medina," he says under his breath.

Medina looms over everything. Of course, Medina and the remains of a manic investigation she left behind is what taints us now when we're just trying to do our job.

Medina had her suspects. Two high school students murdered a schoolmate, but those two kids were caught. The case was closed. But Medina and her noble cause of taking it further, wanting to know the why…when sometimes the why just doesn't matter. Some people blame the death of her partner and my mentor, Detective Van, and the death of the young man she was mentoring, Jordan, on her own stubbornness. What did pushing that case any further get her? An internal investigation and desk duty.

To this day, she maintains there was someone else out at the lagoon with them, that the teen murders at Humboldt Park are more complex than we think, because they will happen again and again, she claims. When she was asked to explain, all she said was, "It's all a fairy tale." Hence, the desk duty, since McCarthy thinks she just needs time to process her father's, partner's, and now mentee's death.

Gutierrez steps in front of me. He is a better charmer than me anyway. "I'm so sorry, but my partner and I just want to understand as much as we can, who was in Robin's life, who she came into contact with…anything that can help us."

She tilts her head. "Why don't you ask Detective Lauren Medina? And why is she still employed by the police anyway? Is the union protecting her? One of my friends is dead."

I wanted to repeat the script prepared by our public relations office: *Detective Lauren Medina has been assigned desk duty. The incident is being investigated by the Civilian Office of Police Accountability.*

Well, if I said that, I'm sure our conversation with this Silent Film Society woman would end right now. Medina maintained that Detective Van fired his weapon first, and that her mentee was murdered by him. Jordan discharged his weapon out of fear and self-defense. Regardless of what happened, citizens of the city believed that Detective Medina was at fault somehow and should be held accountable, as well as the entire department for killing a young man. Medina certainly lost friends on both sides with claiming Detective Van was the aggressor in that shooting, upsetting all of us in the department. It was seen as a betrayal, one of us turning against the other in death.

The woman points to Gutierrez and then me. "Wait, do you have guns on you?"

Our silence is her answer.

"Yeah, I'm not talking to you if you have guns on you. Didn't you see the sign on the door? No firearms allowed."

I throw my head back and sigh. "Miss, we're just trying to do our jobs here."

"My name is not 'Miss.' You can call me Jackie, but first," Jackie points toward the doors, "you can both leave your firearms in your vehicle outside."

I cross my arms across my chest. "We can't just leave loaded firearms in our car." I close my eyes and shake my head. I don't even know what's going on anymore. "Jackie, I'll compromise, why don't we all go outside. Gutierrez and I will place our firearms in our vehicle, and we will talk on the sidewalk. Is that a deal?"

"Yes, but I'm walking behind you, because I'm not walking in front of cops who are armed."

"We're detectives," I say through clenched teeth.

"Doesn't matter," Jackie says from behind us. "You're the same thing. You're part of the same club that let all of those kids get killed last year."

"You know there were a thousand homicides in Cook County last year. Who do you think's gonna get these killers off the street?"

"Obviously not you," Jackie says. "What's the threshold rate again? Fifty percent in this city? That means that half of all killers who killed someone in this town haven't been caught. Maybe do a better job, Detective."

Jackie follows us past the double glass doors outside onto the sidewalk.

Gutierrez glares at me. "Can you try, just try for a second, to not be an asshole?"

"What? I'm a nice guy."

"Jackie doesn't think so."

It is dark outside, and we make our way to our car parked in front of the theater.

I nod for Gutierrez to enter first. "You know McCarthy would have our asses if he knew we were doing this?"

"Yup," Gutierrez says, sliding into the passenger seat, trying to be as discreet as possible as I shield the window with my back. "But then we'd miss out being able to talk to one of the few people who knew Robin."

Once Gutierrez is done, I do the same, knowing the city would probably have our badges for this.

I approach Jackie and open my jacket. "No firearm," I say, and then reach over and open Gutierrez's jacket. "Nothing on him either. Can you now tell us about what the Chicago Silent Film Society is and how Robin was involved? Because I'd really like to solve this before my partner and I lose our jobs."

Jackie shoves her hands in her coat pockets. "The Chicago Silent Film Society is a small non-profit. We're silent film preservationists and we host silent films, not really on a set schedule right now, but Portage Theater is our home for this moment. I met Robin at one of our showings a few years back. We don't get a lot of people. It's usually a small group, but she stood out. I introduced myself and we talked after the movie..."

"Which one was it that night?"

"It was Charlie Chaplin's *The Kid*. I remember because we had live accompaniment."

"What's that?"

"Music. We play live music, piano, sometimes an orchestra, to accompany the film, as they were originally experienced by audiences when the movies were first shown. I remember because I was playing piano that night. I noticed her because I saw that she kept turning her head around, as if she was expecting someone to join her. When the movie ended, she lagged behind, looking up at the ceiling and admiring some of the detail of the space. Lots of these buildings were built in the early 1900s. Many are in desperate need of repair and renovation, but there's so much architectural history and significance in these spaces."

"Admiring this theater?" I say, looking up at the crumbling facade. The brickwork needed some desperate tuckpointing.

"We weren't here that night. We were at the Copernicus Center. We try to offer a showing in a historic movie palace as often as we can."

"Movie palace?"

"Yes, like the Oriental, The Biograph, The Rivera…"

"Copernicus Center doesn't sound like a movie theater," I say.

"It used to be, a long time ago. It was the Gateway Theater. It's a historic building. It was built by Rapp and Rapp, who were famous for designing other movie palaces in the city…"

"The Chicago Theater?" Gutierrez asks.

That's why I like Gutierrez, he's always one step ahead of me.

Jackie's eyes widen. "Yes." She nods. "Exactly."

"What makes a movie theater a movie palace?"

There goes my new partner again, always with the good questions.

"The architecture, certainly. The design detail. The craftsmanship. Most of them were built in the early 1900s in the city, and you have to acknowledge that what they did for entertainment was vastly different than what we do today. A visit to a movie palace like the Gatwick to watch Judy Garland or Buster Keaton, and to listen to musicians play, and to have ushers walking around in these almost military-esq looking uniforms, directing people to their seats, I mean, all of that made a lot of those people feel like royalty, I'd imagine. It was an experience. This was a time in Chicago where indoor air conditioning didn't exist. But places like movie palaces would bring in blocks of ice and position large fans behind them to cool theatergoers from the summer heat. They offered childcare and other comforts that weren't easily accessible to Chicagoans at other spaces in the city."

"Did Robin ever talk about any research she was doing?"

"I mean, yes, she was an amateur silent film historian and enthusiast. She was also fascinated by the history of these spaces, movie palaces."

"Any other interest about films? Which films?"

"She was interested in lost films, especially those of Georges Méliès and all of the silent films that were made in Chicago."

"Silent films in Chicago?"

Jackie rolls her eyes like this is something I'm supposed to know. "Chicago was one of the first places in the world to make films. We had vast production and lots of production companies here. So much of what is standard in the filmmaking business was tried out first in Chicago. Even the very idea of buying stories to adapt to movies was started by William Selig, who created one of the very first film companies here in Chicago. Selig Polyscope Company of Chicago. That was in the late 1890s, and then eventually he and the rest of the American movie making business moved to California around 1919."

"Why was that?"

Jackie shrugs her shoulders. "Look at this weather. You can't really film here year-round, now can you?"

"Why her interest in Charlie Chaplin?"

"He was the biggest name at Essanay Studio in Chicago. Really the world at that time when he was signed. Think of the biggest movie star in the world, and just imagine them living and working in Chicago. It was a big deal for a little while. He was just here for a short time in 1914 and made a few really iconic films but left not too long after."

"Why's that?"

"Chaplin had quite a lot of problems in Chicago. The studio was rude to him, withheld his bonus, which he eventually got after being shuffled from person to person to ask for it. He didn't like the way the studio was run. He thought Essanay Studio was too regimented and weren't open to creativity. Plus, Chaplin knew the technical side of filmmaking and how it should work. So, when he saw that the studio often screened original negatives instead of going through the expense and craftsmanship of making a positive work print, he was horrified. And," she shrugged again, "weather."

"Got it."

"With Chaplin gone, that signaled the end of Essanay Studio. They were no longer tied to a premier talent, the flu epidemic raged, there was a coal shortage, the war in Europe, and they had financial trouble."

"Did she ever tell you about anyone wanting to hurt her? A jealous partner, a stalker, anything?"

"No, nothing. Robin was quiet. She liked movies. She loved the theater. I suppose that's where she lived, and it's awful that's where she died as well."

The wind kicked up and Jackie brought her hands to her scarf, tightening it around her neck. "It's freezing. If that's all, I'm going to head back inside to grab my things and lock up. I really do hope you figure this out."

I walk around to the driver's side door, processing all of this, knowing for certain we are close, and wondering if Robin's killer knew about her research.

At the door, Jackie turns around. "Detectives, one more thing…"

"What's that?" I have my hand on the car door handle.

"I remember now, why Robin was looking around so much that night in the theater. She said there was a story she once heard about how Charlie Chaplin brought a rare film to Chicago from France, and that he hid it in one of the movie theaters here."

"Oh yeah, which theater?"

"That's what she was trying to figure out."

"What's so special about this film?"

She shakes her head. "I don't know. Robin never told me."

"Anything else you got?" I ask.

"Oh, and she was obsessed with Grand."

Obsessed with Grand? Polly told me not to worry, but how could I not be? Polly knows about this film. She knows a lot about Grand. Whoever the killer is, they know about many of the things that interest Polly.

"Why's that?"

"His studio is in the old Essanay Studio building. Robin said just above the auditorium there's the original catwalk that stage-hands would access during filming. She also said deep within the basement there are two original vaults, and one of them still has a label warning about the handling of fragile nitrate film."

"I don't get it. Why was it so fragile?"

"Because once nitrate film catches fire, there's nothing that can put it out."

In the car, I have no idea what to think of any of this. I turn down Milwaukee Avenue when my phone starts ringing. It's Polly. I answer and can't hear anything but screaming, crying, and sirens in the background.

CHAPTER 17

SATURDAY AFTERNOON: LUIS

"It's asbestos," the contractor says as he peels back the old beige laminate tile that was installed decades before. It is cheap material, and I remember when I bought this building what struck me was the beige kitchen floor laminate, how it was raised in the center of the room and how it started curling in on itself along the edges. The woman who lived in this apartment for over forty years mopped this floor daily, until the day she died and the realtor found her dead beside the stove. She kicked over the mop bucket as she fell, the water spilling all over the floor, settling into the laminate tile, and her, for days until she was finally found—still with that mop in hand. They had to peel her corpse off the floor, I was told.

Down the hallway I can hear hammering as new drywall is being installed in the bedroom. Two new men are entering, carrying a large sheet of drywall, maneuvering it through the corners of the door.

I look at the hardwood floor in the living room. Rolls of plastic sheeting are stacked in one corner, and paint brushes and trays in another. A drill lays nearby. There was lots of movement today, and there would be for the next few days. We needed to patch up any cracks in the walls, paint, refinish the hardwood floors, install new kitchen cabinets, and rip out this floor. At least the bathroom had already been remodeled last week.

"Rip it out," I say. Asbestos meant tenant complaints to the city, fire hazards, and fines. I didn't want to deal with any of that.

I was already mentally calculating the additional cost for this rehab. A four-unit building on Wrightwood Avenue in Logan Square could demand a premium. Walking distance to the Blue Line, the farmer's market on Sundays, used bookstore, new bookstore, and however many coffee shops. There was a coffee shop for the after morning drop off mom crowd. There was a coffee shop for the crowd that liked to work remotely. There was a coffee shop where the artists sipped bottomless cups of coffee and would look down their thrift-shop shopping noses at any-one who looked like they played in the consumerism backyard, Canada Goose coat, Apple watch, a Gucci bag, the air of some-one having just paid off their BMW, mortgage, student loans, or worse, the look of someone who lived in Lincoln Park.

That's one thing about Chicago, Chicagoans are pretty good at spotting when one person from another neighborhood crosses into theirs. It's like one gang moving into another gang's territo-ry. Sure, you could do it, but be ready for the consequences.

"This is going to add more days to the job," the contractor says as he tears off a soggy piece of laminate. I wonder if that was one of the pieces the lady died on, but I don't say anything.

Most of my contractors are hired by day, or by project. When I started out, it was manageable to maintain a consistent team of workers, but now that I'd doubled my real estate portfolio in ten years, I needed people quickly. So, I needed them to do the job faster than estimated, because if a unit was sitting unoccupied, it wasn't generating me income.

"You hired me to install the baseboards," the contractor said.

"Can you do floors?"

The man looked over the kitchen. "Sure. I can do it."

I'm sure he didn't have much choice. I usually offered my workers more than the going rate so that they had to stay and finish the job.

"Tear this out and I'll be back with the new flooring," I say.

I turn down the hallway and stick my head in the bathroom where Jose is installing new fixtures.

"Jose, your guy in the kitchen's going to remove the old laminate and install a new floor."

"Tony doesn't know how to do floors." Jose was turning a new shower head into place.

"He said he'll figure it out."

"Alright, I'll keep an eye on it."

Jose steps out of the bathtub and turns the faucet, water spraying down.

My phone rings in my coat pocket. It is the call I was expecting. "I have to take this. Can you pick up the flooring? Vinyl. Something that looks like hardwood, but don't buy real hardwood. That's too expensive."

"Sure. I'll still need another check," Jose says as I walk out of the bathroom.

I race down the steps to get away from all of the hammering and the pounding.

I'm outside on the sidewalk now. I answer. "They accepted my offer." It was not a question.

My lawyer, Glenn, is a loud talker. "That place has a number of violations. I don't even know how it's been allowed to continue operating in the condition it's in."

"It's old. It's nostalgic. It's going to work. Everything I've ever invested in has worked." That place has escaped demolition repeatedly over the years, while others have succumbed to it. It's been the most obvious choice, always there, lights blinking and beckoning, because magick lived and breathed within its walls. I just needed to wait for when it was ready for me.

"Yes, but you have to bring it up to code."

Bringing it up to code could easily run in the millions. I would need help, lots of help, but I am sure I have enough connections in the city to make this happen.

"How much?"

"Initial estimate is four million."

The number didn't matter. It could be one hundred million and I would make it work. The money would come. We could get tax increment financing.

I knew beneath that old plaster and dry wall were original surfaces, decorations, and marble walls, and I had matched old pictures to the current structure. There was a decorative relief in the lobby hidden behind some paneling. The place was screaming to come back to its original grandeur. Walls, floors, paint, lightbulbs, they all absorb energy, the energy of those who have come and gone. Each word uttered, each laugh, and whisper, all of it remains embedded within the space.

Buildings remember. Buildings know.

They stand there watching, waiting, and welcoming, taking in everything you put into them, the joy, the pain, the horror, the possibility of it all.

"Thank you, Glenn," I say, walking to my car that's parked across the street.

"Don't thank me, you're going to pay well for this, and it's all got to be licensed and insured contractors. None of this daily pay workers and cutting corners or the city will have your ass wrapped up in limbo until those violations are fully cleared. Everything has to have a permit if you want to apply for and keep your historic license."

"Sure, whatever they want. I'll do a good job."

"There's one thing…"

I open my car door, already dreading what this one thing could be. I had handled everything as requested. I had provided my assets, a business proposal, and a detailed renovation plan. I had even promised to reserve ten percent of the building's units for low-income housing, something I had never done for any of my other properties, but I knew this would look good and would make the bank more willing to accept my offer.

"The owner wants to meet with you before your offer is formally approved."

"What?" I start up my car. "Why?"

"I don't know. Maybe because he's sad about selling it. Maybe because the place belonged to his family. Go ask him yourself, but do me a favor and be nice for once, because if you mess this up, there's no offer."

"I am nice. I'm always nice."

Glenn laughs loudly.

"Do you know if he's there? I can stop in now."

"I'll text you his number. Give him a call and you two work it out. He just wants to know that it won't be lost, demolished. He had been keeping that old place running for years on his own with the help of an adoptive daughter. The daughter doesn't want anything to do with the place, but just know, the people in the neighborhood are expecting Logan Theater to remain in operation. It's an anchor for the community. Don't piss them off and turn it into some hipster venue for indie bands. The city's already hearing it from residents about the push and pull of gentrification in Logan Square."

"Alright, I'm almost there," I say as I turn left onto Fullerton Avenue.

"Please don't be an asshole." Glenn laughs again.

"I'm a nice guy!" I shout back, but Glenn has already hung up.

As I drive down Logan Boulevard, I think about how all of

this interconnects. These boulevards are some of the most intact stretches of architecture in this city, and no other neighborhood in Chicago has a square such as the focal point of Logan Square, a beaming white marble column with an eagle sculpted at its base by noted artist Evelyn Longman.

Straight. Perpendicular. Intersecting.

Lines.

The patterns they make and the complex meaning within. The alphabet we use to communicate is just a series of lines, straight and curved, and with them people share ideas, create stories, histories are written, and meaning is pulled and interpreted all from these shapes.

And what are words? What are shapes, but magick?

Every symbol has a meaning. Even if you don't know what that meaning is, your brain settles on those markings, trying to connect the neural pathways to make sense of the world. I know this, and before me all of the greats knew this too, and all we had to do was listen and go within, but many refuse to see the power they truly have, and that there's ever more power to tap into.

I'm parked now in front of that great vertical line that greets people to this gateway, this corridor.

L
O
G
A
N

A neighborhood named to honor Civil War general John Logan. A neighborhood built using Gothic, Châteauesque, Arts and Crafts, American Foursquare, Classic Revival, and Prairie School architecture. A neighborhood that welcomed thousands of displaced people from Eastern Europe after the Second World

War, and a neighborhood that continues to welcome those in motion and movement, looking for a place to call home, looking for a spark of magick, looking to feel something.

And little have they all known, that magick has lived here for a long, long time.

CHAPTER 18

SATURDAY AFTERNOON: PALOMA

The letters above the door read ESSANAY. On either side of the arches is a hand-painted Native American in headdress with brown, pink, and blue painted feathers. The sculpture is dated and offensive and would never work today as the logo for a movie production company. Then again, many silent films and early cinema portrayed offensive images and stereotypes, and hateful and hurtful depictions of people. Vaudeville did as well. It's a sting that lingers from those early years, something I hoped modern horror was working toward eliminating.

The commission of Chicago Landmarks assigned the building monument status, and so the original designs remained, a historic marker and reminder of what Chicago once was to the world of moviemaking. Each of the logos in profile face the doors leading to the once-famed Essanay Studio, a fitting place for Grand to live and film his long-loved program.

As soon as I turn off my car, and the heater, the cold creeps in. With the windchill, it is well below ten degrees, and in this weather, exposed skin, noses, fingers, cheeks, anything, would first feel that sharp stab of cold, followed by the burning spread of needles pricking skin. The sensation was unpleasant after a few moments, and after longer, ten or twenty minutes, nearly unbearable.

I open the door. The cold bites so bad I immediately close it and turn the car back on and crank up the heater. I don't feel like going outside just yet.

Ask the heartiest Chicagoan about winter, they'll surely say something along the lines of it sucks or it's painful, but we get through it. We'd complain. That's Chicagoans for you, we have been conditioned to live through situations that just suck or are painful, but we survive. We are unquestioning and unforgiving, and, ultimately, we do not position ourselves as victims. We are people who survive.

We aren't the aesthetically put-together West Coast, driven by image, and we aren't the brusque East Coast, driven by status. We are hearty Midwesterners who eat Polish sausages at White Sox Games and drink cold beers in coffee tumblers on North Avenue Beach so the cops don't confiscate our drinks, and who shovel our elderly neighbor's sidewalk after a snowstorm because we know they can't do it, but we can and so we help.

That is what we do. That is who we are.

We're not self-important people in this city.

Like Carl Sandburg said in his poem *Chicago*, we're "stormy, husky, brawling, City of the Big Shoulders" sort of people. So, a little frost and a few flurries dancing off Lake Michigan and cascading along the town can't slow us down, not by much at least.

I turn the car off again and reach for my bag. I look in the rearview mirror and pull my coat hood over my head and push my hair inside.

I look back at the entrance steps, steps that so many silver screen stars had walked, including the legendary Charlie Chaplin, who worked here for a year. Chicago was a center for film production in the early 1900s. We were Hollywood by the lake, before there was even a Hollywood. The first film completed in Hollywood was in 1908. The first movie shot in Chicago was in 1896. Chicago's contribution to film history has been forgotten—or ignored—by most, but not Grand, who often spoke affectionately of the city's silent film era.

From its founding at the massacre of Fort Dearborn, the Chicago fire, and beyond, Chicago likes to pretend bad things did not happen here, as if it were all a dream, or a movie. Chicago likes to hide its bruises, its history of disaster and violence. But it's true, bad things happened here. Bad things still happen here. Sure, bad things happen everywhere, but there's something about this city, as if it's a magnet for destruction and despair. Or maybe it's not a magnet at all. Maybe there's just something here, embedded deep within our foundation, that vibrates on some perilous frequency. Bass sees it. I've seen it. I've lived it. But it's also within those threads of tragedy where I found happiness.

The sun had set over an hour ago. The other cars parked around me were already caked in white, their owners probably not having any intention of moving their vehicle out of their spot for the rest of the weekend. Small flakes float down gently from above, glimmering against the streetlights. The black sky sparkles with snow crystals.

Bela loves days like this.

This morning he rushed to his window and shouted that there was more snow falling. When I made it to his room, he was right, there was new snow falling outside, and blowing into his room.

His window was once again open.

Bela insisted he did not open it. I felt guilty waking Bass, who had just fallen asleep, but he had to see for himself.

"I have a window lock I can put in," he had mumbled, still lost in his sleep. "No one will be able to open the window."

"Can you do it now?"

Bass rubbed his messy hair, nodded, and I heard him walk out to the enclosed back porch where he keeps his tools.

Bela once again continued his protests, "I didn't do it. I didn't do it," until I gently shushed him and told him it's alright, that we believe him, even though I really didn't.

Bass returned and looked out the window, inspecting the sides, and said, "Romero would have barked if he heard that much noise. Plus, the camera would have caught something." This was true. We had security cameras in the front, back, and sides of our house. It was Bela, whether intentionally or not.

Bass installed the lock, hammering it in. Once he was done, he pulled at the window again to be sure it would not budge. "I'm going to try to get some more sleep." Bass kissed me on the forehead, balancing his tool case beneath his arm. "I need to talk to you when you get back."

"Sounds ominous. Everything okay?"

He scratched his head. "Yes, just…some things came up yesterday that I'm hoping you can help me with."

"Maybe now isn't a good time? With…Noel and the meeting with Grand," I say. After Noel, I rushed into theater number five and whispered to Bruce to keep Bela inside, that there had been an accident. When it was time to leave, I took Bela through the back of the theater. He did not need to know what happened. My brother, who I had seen for the first time in years, was pronounced dead at the hospital. And I just didn't know how to feel, because all I could keep hearing were his words to finish the evocation.

I close the car door, and as I step out into the unplowed, snowy street, I smell the sharp scent of burning wood from a nearby fireplace. Birds caw above me, which seems strange considering how cold it is, but as Bela brilliantly reminded me before, all birds don't migrate for winter. Some of our local birds, like robins, goldfinches, cardinals, and red-tailed hawks, stay around during the cold months, while other birds actually migrate here for the season.

The sidewalk has not yet been shoveled, so my feet sink into the snow. I shove my hand in my bag, feeling for my tablet, phone, and wallet, and find them all there. I take another step and then feel something bulky under my foot. I lift my boot out of the ground and hear a ripping chirp. I look down and find a black bird on its side.

The animal flaps its wings wildly and kicks its feet back and forth, struggling to stand in the depression where my foot had been. Small black, cottony feathers shake free from its body, scattering around itself.

Something falls from above, passing inches from my nose and landing on my foot. A black mass crashes on top of my boot. It's another bird. It rolls off the top of my foot, falling onto the ground. Its wings outstretched and unmoving. It's beak opening and closing, as if gasping for air.

Two black spots struggling for life on the cold ground.

It sounds like applause coming from above, and before I can look up, a hail of dark wings and talons come crashing down, knocking me on the top of my head, their claws scraping down my jacket, fighting to grasp onto something before colliding into the earth. One of their talons catches the ridge of my ear. I scream, swatting the bird away, and when I feel it fall, I raise my arms, close my eyes, and shield my face. I sense warm liquid pouring down my ear. It must have broken skin.

My lips tremble, and I am frozen here, unable to move. My breath feels trapped in my throat. Was I even breathing? What was happening? I am too afraid to open my eyes for fear of them being punctured by crows raining down all around me. I imagine my eyelids being clawed, corneas sliced open and milky white vitreous eye gel flowing down my cheeks. I feel another bird crash down on my head, and when I adjust my arms to try to cover myself more, someone's hand is on my shoulder and I'm being pulled away.

"Come!" It is a woman's voice.

Without realizing how, I am walking up the steps of the former Essanay Studio.

The woman who brought me inside is now standing at the door, facing outside, brushing large fluffy snowflakes off the arms and shoulders of her black tweed coat, and dusting off the front of her pencil skirt. She turns over her shoulder and gives me a sweeping look, before returning her gaze to the window. "I hardly think a few birds are going to bring about the end of the world."

"Excuse me?"

She runs her fingers through her short bob. "It's a quote from Alfred Hitchcock's *The Birds*. Have you seen it?"

"Yes," I say, picturing that famous press photo of lead actress of *The Birds*, Tippi Hedren. In it, she's wearing a white spaghetti strap A-line dress. Her right arm is bent at the elbow, where she balances a large raven perched on her forearm. She looks at the camera defiantly.

"He spent some time in Chicago," I say, trying to catch my breath, and waiting for feeling to return to my face.

"Who did?"

"Alfred Hitchcock. He filmed parts of *North by Northwest* here."

The woman ignores my answer, acknowledging only the birds outside. "They're just silly things, really."

A collection of crows lay on the ground. They look like large, shiny black apples shaken out of a tree. Their wings whip and flap about them, struggling to right themselves. It is as if they are magnetized to the cold ground.

The woman reaches up and taps the glass with a finger of her black leather gloved hand.

Tap. Tap. Tap.

In that moment, it is as if all the birds outside are awakened from their trance, resurrected by some invisible electric current. One by one they break free from whatever spell they are under. They tear themselves away from the ground. Their great black wings open, and their bodies launch into the air. They flock up to the tree from which they fell. The birds perch on branches and gather closely together as snow gently accumulates on their rainbow obsidian feathers.

I look down at my jacket, expecting to find the fabric of my black coat torn open, white stuffing spilling out, but there is nothing. I touch my ear, running my fingers down my neck, but feel no moisture as I had just felt moments ago. I reach for my phone, open the camera, and point the device at my face. I angle my head just so in order to see my ear and neck on the screen. There is no blood as expected.

"They're just being overly dramatic, but don't worry. They can't do you any harm, unless you allow them," Wren says over her shoulder, a hint of a smile on her lips.

I want to tell her that I thought I saw her yesterday morning, walking away from Bela's school, but it seems like such an out of place thing to say at the moment. I knew that jacket and that dress and this form. It was the same sunburst color hair and Giallo gloved hands. Wren had been Grand's assistant for years, often appearing in skits with him before and after commercial breaks.

Before I can fill the silence between us, she says, "A Grasshopper frolicked while an Ant stored food for the winter. When winter came the Ant was comfortable; the Grasshopper not so."

It made absolutely no sense given what just happened.

"What?"

Wren returned her focus outside the window to the birds.

"It's an Aesop's Fable. It means, prepare for the future. The crows don't seem to be preparing for the future."

There it is again, these fables with their strange meanings and lessons I felt like I was being called to interpret. Days before I had rarely ever heard of them, and now it seemed like they were seeping into every aspect of my life.

She turns back to me, looking me over with scrutiny. "You do look like her," she says, sounding disappointed.

"Like who?"

"Your profile picture from your channel. Never can be too sure with internet strangers these days."

"Should we call someone?" I say, pointing outside and feeling stupid as soon as I say it. How would that call to animal control really go? 'Hey, I was attacked by some crows, but they're all back in their tree now. Can someone maybe come by and check and make sure they don't have motive to do it again to someone else?'

"One should never provoke a crow. They remember faces and can hold grudges."

"Is that another Aesop's Fable?"

"No." Wren raises her eyebrows. "It's an important life lesson. Come, follow me. Grand is looking forward to speaking with you. He said it's as if he's been waiting to talk to you for years and years."

I follow her down a dimly lit hallway where we turn right.

"How long have you worked for Grand?" I ask, already knowing the answer to the question, but needing to talk, to do anything, to lower my heart rate after being attacked by a black-feathered mass.

"I've worked for Grand for thirty years."

We come up to a short hallway painted black. Glass sconces line either wall, softly illuminating not just the way, but shinning a light on the vintage horror movie posters on display.

"They're all original," Wren says, knowing exactly what it is I'm thinking.

Frankenstein, The Bride of Frankenstein, Son of Franken-stein, The Ghost of Frankenstein, Frankenstein Meets the Wolf Man, House of Frankenstein, and *Abbott and Costello Meet Frankenstein.* Grand has each movie poster from Universal Studios's *Frankenstein* series. At least once a year he would show a few from this series and, like every film, delve into the historical background of the movie, as well as an overview of the career of the actors involved. His love and enthusiasm for the adaptations of Mary Shelley's masterpiece have always been evident.

"Mrs. Ramos," a voice calls.

The room at the end of the hallway is as I and audiences everywhere have seen before, classic Hollywood Gothic maximalism, like a movie set plucked from a Hammer film. The majority of his program was recorded in front of a set, but sometimes Grand would read viewer mail from this space, his office.

Grand is standing in the center of the room, in his signature black tuxedo. He has wavy black hair that rests just at his shoulders, and a black mustache and small goatee. He's much, much taller than me. He reminds me very much of the youthful Count Dracula in *Bram Stoker's Dracula,* starring Gary Oldman, Keanu Reeves, and Winona Ryder. Yet basic math tells me Grand is not youthful. Grand must be in his seventies, and his face indicates that, with deep, heavy lines across his forehead and around his eyes. Still, there's no separating Grand from the black, white, and gray paint that produces his mask for the outside world. He is the character he plays, in many ways. And even now, as expected, he is in full stage makeup.

The office is decorated in deep reds and blacks and golds. An intricate crystal chandelier hangs from the center of the room. In one corner, there is a deep velvet crimson settee and displayed above that are shelves showcasing antique broadcast microphones, a nod to Grand's past as a radio reporter. Above those is a row of antique desktop radios, a Crosley art deco mid-century, what looks like a General Electric from the 1940s, and two small square Zeniths. Before I can ask where the film antiques are, I spot them on the opposite wall. Grand has several vintage projectors positioned on top of sturdy cabinets. Above them are old film reels displayed on the wall.

"Those are empty," Grand says of the wall display. "Those, however, are not." He points to a massive glass case holding several film reels in which large metal discs appear in various states of rust and decay.

"Is that fire damage?" I ask, approaching the case and pointing to one reel whose steel polish is hidden under a layer of black ash.

Grand nods. "We had this case custom built with fire protective glass. I didn't like the idea of these beautiful things sitting inside a vault."

He moves to a wooden chair, I assume where he will be seated for the interview, and his movements surprise me. He is faster than I expect someone his age to be. Another chair sits directly in front of his, where I will be seated. The lighting equipment and a camera are stationed and ready for our interview. He had offered to supply me with all the technology I would need for the recording, so long as he reviewed and approved the recording first.

All I needed to do was to be present and ask him questions.

His eyes meet mine, and suddenly he is standing a foot from me, a hand extended toward my cheek. "The birds attacked you, didn't they?"

I reach up but then drop my hand. How could he have known that? There was no scratch and no blood. "It's fine. I'm fine. I've never seen birds act that way…"

"They just want to be a part of the show, but once they see there's no room for them, they spring back to their branches."

"None of that makes any sense, just like this…" I dig into my bag and produce the book.

Grand's face beams, and I can't help but think about what he looks like under that layer of stage makeup. He claps his hands together once. "I'm so glad Master Bela received this book."

"How did you know where I live and that I have a son and that his name is Bela?"

Grand takes the copy of *Aesop's Fables* he sent to Bela in his hands, admiring the leather-bound green cover. In the center there is an image of a lion with a tiny mouse resting on his paws. Beside him is a peacock. The branches of a tree extend across the front and a cat rests there snugly. There is a hare and a turtle, a bright sun, and just above it a crow.

"Everything is easy to discover on the internet. Do you really think I would not research a stranger who requests to meet me in my home?"

That was fair. I realized also I had mentioned Bela by name in many of my videos and he had even appeared in some. I suppose Grand was right, anyone could stitch together aspects of my life just by watching my previous shows.

He hands me back the book. "I'm sorry I've upset you. That was not my intention. I do hope you accept this gift from me and my admiration of you and the work that you do in horror. I also find it a joy to see that you involve your son in the genre you love so much. Horror is a great teacher, and this book holds many lessons, sometimes the lessons come after something terrible has happened, much like horror. I hope I have not offended you. I only wish you and Master Bela well."

There he was again with "Master Bela," and while I found it silly, it was strangely endearing.

Once known as broadcast journalist Konrad Jonas, one Saturday evening in Chicago in 1979, audiences turned on their television sets to discover a new horror host. A man dressed in a tuxedo and hat. His face was covered in white and black makeup, his eyes and cheekbones appearing sunken. His lips red.

"I am Grand Vespertilio, and I am here to show you things that will sicken you, disturb you, that will terrify you, and, let's hope, make you descend into a rich madness from which you never return. Sit back and welcome the fear."

He then proceeded to lay down on a wooden table. A woman in a black dress stepped around and stood next to his head. She reached down, produced a machete, and brought it down on Grand's neck. Blood squirted out from the stump, and the camera zoomed in on the woman's face we were later introduced to as Wren. She calmly looked into the lens and said, "Welcome to our show."

The censors were bombarded with complaints. The violence was too realistic, with many believing what they saw really unfolded, until, of course, when Grand returned looking fine after a commercial break.

"Some horror hosts incorporate humor," Grand had said on that famed 1979 debut. "We here celebrate Le Théâtre du Grand-Guignol while honoring the special effects mysteries of the early makers of film."

Le Théâtre du Grand-Guignol was an addictive and unimaginably gory Parisian theater of horror and terror. Life-like depictions of murderous and criminal exploits drew locals and tourists. Grand had alluded that he had spent time at the theater at the end of its existence in the early 1960s. Many people always assumed that's where Grand got his stage name, but he never confirmed nor denied. Still, somehow, he wound up in Chicago, a man with a love of horror and its history.

I flip through the pages, not really knowing what I was looking for.

"*Aesop's Fables* and horror, I would not have made a connection there." I shove the book back into my bag.

"Do you know the history of *Aesop's Fables*?" Grand asks.

I try to think of anything, but all that comes to mind is: "All I really know is "The Goose That Laid the Golden Egg." That's as proficient as I am in fables," I say

He points to the chair positioned next to the camera, and I take a seat.

"The author's name was Aesop and he was born around 620 BC. He was a slave on the Greek Island of Samos. It's said that early in life he was not able to speak, but after doing a good deed for the Priestess Isis, she prayed for him, and he was thus granted the ability of speech. Shortly after, he was freed. Aesop enjoyed telling stories, highlighting the lessons they taught. He was famous for his tales, and because of his talent, was resented by many. He was sent on a mission to visit the Delphinians by King Croesus, and it was there that he was accused of stealing a golden cup from the temple at Delphi. He was accused of blasphemy against the god Apollo, and as his punishment, he was thrown from a cliff."

"Well, that is a horror story," I say, but my thoughts return to yesterday. The street. The accident. Why am I here? My brother was killed and I'm so driven to learn about this film that I won't even allow myself to mourn him, but maybe I mourned him long ago, when I was younger and any normal person would have canceled, been home with family after watching their brother, even their estranged brother, take his last breaths, mangled and bloodied on a cold, snowy street. But I knew it was getting closer. Last night proved it, as did this morning's new emails demanding I provide the location to the film. If I didn't figure out where the film was, I knew I would be next.

"Are you alright?"

"Yes," I lie.

Grand leans back into his seat. "Fables are stories I find comfort in, even as horrible things happen around me. I hope they bring you comfort as well." Grand nods at the camera beside me. "Are you ready, then, to talk about the history of the horror host?"

CHAPTER 19

SATURDAY AFTERNOON: BRUCE

I dig out the ladder from the cluttered back room, crowded with stuffed cardboard boxes and old posters and empty frames. The ladder is rusted and the paint is chipping in parts. An old, worn thing that creaks and moans occasionally, but still it works, much like me.

Polly said it would be too cold to be outside, but a little cold didn't scare me. The bitterness of our winters had long ago burrowed deep into my marrow, an infection I could never shake. When she insisted I get rest after what had happened, I asked her if she would be staying in and resting herself.

Silence was her answer.

I needed to keep busy after Noel. As did Polly, because that's what we did. We kept moving through the tragedy of it all, the tragedy of life and living, of never knowing when and where we'd take our final breaths. And never knowing when we would be present for the final gasps of air from someone else. I never imagined Noel would die just feet from the theater and the apartment he called home for so long. Sometimes something inside us warns us not to return home for a reason. The unfairness of it all, of losing him after he had reunited with Polly after so many years.

It is the right thing to do. To take this ladder out and paste up those letters onto the marquee and announce to the old community that I was leaving and the theater would be under new ownership. The bloodstained asphalt in front of the building is a reminder enough that it is time to leave. I thought I'd die here too, but maybe it was okay to let Chicago go before she dragged me in, encasing me in the frozen dirt of Graceland, Rosehill, Oak Woods, Bohemian National, Calvary, Burr Oak, Forest Home, or another one of its local or surrounding cemeteries.

It was time to allow my story to come full circle: a man once left his country by boat to tour and settle in a great city by a lake and then was lucky enough to do what he loved, sharing the wonder of movies with his neighbors and children. That man then had a family, and that family had a family, all of them continuing on in the movie theater business. But either I didn't love it anymore or it didn't love me. I felt the tug leading me away. It was time to hand over the theater to someone who could care for it the way it wanted and needed to be cared for.

This building had played host to millions of memories in the form of first dates, a chorus of laughter, and a sea of tears. It was once called the Paramount Theater, but that was a long time ago. It wasn't fancy like a Balaban and Katz theater. But people from that time no longer existed, and names like Paramount and Balaban and Katz no longer registered in the minds of patrons seeking sweet and salty snacks, a cocktail or two, comfortable seats, and sound system that swept them into another reality, so that they could escape their own—if even for a little while.

Sometimes I wondered if I held on to the theater too long, but what I was holding on to was Polly and Bela, my family. I would have loved for Polly to have taken over the theater. I begged her. "Here are the keys," I told her. "I don't want a penny from you. Take it. This place is your home. It's Bela's home too." But she refused, saying it was best I sell the theater and use that money for my retirement. I felt that response was wrong as soon as she said it, but I respected her answer, even though I knew Logan Theater didn't just belong to her, but to Bela as well.

Before long, people around the neighborhood would forget me. Eventually, there will be no one from the old neighborhood, and so there will be no forgetting. All of our second deaths are coming, a day when there will be no one to remember us. A great tide of unknowing. Newcomers moving in, settling in, and making this place theirs.

And I know the new ownership of this building will contribute to the erasure of my memory, and of Noel's and Polly's. That is the danger of newcomers, their unsaid position that their existence is the superior one, but we all must end. None of us are immortal and we have to reckon with the love and suffering of our lifetime one day meaning nothing to no one. As we live, we are all old movies in a way, a collection of prized memories that we recall and play back to ourselves. But newcomers, new buildings, even the tragedy of gentrification, it's the promise of a nitrate film catching fire, and the raging inferno dancing around it, swallowing up everything that came before.

I drag the ladder down the lobby carefully, its edges leaving an impression in the carpet. My back didn't like me doing this so much, but I won't tell Polly she was right, that I should have waited for Bass to have a moment to do this for me. I stop at the glass doors and lean the ladder up against the wall so I can pull on my gloves. The sidewalk doesn't look too slippery. I had scattered some rock salt early this morning, but maybe it was a good idea to toss some more on the ground.

I reach for the white bucket beside the door and step outside. The wind stabs my face, and I smile. How I cursed the cold for so many years, and how I know now I will miss that brutal wind that reminds me each time it sweeps across the deep lines on my forehead that I am alive.

I set the bucket down and open the lid.

More snow fell last night, a dusting, but still enough to give us work. Many people from the apartments above came down early this morning and brushed off their front and rear car windows. Some parking spaces were already empty, people who drove off for the day to work. But before they left, many were sure to place plastic chairs, cones, or anything large enough to take up space in the parking spot they had dug three feet of snow out of the other day. Dibs, one of the other uniquely Chicago things I'll miss. People respect that around here. If you dug out the snow from a parking spot, it was yours, until the weather warmed up enough and surrounding snow piles melted and the city came around with garbage trucks to throw out your old lawn furniture used as placeholders. It's like that all over this city; all you need to do is lay your claim to a space and call it. People are smart around here not to disrupt someone's position, even a dibs spot. Doing otherwise could easily get you killed.

I reach for the scoop inside the bucket and gather some rock salt, starting right in front of the theater and working my way down to Intelligentsia next door. I stop, my head tilting back, and I admire that white marquee, bordered in red and a double row of lights. Suspended just above is our beacon, that vertical LOGAN sign that has welcomed so many here to my home.

I liked all of the movies we played, romance, action, mystery, comedies, horror. I loved stories, and I just felt so grateful each time to sit in one of our seats, and as the lights dimmed and the screen illuminated, I felt complete in knowing that this was my life's work.

I will miss it all.

The early showings. The late showings. And every year when Halloween would roll around and Polly would pull together another horror movie series. People would come from all over

188

the city to see what she thought were the best films. Audiences enjoyed our horror offerings because Polly showed independent, big budget, and silent films, ranging from slashers to monsters to psychological horror to ghost stories. She knew each of them had an important story to tell, and if anyone could understand how to process horror and horrible things happening, it was her.

Our ghost stories were always shown in theater number five. I didn't really believe in ghosts, not in the rattling chains and moaning down long, dark hallways looking for vengeance or peace kind. I didn't believe in those theater number five ghosts like Polly and Noel did when they were kids, but I couldn't deny that they and other people believed something happened to them in that room.

What I did believe in were the memories of places and people. Those people, those movie stars on silver screens. Could any of them who performed in silent pictures so long ago know that they would be immortalized, frozen in a fragment of a moment of their life? So many of them are stuck with us, playing a part on repeat, forced to perform again and again for audiences when we hit play. We are all time travelers to a reluctant past when we sit down and watch an old movie.

Those are ghosts that grace our screen, the actors of old movies who died long ago. We're watching an essence of them caught in a loop. Film as purgatory. As those performers approached and faced death, did they find some level of calm, or even panic, in knowing that they would not really ever be gone? There is no facing a second death when your doppelgänger sits and waits in celluloid.

I watch a flickering bulb overhead. The L will give out soon, which is fine. It had to be fine. I could no longer climb up that far to make sure those fluorescent letters would burn bright down Milwaukee Avenue. My hands are no longer steady, and the glass bulb would surely slip from my fingers.

My back ached from spreading out rock salt. I place the bucket back in the entryway. I push the front door open and lock it into place and retrieve the ladder, pushing it outside.

I look to the windows. I cleaned them myself this morning, even though my fingers ached throughout the motion of moving back and forth. It was in this discomfort, of the biting scent of Windex and the sounds of cars moving along behind me on the street, that made me remember not a specific moment, but a feeling of excitement. That excitement was planted and rooted in this very place, and in this very spot. Perhaps it came from knowing I held that door open for thousands of theatergoers. Perhaps it was in knowing that I sold tickets to many a couple on their first date. Or perhaps it was knowing that magic, real and true magic, erupted on those screens for decades.

There was wonder here once. Grandeur, in fact. But it all feels like it's not even my memory anymore, like it is a story told to me by someone else that I keep trying to recall.

The posters are faded, as is the paint on the walls. Plaster continues to crack throughout rooms, a spiderweb that grows with each passing night. The carpets have come into contact with a variety of human fluids that no matter how many times I scrub or shampoo the material, a heavy sour stench remains.

All of this and the neighborhood is changing. There is no denying that. For sale signs were followed by joggers, and then people walking their dogs at times of night you once would never see anyone outside, unless they were looking for trouble. Coffee shops opened and offered a warm greeting to newcomers, but cold stares to those of us who were born here. I know the movements and the names—revitalization, urban renewal, gentrification—but all of that ultimately meant displacement for those that already lived here.

In the coming days and months there would be community meetings demanding affordable housing remain in the neighborhood, and the newcomers would nod and press their lips together as if in deep thought, and then shout their buzzwords like "unity," "diversity," "intersectionality," "defund the police," and cheer that they are excited to meet their "brave" neighbors. But were they really? They pin up their BLACK LIVES MATTER signs in their all-White neighborhoods but won't step foot in Black Chicago neighborhoods, and they certainly don't make their own White neighborhoods welcoming to Black Chicagoans. They speak of acceptance of all cultures but clutch their designer bags when a Latinx or Black person walks past them. They speak their White liberal trending words when they move into diverse neighborhoods to ease their own guilt that they are pushing diversity out. Then they have the audacity to call themselves Chicagoans. This city was made by Jewish, Black, Greek, Czech, Italian, Polish, Mexican, Puerto Rican, Chinese, Indian, Filipino, Ukrainian immigrants, and more.

Everyone has a right to live where they feel safe and comfortable. What pains me is feeling like a stranger in my own neighborhood. Yes, I have Polly, Bass, and Bela. There are also a few regulars who still watch a movie here and there. And also those who stop in when they are in town visiting from out of state or the suburbs. They come in chasing nostalgia, hoping to sense the specters of their younger selves here in the lobby or in the seats.

But I see how their eyes gloss over the place, and how they cringe when they note the widening stains on the carpet and crumbling plaster. I tried to keep up with the building as best as I could, but it's grown far beyond what I can manage at my age. Very often, our passions don't pay. Too frequently, maintaining these passions requires financial security, and, well, between my small savings and social security, it's an impossibility to give this place the financial commitment it needs.

Because of that, I feel like a failure some nights. In a way, I am abandoning the family business because I had not been able to save as well as I should have. There's no money in owning a small theater, especially when for decades I looked away when kids snuck from screen to screen, or I gave an extra bag of popcorn or box of candy here or there. What was most important to me then was that people came here and felt, if even for a few hours, they could escape all of the troubles that were awaiting them outside in the streets.

Inside Logan Theater, I promised them an escape. All they needed to do was sit down in a seat and gaze their eyes upon a screen, and for just a little while they could be transported away from the cold and the ever-increasing taxes and political corruption, alderman who sold their souls to corporations and lined their pockets with donations, and the gangs and the gunshots and the long commutes on the El or Kennedy Expressway to their awful jobs and abusive bosses and those fragments of desperate dreams they just could not grasp.

All my patrons needed to do was leave the heartache outside, because inside, I promised them magic.

I look down at my watch and then up to find a black car parallel parking in front of the building. The car is silent and the cleanest thing outside where everything is covered in sludgy, dirty dishwater-colored snow. It is one of those fancy electric type vehicles with tinted windows. I know this is the man I've been waiting for.

The man approaches, looking as fancy as his car, all black clothes and polished shoes. He is elegantly dressed, but misplaced all the same.

"I remember you," I say.

He removes his sunglasses and smiles. "And I remember theater number five."

CHAPTER 20

SATURDAY AFTERNOON: PALOMA

I rest the notepad on my lap, look down at the first question, and begin. "What was the first horror movie you remember watching?" I glance at the camera to make sure it is recording.

His lips part, and in that moment, there's something about how the light falls on his face that makes him seem much younger than he is.

"That was indeed quite a long time ago. I'll instead talk about how horror has been foundational to me."

I don't object, why would I? I'm curious to know what brought him to this career, because in a way I saw much of myself in him.

His legs are crossed, and his hands are folded on top of his knee. He's draped in dark shadows, except for a single light focused on his face and chest. "The horror genre does work that no other genre can do. It explores the depths of our hopes, fears, nightmares, failures, guilt, revenge, and love, and it does so through the lens of a ghost story, monster mystery, demonic possession, or slasher. Modern horror viewers have grown the genre into all sorts of directions I could have never previously imagined. Ultimately, horror is art, with all of its fangs and sharpened blades, racing hearts and disembodied cries in the night. Our art is the movie set and its props, fake blood and the actors who allow themselves to be covered in red corn syrup at sweltering film locations. They do this for us. The films that moved me to want to explore the genre include *The Cabinet of Dr. Caligari*, *Haxan*, *Nosferatu*, *Faust*, and *Vampyr*. Earlier works as well…"

"Earlier than 1920?" I can feel my eyebrows drawing upward. He was certainly reaching far behind the curtain of the golden age of silent film.

"Of course," he says, his eyes wide. "Horror cinema stretches back to the founding of film itself. The first movies were made by the Lumière brothers, and those were shown in Paris in 1895, twenty-five years before *The Cabinet of Dr. Caligari*."

"But the Lumière brothers didn't make any horror movies."

He leans forward in his seat. "Ah, Mrs. Ramos, I knew I would enjoy speaking with you. The Lumières may not have created a horror movie, from what we know. But it's because of them that we have horror movies. Their invention of the cinematograph inspired others to create. And it only took one year, one single year, since the invention of the cinematograph for the first horror movie to be made."

"The idea of projecting an image actually existed long before the Lumière brothers, Auguste and Louis, patented it in the late nineteenth century. The brothers were inspired by William Kennedy Dickinson and Thomas Edison's Kinetoscope. In Dickinson and Edison's design, a film strip was passed quickly between a lightbulb and lens. The viewer would then look through a peephole to watch the images unfold. Edison didn't see the possibility of this design and viewed it merely as a toy, and perhaps because of this he failed to have the motivation to obtain copyrights beyond the United States. When most people in America and abroad witnessed the new invention, they were in awe. Others, including some in Chicago, saw the new technology as a means to make them rich."

I look down at the notepad on my lap and the questions we had agreed upon, that I was surely going to deviate from. "I heard you were a board member of The Silent Film Society of Chicago. Is that true?"

"Yes, that was a few years back. At my age, it's difficult to manage so much, but I do what I can from afar. I try to visit Portage Theater, The Music Box, and other theaters where their screenings take place. I do prefer the live accompaniments, but those rarely occur."

Not many people today would associate silent film with horror, but I suppose not many people would even think to watch silent films, or black and white films. I can't imagine many young people look forward to watching Grand host a vintage film on Saturday night when they can just stream an endless catalogue of high action or high gore horror on a number of subscription services or watch free content like horror shorts or even my show online.

Content is constant and unlimited today, including horror. It never ends. We have options. If something doesn't appeal to us, we can turn to the next channel or device or app. So, when someone turns to Grand's show or mine, or especially a silent horror film, that's an interesting choice they are making. They are choosing to engage with something often aligned with the creation and foundation of horror.

"Do you know a lot about movie making, Polly?"

"A little. I know about cameras and filming. I worked first at WGN studios for a bit and then for some local television shows, but…" I stop myself from saying it because I hated recounting those days on the sofa in which I thought I'd never get up. "I got sick and needed to stay home. I used what I learned between my old jobs and school for my own show."

Grand's eyes are intense. The whites of his eyes are bright, not clouded by age. "And about film history as well?" he presses.

I know enough. I know that one of the earliest recorded films by the Lumière brothers is a forty-six second movie called *Workers Leaving the Lumière Factory*. A camera is pointed at factory gates, and we watch as women in long dresses and wide hats, many clutching lunch pails, exit a building and then move out of frame. It's just a mass of people, moving with intention, similar to images we have seen many times before in commercials, on television, and in theaters. A swarm of people in motion with purpose. Today there's really no reason to take notice of such a scene, but long ago there was. These images left audiences mesmerized.

"It wasn't the Lumière brothers who we can thank for modern horror cinema," Grand says, pulling me away from my thoughts. "But a persistent young filmmaker named Georges Méliès. Méliès was experimenting with film around the same time, and it wasn't too long after he acquired the technology to create movies that he filmed a horror movie—"

"*The House of the Devil*," I say, finishing his sentence.

Grand's eyes light up with amusement, and I see the cast of what was once a boyish face beneath the deep lines. "I'm very glad to see we have the same interests."

I feel myself gripping the notepad, searching for anything to hold on to as I move on to the next unapproved question. "And it's the one film you have avoided speaking about publicly. Why is that?"

Grand relaxes back into his chair, his eyes turning up to the ceiling. "It's three minutes and no one can adequately summarize what happens in those three minutes."

In this moment, it's difficult for me to ignore that a replica poster of *The House of the Devil* appeared at the Chicago Theater, stabbed into the theater manager's chest. Was it coincidence? Or was it synchronicity? The occurrence of two events appearing connected somehow but aren't.

My focus moves past Grand to his desk and to a single framed picture that I can't look away from. He notes my distraction and doesn't even need to turn around to see what has caught my interest.

He lowers his head, once again meeting my eyes. "I see you found her."

"Is that...?" I say, already standing.

Grand meets me at his desk. His movements are smooth, quick, a young man. He extends a hand toward the frame, motioning me to come closer, and that's when I note his fingers are not spotted, or gnarled nor twisted with time. They're smooth and youthful. He pulls his hand away.

It's a small wood-framed black and white photograph with a signature in the bottom right-hand corner. "How'd you get a signed picture of Maila Nurmi?" I reach for the picture and hear someone behind me say, "Please don't touch his things."

I'm not surprised that Wren is this protective of Grand.

"It's fine, Wren," Grand says. "Did you need something?"

She holds her hands together in front of her waist. "You have ten more minutes."

"Yes, we know. We can keep time."

"Well, the knives are ready. I've picked them out since you two were taking so long." She shoots me a look I can't quite interpret and then exits, her heels hammering into the floor as she departs, signaling her frustration.

I return to the picture of Maila. "I've never seen her like this before," I say. "She's beautiful. As Vampira and here just as herself."

"I was and am a great admirer of Vampira, and the woman behind Vampira, Maila. Every person who has come after to host audiences of horror has her to thank. She was the first to step out onto this great stage and all of us who have come after should be grateful for her work." He looks from the frame to me and then says, "You do look like her."

I suppose I do. Not the character of Vampira, but the woman who played her. My focus moves to the cabinet beside his desk displaying metal discs and boxes of all sizes.

"And these films in the protective case are?"

"Rare prints of silent films recorded in Chicago."

I can feel my heart start to race. What Grand has here is beyond rare. It is historic and priceless. "Are these from Essanay?"

"Some from Essanay. Some from Selig and others."

"Aren't you afraid of a fire?" I ask.

Grand returns to his seat while I stand there, entranced by the possibility of what lived within those metal disks. I am transfixed by that cabinet, inspecting every detail of the film reels within. The dents. The rust. The peeling and yellowed labels. The swooping letters written in blue-black ink long ago.

What was captured on those rolls of 35mm?

He continues speaking behind me from his seat.

"Much of the lore comes from this idea that the material itself will self-combust. That's not necessarily so. Nitrate film, used often in the 1920s, was indeed highly flammable. The problem was not so much that it would erupt spontaneously into flames, but that if it should catch fire, then it was nearly impossible to extinguish."

I think of the fire that decimated the Irving Park and Western Avenue movie production lot. "Which is what happened at Selig's studios."

"Indeed, and which is why we are not only a city whose history of silent film is forgotten, but we are a city forever tied to hundreds, possibly thousands of lost films."

It wasn't long after moving pictures were invented that Chicago took part in the new technology. William Nicholas

Selig was born in Chicago and moved around for some time, working in the world of vaudeville and sideshows. He turned to stage magic for a while and was a successful performer. While traveling through Texas, he visited a kinetoscope parlor, a small storefront where people would pay a few cents to press their face against a small machine, turn a crank, and watch images float by. Selig was enchanted. He believed there was huge potential in this new technology. He returned home and rented office space on 8th Street in the Levee District, Chicago's once infamous red-light district.

It was around 1895 that Selig saw an exhibit of the Latham and Lumière machines at the Schiller Theater in Chicago. He saw the financial opportunity this new invention presented and wanted access to it. He tried experimenting with projection technology in his Peck Court office, but he became frustrated because he was unable to create his own device. In true Chicago spirit, Selig got what he wanted via questionable means. He went to a guy who knew a guy.

Selig turned to Union Model Works, a Chicago machine business on Clark Street. There he met Andrew Schustek. When Selig explained to Schustek the machine he was trying to build, Schustek confessed to him that he had been working with a foreign customer, a gentleman who had been coming to his shop asking for Schustek to reproduce certain items for a mysterious mechanical device. The enigmatic stranger never revealed the full scope of what the machine was or its purpose. Still, Schustek took interest in the project and made sketches of the pieces he had been asked to produce.

Soon, Schustek learned that his customer was from France and had been directly involved with the demonstration of the Lumière machine at the Schiller Theater that had initially inter-ested Selig in creating his own machine. The French client paid a premium for each piece that was reproduced, and never left a name. But what he did leave behind was a perfect set of plans that Schustek used to recreate a motion picture and projection machine, which he made for Selig.

Who was the French stranger in Chicago who commissioned a replica of Lumière's film machine to be made? There are rumors it was Georges Méliès himself, but what would Georges Méliès be doing in Chicago in 1895? Some may mistakenly believe he was attending The Chicago World's Fair, but that was two years prior in 1893. There's no account of him visiting the fair or Chicago around that time. By all accounts he was still in Paris. What we do know is that Gaston Méliès, Georges Méliès brother and filmmaker, set up a studio in Chicago in 1908.

I return to my seat, sensing Grand following my every shift and adjustment as I try to make myself comfortable.

Schustek left Union Model Works to work with Selig who opened a second office at 3945 N Western Avenue. Together they recreated the cinematograph, applying small enough changes to the device in order to avoid patent infringement. That machine was named the Selig Polyscope, and it's because of that machine that they would go on to create one of the first major movie studios, spanning thirty-two acres. It was from that location that hundreds of movies were recorded and distributed.

Grand drops his chin gently, and he's focused on a point on the wooden floor. His voice grows softer. "That former movie lot today is just a collection of overpriced modern houses, shaped like boxes, built cheaply and quickly surrounded by streets plagued with congestion. Most people in this city don't realize that much of what we consider the key aspects of a movie production studio lot were developed and refined here on the Northwest Side. The history of cinema is intertwined with the history of Chicago, but many people refuse to acknowledge that."

I'm still trying to grasp how all of this can be connected. "Around the same time Méliès is filming movies in France, Selig is making movies here in Chicago. Don't you think it's strange that both of them are stage magicians turned filmmakers?"

"Synchronicity, Polly," he says. "Oh, how you find so many synchronicities. There are many throughout the history of film who were magicians."

"Why would magicians be drawn to filmmaking?" *Was it the power of illusion or something more?* I think to myself, wanting to hear Grand's answer undirected.

"Just look at Méliès, he was a stage magician before filmmaking and after. He owned his own theater, and he was a master of illusion, knowing how to make things appear and disappear."

The question waiting to be asked is cold space between us. "So Méliès was a stage magician. Selig was a stage magician. Maybe you were a stage magician before you started your broadcast career?"

Grand smiles. "Did you once live in the Shoemaker's Loft? It was once the old Florsheim Shoe Factory?"

It seems like Grand knows a lot about me. "You know where I used to live?"

"You mentioned it once on one of your programs. It's funny, Méliès's father was a shoemaker. You have to understand that not everything will be a hard coincidence. Synchronicity is just a hint, it's a breeze, a wink that there's something there, something you should be listening to, paying attention to. Why did the universe pull you to live in the Shoemaker's Loft? Was the universe trying to tell you something about a certain shoemaker you may have something in common with? We're drawn to things and people and sometimes we don't even know why, but that's the fabric of reality—pulling us together, placing us where we are meant to be. And so, to answer your question, the stage is magick. Film is magick. I know that. And I believe you know that as well, just like Méliès knew that, a man who was the son of a shoemaker who turned magician. The Shoemaker's Magician."

I don't even refer to my notepad anymore. It's a farce and we both know this has nothing to do with a school project. "Can I assume that the rumored print is not just a rumor?"

Grand draws in a deep breath. "Where did you hear this?"

"It's Chicago. Everyone's got a tale to tell. Someone in some pub on some cold night mentioned it to me when I told them I was studying the history of horror movies."

A grin spreads across his face. "You hold your playing cards very close, Polly."

Even the reference seems coincidental. I think of Méliès's first ever recorded film, *Une Partie de Cartes*, in which a group of men sit around a table in a French park playing cards. The film was once thought to be lost but was discovered in the 1980s. Maybe I needed to stop thinking of these things as coincidence. It was all, as I was quickly discovering, synchronicity.

"Polly, people romanticize the possibility of a cursed film, that images flitting across a screen can compel us into some wicked action. It's similar to this idea many monotheistic religions hold with regard demonic possession, that an entity can take hold of someone's body, pulling them along like a puppet. Or maybe we should think of possession as a greater violation. It's as if someone breaks into your house, ties you up, and is allowed to assume your entire identity, slipping into your life while simultaneously upending it. People often point to the supernatural to explain away their monstrous activities. 'I didn't smother my child in their sleep. The demon did!' Or, 'I didn't put a bullet in my husband's head, I was possessed by evil.' No film can make a person evil. People just are evil."

Hundreds of emails sit in my inbox from Quasimodo.

A body found in the Chicago Theater.

And my own brother was killed.

I know none of this was an accident. This is all happening because of that film and because of what I had done so long ago.

I would not allow it to take me or Bela.

"Some people have said that you have a copy of one of Méliès's films in your private collection. The print that we have of *The House of the Devil* was discovered just in 1986, and there's a rumor that there is an original recording of it."

"You speak to people who spread so many rumors, Polly. That can be dangerous."

"I need to know if it's true."

"Maybe. Maybe the first ever recorded horror movie is a cursed film, and maybe actor Charlie Chaplin brought it with him to Chicago from Europe after he came here to Essany Studio to film several movies," he said.

I imagine Charlie Chaplin walking through this space, carrying a large film reel one evening, making his way to the vault. "Then this building, and perhaps the vault downstairs, would be a perfect place to hide it."

He shakes his head. "You're more than welcome to visit the vault, but I assure you it's empty save for dust and cobwebs."

"Then the film could potentially be anywhere in the city? S theater, perhaps?"

He shrugs. "Perhaps."

"You're not denying that it exists?"

"Polly, I think you know I'm saying that and much more."

This was taking too long, a winding road with no end, but I know I have no choice but to sit here and ask more questions. I wonder now if Grand had known this entire time why I was here. Is that why he accepted my interview? "I feel like you're telling me the film is real and it's as dangerous as I thought. Like some sort of supernatural virus."

"Perhaps, but then we both likely sound a lot like that detective woman from last year…"

"Lauren Medina."

"Indeed. Detective Lauren Medina, who believed in an evil ·

so all-consuming that it traveled through the ages here to kill the children of Chicago. It sounds quite mad, doesn't it? And then doesn't it sound mad, then, too that the first horror film, which is also the first cursed film, is being stored here in this city and that it poses the power to cause massive death whenever it is shown?"

I feel a tightening in the center of my chest. "I'm starting to believe she wasn't mad."

"That's probably a good assumption. It's probably also a good assumption to know that some things are kept hidden to prevent disaster. Some things are difficult to contain. Sometimes a special person is required to guard these things from those who will misuse them. Unfortunately, sometimes evil seeps out from between cracks, causing an accident, a murder, an explosion, a war, and then it must be sealed and contained again."

Before I can ask my next question, there is a knock at the door. Wren.

"We have to prepare for the intro and," her eyes dart to his hands, "we need to finish your makeup."

"Ah, indeed." Grand rises from his chair and waits to move until I walk past him and meet Wren in the hallway. "I wonder, Paloma, have you seen the 1910 version of *Frankenstein*?"

"Was that filmed in Chicago?"

"No, the Bronx. But in it, the monster is not killed by man. Instead, the monster looks into a mirror and then fades after seeing its reflection."

"Why is that?" I say, clutching the notepad to my chest.

"Because he's protecting people from himself."

CHAPTER 21

SATURDAY EVENING: PALOMA

The studio is smaller than I thought it would be.

Two cameras point at Grand's set, which consists of a large desk, a leather chair, bookshelves displaying horror movie memorabilia, a door in the far-right corner as well as a small piano, and then, of course, his signature coffin from which he would emerge and return to at the end of each show.

No one introduces themselves to me or suggests where I should sit or stand. It feels as cold as the *Chicago PD* and *Chicago Fire* sets I had worked on.

A light beams on the coffin and people move quietly to their places. The theme song begins to play. It is an original score inspired, he said, by reading *The King in Yellow*. The play was rumored to induce despair and madness in anyone who viewed it. Grand wanted a theme song that would generate the same wave of emotions.

I watch on a small screen nearby what audiences at home are viewing. It begins with an animated entrance reminiscent of Vampira's show over sixty years ago, with a long, dark corridor rolling with fog. On the walls on either side are posters of the great Universal Monsters, the Creature and Wolf Man, Frankenstein and Dracula, the Mummy, and then the camera approaches the coffin. The live recording begins.

Grand pushes open the door.

"Good evening," he says as he steps out.

"The cursed movie. It sits on our consciousness as a horrifying possibility…"

Does he plan on talking about cursed films? Or is this just another coincidence? A day dotted by events and occurrences related. There it is again, more synchronicities.

"Very often our idea of cursed films is related to movies about the demonic, like our unofficial Satanic trilogy, *Rosemary's Baby*, *The Exorcist*, and *The Omen*. There are others in this subgenre of horror. Satanic themed films, with possessions and cults that appear to take away the babies of pregnant women, is still a steady category. Why do you think that is, dear viewer?

"And why are these three films, *Rosemary's Baby*, *The Exorcist*, and *The Omen*, thought to be cursed? Or is it that people are just so frightened by the possibility of the Devil that anything evil is somehow related to him, and the demonic?"

Grand winks. "What is the saying? Speak of the devil and he'll appear? Let's go ahead and speak a lot of the devil, then, and hope he arrives."

Perhaps today's audiences would not faint in the front row as young Regan, played by Linda Blair, spews green vomit, but in 1973, when *The Exorcist* debuted in theaters, many were gripped with such terror they collapsed in their seats. Others were rushed out of the theater, whisked directly to a local priest who prayed over their poor soul under attack by the diabolical.

Are the rumors true? Can an image on screen compel us to do something outside of our control? Or are we placing blame on something that does not exist, all to shield us from our own intended cruelty? Perhaps it's just all urban legend wrapped in tragedy that allows us to simply separate our lips and whisper the word "cursed" to explain the awful things associated with these images on film we believe exude evil power.

"I ask you, dear viewer, are you prepared this evening to sit with me and watch a film that's been claimed to be…" Grand pauses and looks from side to side, and then whispers, "… cursed?"

He walks slowly toward the camera. "Don't worry, I promise you that *Rosemary's Baby* cannot harm you."

The cameraman raises a hand, signaling the introduction is complete and we are now in commercial break.

Grand isn't Chicago's first horror host, that honor goes to Terry Bennett. Bennett appeared on WBKB in 1957 wearing thick, dark-framed glasses, a black jacket over a black turtle-neck, and black slacks, embracing Vampira's all-black attire. But Mad Marvin didn't embody a romantic Victorian Gothic aesthetic like Vampira. Mad Marvin was a horror host of his time, a demented beatnik. On his show, Shock Theater, Marvin pushed the macabre humor, once claiming to swallow poison and slowly describing the effects to a horrified audience at home who believed he really was dying on live television. Panicked viewers flooded phone lines, demanding someone help him. He didn't really swallow poison, but the power of the horror host proved to be very real that night. Marvin's stunt translated to a spike in ratings, proving people wanted to be scared.

While many recent horror hosts aired recorded episodes, Grand pushed for and maintained a live format, which made him not only the one of his kind in horror today, but the only one of his kind in all of American broadcast television. The popularity of American variety shows long ago died, and live television showcasing performances and sketches exist only minimally in late-night talk shows.

The lights dim, signaling the return from commercial break. I notice once again how none of the crew speak or even acknowledge one another. I understand the need for quiet, but it is strange not to hear anyone's voice, other than Grand's, especially with other people in the room.

On television screens in homes, audiences have already been introduced to Rosemary and Guy Woodhouse, who just moved into their new apartment in the Bramford building in New York City. This is the part of the segment where Grand gives a brief overview of the lead actors in the evening's feature. I check my social media feed, and like each week before, viewers at home are posting their viewing experience live.

"It's DEVIL BABY NIGHT!"

"This movie always freaks me out #Grand"

"What death scene is Grand going to play out for us tonight?????"

"Watching Grand! #GrandVespertilio"

The hashtag #GrandVespertilio is a top twenty trending item in the United States this Saturday evening, like so many Saturday evenings before.

"Rosemary's Baby is based on Ira Levin's 1967 best-selling novel by the same name. The film adaptation came later that year, with lead actress Mia Farrow playing Rosemary Woodhouse and John Cassavetes playing Guy Woodhouse.

Grand paces the stage, his hands behind his back. The camera follows him.

He stops and faces the camera. "Synchronicity," he says. "This film, from the beginning, was already full of so many synchronicities. Coincidences, or curses in the making? Or maybe we can just call it damnation by design?" He walks over to his black leather chair and sits down, staring at the camera, connecting with his audience at home.

"Even the neighbor being named Roman, like infamous director Roman Polanski, is somewhat curious. It's no coincidence that both men, the fictional character and the director, are abominable people."

Grand reaches over to the coffee table beside him and picks up a copy of *Rosemary's Baby*. It's at that moment I notice on the bookshelf behind him that familiar hardback with a leather green spine, a near identical copy to the one in my bag right now. The letters from here are clear, *AESOP'S FABLES*.

"What is the legacy of *Rosemary's Baby*? There have been remakes, like a 2014 miniseries with Zoe Saldana, and there was even a sequel published by Levin, *Son of Rosemary*, in 1997, but nothing in the same category has been able to horrify moviegoers the same way. Have we been desensitized? Is it a tired trope? The devil's offspring is no longer original? Perhaps. Now back to *Rosemary's Baby*."

The cameraman standing in the center raises a hand, signaling the end of this segment, and the film continues where it left off, with Rosemary in the basement doing laundry. Once again, the set goes quiet. There is no chaotic flurry, no chatter, no loud positioning of any equipment or questions for Grand about his next segment. His workers fall back into the shadows and remain silent until it is time to reemerge.

Grand approaches and takes a seat beside me. "I think this movie is a good example of the panic that can grow around a film dealing with tragedy. I don't believe as much interest would have arisen had it not been about the occult. I certainly don't believe any horror movies have dealt with the occult accurately. Wouldn't you agree?"

His eyes are fixed on me and waiting for an answer. I thought about the hints to the occult throughout the film. A pendant full of herbs, Rosemary waking up from sleep with scratches down her back, the image of her nude on a mattress surrounded by naked men and women, and finally the black cloth covered bassinet with an upside-down cross hanging from above. When Rosemary approached that bassinet with knife in hand, she demanded those people seated in the apartment tell her what they had done to the baby's eyes. Rosemary then discovered that Satan was really her baby's father. The cult raised a toast and cheered, "Hail Satan."

In 1968, these images shocked a largely religious public, but today, these scenes are mild and tame, silly even, for the average horror moviegoer. Yet, even though what images we find terrifying on film has shifted, the allure, the legend, and the mystique of the cursed film remains. We want to believe that something we can view has the power to manipulate our actions against our will.

I feel like the show should have returned from commercial break by now. Time slows. I answer him. "Not many horror movies know how to deal with the occult. Some have witches who practice low magick consult on set, but there hasn't been a single accurate horror movie made depicting high magick. Wait," I think, "I take that back. *A Dark Song* tried." I remember the fasting, the purification, the chanting, the sigils drawn on bare wooden floors with chalk, and the commitment the protagonist, Sophia, made, all to complete one simple spell that took a year to execute.

Real magick isn't instant. It's not a few words chanted or a puff of incense. Real magick pushes our physical, psychological, and emotional limits to places we could not previously believe were states a human could achieve.

"Ah yes," Grand says, placing a finger to his temple. "*A Dark Song*, a film about a grieving mother who conjures a Holy Guardian Angel via the The Abramelin Ritual. It's such a powerful message, a moral lesson—the lengths a mother will go for her child. A mother would do anything for the love her child. I'm sure you will agree with this?"

"Bela's autistic, high functioning. He's had some challenges, but he's had the right social and emotional supports in school and at home…" I stop myself, realizing too late I was oversharing. That was one of the drawbacks of being alone so much, that once I got around people, I just didn't know what to say, how to say it, or when to stop. "He's fine. It's just…he's my only kid. I love him and want to protect him."

"What do you want to protect him from?" Grand asks.

I can picture his bedroom window open and the curtain flapping in the wind, snow rushing in. I can see his floor undulating with the movement of black birds packed tightly, covering the floor like a great, black carpet, all inching toward him asleep in his bed.

"I want to protect him from everything and everyone."

"I'm sure you will do just fine protecting our Master Bela," he said.

He's really committed to this role. How could he wear this makeup all day? Speak like this all of the time? Did Jonas even exist anymore beneath that mask of latex and paint? I want to ask him that, but I have so little time and I need to know about the film.

"Will you be exploring the occult on your program any time soon?"

I know enough about the occult to know that people do not want to really know about the occult. People didn't want to know about Enochian magick, Kabbala, the tree of life, angelic conjuring, demonic conjuring, the lesser banishing ritual of the pentagram and the lesser invoking ritual of the pentagram. People didn't want to know about the middle pillar and the rose cross, the shem operation, and all of the other rituals, designs, and sigils I had studied and performed for years. Could a casual reader even understand the writings of Crowley, Warrick, Regardi? Never. Because people expected and wanted life to happen for them easily. Real magick demanded commitment.

This took time. This took study. This took devotion.

I've read *The Golden Dawn* cover to cover, twice. I rewrote it all by hand once, all one thousand pages. I know the timelessness of this all, of us, and I don't think people really care to know.

The occult in horror movies is often relegated to some weak bastardization of what writers and directors in Hollywood *think* is the occult. There are often groups of people chanting in Latin or some made up language, dark robes, nudity—lots of nudity—use of herbs or symbols or sigils that didn't really have any meaning, and, of course, astrological symbols, references to planetary movements, and, for good measure, pentagrams or pentacles, because modern movie makers often didn't know the difference between the two. And don't forget the sprinkling of some demonic-sounding names in there.

"No, I won't be exploring the occult in films," I say. "Right now, I'm focusing on the Universal Monsters and also the Shock Theater package."

"Shock Theater," Grand nods impressed. "That's a phrase I have not heard of in quite a long time."

In the 1940s, major movie studios were more focused on their latest releases rather than their older titles. There would be an occasional re-release, but generally little was done with them. Sometimes these older films were sold to smaller companies in reissuing packages. None of these distributors, like Film Classics or Astore Pictures, were as successful as Realart Pictures. Realart Pictures secured reissue rights to the Universal Pictures library, which included *The Wolf Man*, *The Invisible Man*, *The Mummy*, *Frankenstein*, and *Dracula*. Realart showcased these horror "thrill-bills" in small theaters across America. In Chicago, these fright films played on neighborhood screens throughout the city.

At first, the motion picture industry feared television. Then, after they saw the success of older films being reissued on smaller theater screens and the success of television, they turned to TV as a place they could send their older titles that were gathering dust in vaults.

Local TV stations acquired film packages that were often associated with a specific series, giving them such titles as Family Classics, Sherlock Holmes Theater, Gunslingers, and Mystery Theater. What proved to be the most popular among TV viewers was horror. With so much old horror hitting televisions, a revival of vintage horror pictures gripped the nation. Then in 1956, Screen Gems secured the broadcast rights to six hundred movies from the Universal Pictures library that debuted before 1948.

Many of the horror movies from this acquisition were packaged together and called "Shock," and over 142 markets in the US aired a late-night Shock Theater series. And soon, horror hosts donning black clothes and sitting in dark rooms would appear on numerous local stations, from Los Angeles to New York.

"Well, right now I'm really looking just at those vampire films from this package and then I'll expand to the rest of the films in Shock Theater, expanding to all of the Universal Monsters."

"What does your audience think so far about all of those dusty, antiquated movies?"

"I think most people get bored of them, but I don't care what people think. They can watch something else. They don't have to watch me. I enjoy talking about these movies and so that's what I'm going to do."

Grand leans closer.

"And you don't get bored of old movies, Polly?"

"Old horror movies are not scary, but I don't think the purpose of a horror movie is always to scare. A lot of people come to horror seeking an extreme experience, to witness something taboo or to be frightened so much so they'll remember that scene or that moment from that film forever. That's not really what

213

horror is about."

It is as if his eyes flicker in the dark room, a small spark of electricity within the stillness. "What is horror about, then?"

"That, I'm still trying to figure out, but it's beyond fear. I grew up in an apartment upstairs from a movie theater that used to show old movies, so if I wasn't watching them on my television set, I'd sneak downstairs and the owner would let me walk into whichever screen I liked. He used to show a lot of horror movies, and for me, they were a way to process the horrors around me."

A buzzer sounds, noting that Grand is expected on set. This time he takes a seat in his leather chair. The cameramen return to their positions and Grand begins.

"*Rosemary's Baby* is infamous for several reasons," Grand says. Atop the bookshelf behind him there are framed pictures of what seems like all of the Universal Monsters, Dracula, The Wolfman, Frankenstein's monster and his bride, the Creature from the Black Lagoon, and beyond. On his desk are figurines of modern monsters, Freddy Krueger and Jason, Michael Meyers and Jigsaw.

"It's been quite some time since we've shown *Rosemary's Baby*. The last time we did, we received some angry responses from viewers saying that they find this film uncomfortable because of its demonic subject matter."

Wren takes a seat beside me. I hadn't even heard her enter. Her gaze is focused on Grand.

"This is true," she whispers.

Grand raises a picture on the desk. "Composer Krzysztof Komeda, who was a friend of director Roman Polanski, wrote the score for the film. Komeda was accidentally pushed over an escarpment by his friend Marek Hlasko. Komeda would die in a coma four months later, and his friend eventually took his own life."

Grand places the picture face down on the desk and raises another. "This is producer William Castle, king of the B-movie, and director, writer, producer, and actor in dozens, from *The Old Dark House* to *House on Haunted Hill* and *13 Ghosts*."

He places this picture face down.

"William Castle didn't die during *Rosemary's Baby*," I whisper.

Grand clasps his hands together, and as if he heard me from the far back, dark corner of the studio, he says to the camera, "Now, William Castle didn't die during the filming of *Rosemary's Baby*, but he was hospitalized with severe kidney stones and almost died during production. Because he was gravely ill during filming, and also because Komeda had just died, people associate this with perhaps being connected directly to the movie, and by that, connected to the film's association with Satanic worship."

"I think he's trying to upset people again," Wren says, crossing her legs and sitting back in the chair. "He likes to do that. To make them see how small their fears really are. Demons and witches and ghosts. The things of childhood nightmares. What they need to fear is each other. A movie can't hurt you."

I hold back a laugh. "You don't believe that yourself."

She eyes me up and down, then returns her gaze to Grand. "Only if you let it in. We knew you'd come, by the way. That's the only reason he accepted your invitation. We know this isn't about school, some silly scholarly pursuit. We know what you suspect."

"I need to know if what I saw was real."

We both go silent, listening as Grand leads the audience into the next segment, doing what he loves and what he has done for a long time.

"It was indeed very real."

CHAPTER 22

SATURDAY EVENING: SEBASTIAN

"What's that?" I point with my chin toward the abandoned building.

"It's called a street," Gutierrez says.

"No, seriously. I saw something." I'm already unbuckling my seatbelt, and I push my door open.

"Whoa." Gutierrez reaches out his right hand. A car speeds past my door, and slams on the horn.

"I saved your life, you know that, right?" Gutierrez says.

I'm ignoring him as I'm already approaching the building.

"Isn't this technically trespassing?" he says, his voice cracking, and I get it. He is probably scared of rats and broken glass, and floors that can give way, and a sprinkling of mold, probably asbestos too, and squatters.

My hands are on my hips as I inspect the entrance. Scaffolding and layers of posters for events that have long passed cover the walls. The windows are grimy and clouded with years of dust. According to Robin's notes, this used to be one of the most magnificent movie palaces in Chicago. Today, it sits empty on a premier piece of city real estate that would probably cram hun-

216

dreds of condos into this area if this building was razed.

"I like to call this taking initiative," I say.

Gutierrez is standing back by the curb. He's paranoid and showing it, looking around him, eyeing each car that passes us. "Can't we lose our badges for this?"

I shove my hands in my coat pockets. It's colder than I thought. "Only if you shoot someone. So don't do that."

"Does anyone know we're here?"

"Of course not." I spin around. "We'd lose our badges."

Gutierrez looks back at the car. "Should we move it? It's just out in the open."

"It's fine. In case anything happens to us, they'll at least know we meant to do this."

"In case anything happens to us?" he repeats, and I roll my eyes.

"Welcome to homicide, detective, where we risk our lives every day knocking on doors and tracking down suspects."

I try the front door. It's covered in plywood, but I run my fingers down the sides of the edge of the material until I can find a good grip. I pull, but it won't move. I grit my teeth. Urban explorers have been getting in this place for months, it seems. They wouldn't try the most obvious point of entry, but it was worth a shot.

"How long has this place been abandoned?" Gutierrez asks. I can tell he's nervous and trying to keep his mind occupied. I walk to the side doors, figuring I should at least try those before heading to the back.

"Seventies? Eighties?" I say, trying the door to the very left of the main doors. It too is covered in plywood and the material does not budge.

"I hope the owner rehabs this place," Gutierrez says, taking a few more steps back and looking up, admiring the building's façade.

217

"What? You don't like your overpriced condos, cocktails, and coffee?"

"Condos aren't all that bad. Hector and I live in a condo. The city's changing, you're going to have to get with it, Bass."

The city was changing, had changed. Some days I didn't recognize it. People moving in. People moving out. Most of the people I grew up with in the old neighborhood moved to the surrounding suburbs. They went to communities like Evanston, Naperville, Arlington Heights, Schaumburg, or Tinley Park, places where they'd turn their nose up at the city and say, "I'd never live there again," but they sure did like to visit our restaurants and attend Bears games here.

If you've lived in Chicago, you'll crave it. There's no escaping the taste of her. Chicago is that relationship you knew was bad for you, but you needed more of, even though you knew it'd ruin you forever. But you'd let yourself enjoy the rush of it as everything around you burned down to the ground, and once you lost everything, you'd beg for those flames to consume you too just so you could feel her again. That was Chicago, and Chicagoans. Sometimes we didn't care how bad it got. We wanted it to be bad, because that is all we knew and there was no disconnecting from it. This was our identity. And so we burn, and so we stay.

Gutierrez is standing under the scaffolding now, looking up at the rusty, empty sockets. Decades ago, hundreds of lightbulbs lit the way for patrons to the box office of the Uptown Theater.

Next, I try the door to the right of the main entry doors. The plywood barricade here seems to be peeling back along the edges. "People used to get in this door," I say. I pull the material back a bit, but I can see the glass door beneath has been covered with plywood from the inside as well. We're not getting in that way either.

"Let's go around the back," I say, already walking down Racine, Gutierrez jogging behind me to keep up. We turn left and go down the alley until we come up behind the theater.

"What are we even looking for?" he asks.

It hasn't been shoveled back here by a person or service since the snowfall began. We trudge through mounds of frozen and packed snow until we reach the building.

"Not what. Who," I say as I reach the back door. "One of Robin's notes said there was a guy living here when she came searching for the movie. That man told Robin about someone else who'd come to the Uptown searching for the same film. Two people come to this theater searching for a rare silent film, and one of them winds up dead. Murdered. Where's the other person? That's who we need to talk to next."

"How's this guy even going to remember that? If he was asleep when Robin entered, it was probably dark. It was probably dark when that other person came before her looking for that movie too."

It felt like the temperature was plunging. Gutierrez's words were starting to come out strained as he fought through the cold.

"Even if we find him in there right now, how can we trust what he tells us? How can we trust he's reliable? We're probably the last people he wants to see. He's probably going to get really upset thinking we're going to remove him from the property," he said.

I assess the door. It's red and rusted over in a scab of time. It's cold as hell right now, and anyone in an abandoned building was taking a major risk with their safety occupying a structure that was probably not sound. If there was someone in here, I'd rather they be in a warming center with some hot coffee, but I was not going to remove any of Chicago's homeless tonight or ever.

I speak over my shoulder. "We'll tell him we can get him transportation to a warming center, if he wants and only if he wants, but we're not removing anyone."

I turn the doorknob and it moves. I hear the door separating from the frame. I pause. I take one more deep breath. I tighten my grip around the doorknob once more and then pull. There's a loud clang, and a pop as the door opens and I nearly fall backward. I exhale, pat the front of my coat, searching for my phone, and feel it in my left pocket. I remove it, activating the flashlight, a beam of light into darkness. A swirl of dust motes welcomes our arrival.

"We won't know anything until we find him and ask," I say, entering the building.

Inside, the light leads me along a ground covered in dust, dirt, and warped and mold-dotted sheets of plaster that had been ripped off the walls. Red, blue, green, and black graffiti cover every surface down this corridor. It's pitch black and the only light is the beams coming from our phones. Gutierrez is silent, but I hear his breath. I also hear the wind outside and inside, as nature has crept in through broken windows and collapsing walls.

We step through shattered glass, food wrappers, kick over empty cans and other debris as we make our way in further. I sense moisture all around us. Rain and snow have found their way inside. There is no concealing our approach. If there is someone here, they will hear us. If there is someone here, they also have an advantage over us, because they know this space better than we do.

A quick Google search on our way here didn't tell us much about the interior. The Uptown is listed as one of the state's most endangered historic buildings. When it opened in 1925 it was one of the largest freestanding theaters built in the country. More than one article called it one of the nation's grandest movie theaters. After a series of burst pipes and flooding in the 1980s, the Uptown shuttered. It's been decades since the auditorium with seating for over four thousand was fully occupied. But tonight, I hoped we'd at least find one person in those seats.

We continue following the hallway, moving further into the building. Once we reach what seems like the end, I raise my right hand, signaling Gutierrez to pause.

I can feel his breath on my neck, he is standing so close. Before I can say anything, he does.

"Did you hear that?" he asks.

I brush the thought from my mind. We are cold. Our feet are wet. It is dark. We had broken into an abandoned building. Debris is scattered all over the floor, left behind by people who either came here seeking adventure, or a glimpse into the past. Then there were those who'd lost everything and likely came to this dilapidated beauty hoping to gain shelter. The night, the darkness, and all the unknown things we step into right now spin ribbons of dread and worry around our senses, hearing, sight, smell, taste…

There is no need to strain to listen to the Uptown Theater tonight, because here, phantom sounds are the orchestra and, whether or not we want to, we have to listen.

"It's the wind," I dismiss, but then I hear it. The crackle and pop of speakers. A steady, electric hum.

"You hear that too?" Gutierrez steps ahead of me, aiming his light into that infinite pit, the light penetrating nothing but layers of shadows. It feels as if we are standing at the mouth of a great cavern deep within the earth.

"It sounds like…"

His words fall away, and we listen. Static crackles and then a faint tune fills the void. It sounds like something I have heard before. It is bright and jovial, almost like a children's song, but here at this time and in this space it feels sinister. Someone is here and they want us to know they are with us.

We move carefully, taking small steps, until the sound erupts all around us. Music that sounds like something from long ago, muffled and aged.

"Let's all go to the lobby,
Let's all go to the lobby,
Let's all go to the lobby to get ourselves a treat.
Delicious things to eat.
The popcorn can't be beat.
The sparkling drinks are just dandy;
The chocolate bars and nut candy.
So let's all go to the lobby
To get ourselves a treat.
Let's all go to the lobby
To get ourselves a treat."

The music stops.

Gutierrez gasps. "What the hell was that?" He's already reaching for his weapon, and I stop him.

"Our badges," I say. "If we mess this up, it will be bad."

"Ramos, should we call for backup?"

We can't mess this up.

I remember my days on vice. I didn't get most of my information by intimidating suspects or bringing them down to Grand Central Police Department for interviewing. I had to reach out to them in their environment in the hopes that they'd share whatever pieces of information they could so I could get another murderer off the street.

Here's the thing: sometimes my own informants were murderers themselves, and I knew that walking in. They were known for ordering hits on their rivals, or anyone encroaching in their neighborhood. But that's what people didn't understand out here—that sometimes you needed to shake hands with someone else's grim reaper to grant another peace. People wanted to believe in the myth of the hero. People wanted to believe that all humans were governed by an unwritten book of morals. What they didn't understand was that book was being revised and re-written each day. We did what we could to set the dead free from their purgatory and to prevent any other lives from being lost.

What is justice? Where do we draw the line? Sometimes there's no black and white in the streets, and that's hard to internalize for some people who want to believe in a fairy tale that there are mostly good people in the world. There aren't. Boogeymen don't just exist on your screens or between the pages of your books. Your boogeymen live right in the world and breathe the same air as you. They are the people who will break into your homes, demand your credit cards, and slit the throats of your children because you took too long to get them what they want. They are the people who will walk up to your car at a red light at one in the afternoon, raise a gun to your face, and even as you open your car door to let them have your vehicle, they'll still put a bullet in your mouth. Why? Because morality does not exist within the structure of monstrosity, and monsters do not care about any of us.

And sometimes there are people who wield a strange sort of street justice, pulling the strings of a moral code and compass they have designed for their followers, and these are the people I need to turn to at times. Some of us have to walk the gray line, sometimes no line, in order to keep others safe there in the light.

The music continues to play, an endless, menacing loop reminding us that we are not alone and whoever is in here with us knows exactly where we are.

"No, we're not calling backup or anyone."

We take cautious steps forward, our footsteps echoing around us. The space feels massive, expansive, endless. I'm afraid to take another step, fearful my next move will leave me tumbling into a bottomless black pit.

"I think we're in the auditorium," Gutierrez says, taking two steps forward. His flashlight lands on the wooden back of a seat.

He scans it left and right.

"Looks like we found the back row," I say. I've had enough of this and that awful tune. "Police. Who's there?"

My voice reverberates across the weather-worn carpeting and crumbling plaster, but no one responds.

"We just have a couple of questions," I shout above the song, out into open black space. "A woman was here a few weeks back. Do you remember her?"

The music pauses mid-tune.

A piercing bright white light flashes before us.

A glowing rectangle appears, suspended above as if floating in space.

"How is that possible?" Gutierrez asks.

My fingers grow numb from the cold. "I don't know. There's no way the electricity is on in this place."

I had read a compliance agreement with the city which required that the Uptown continue maintenance and upkeep on the structure. The white movie screen before us stands in direct contrast to the decaying elegance it illuminates. The screen goes black, for just a moment, and reemerges. There's a soft crackle. The floating white rectangle reappears and wisps of black dirt form in the corner and then disappear. The intermission song plays once again, but this time we see the characters appear on the screen before us. Four animated food package items are on display—a box reading "candy bar" holds a baton, a bucket of popcorn holds a "REFRESHMENTS" sign, a box reading "candy," and a drink—singing, "Let's all go to the lobby…"

"That damn song never sounded so creepy," Gutierrez says.

I step forward and then turn my back to the film. I see light on in the projection box above.

"We just want to ask a few questions and we'll leave. Then you can get back to whatever it is you're doing here."

There is no response and no movement from above. I sigh.

"I really don't want to go up there," I tell Gutierrez, but I've brought us this far. I follow the line of back row seats, searching for a stairway to take us upstairs. I can feel Gutierrez's back practically against mine as he's walks backward now, keeping an eye on the booth above.

"I don't see anybody moving up there," he says.

"And they're not going to until we come to them," I say, already knowing what kind of person we're dealing with. Whoever is up there craves power and is not going to bend to the command of anyone.

I have no way of knowing how to get up there, and safely. Railings could give way. Floors could sink beneath our feet. I feel Gutierrez pause.

"I don't like this, Bass. Something's not right here."

The song ends. The screen goes black once again. I locate the exit into, of all places, what seemed to be the lobby. There should be a stairway leading upstairs.

"Bass!" Gutierrez loud whispers and grabs my arm.

The screen once again explodes to life, glowing, but silent.

"What is that?"

A black-and-white scene appears. A woman in a dirtied and dusty white silk dress emerges from a doorway of a building that seems to have been burned or collapsed or both. She brings her hands up to her face as the sun falls on her, her features twisted in anguish. The camera moves over to two men on top of a pile of ruin, crushed and pulverized bricks and stone.

This is the end of a struggle. One of the men stumbles off and the other remains immobile. The camera zooms in on the face of the unconscious man. And slowly, his nose, lips, and cheeks begin to dissolve in the harsh sunlight, first into a foamy, liquid, before evaporating to gas.

Thick black tendrils of smoke emerge from the ruins, like fingers, reaching out to pull the decaying man into the earth.

225

"*The Return of the Vampire* from 1944," a voice booms from someplace above.

"That's nice," I say, annoyed. "We heard you may have talked to a woman a few weeks back who came here looking for a movie. Her name was Robin. Do you remember anything about your conversation?"

"Do you watch scary movies, detective?"

"We can talk all about my likes and dislikes when you come down here."

"What fun would that be? We need some of this build up. Some of the anticipation, don't we? Tell me, what's your favorite horror movie, detective?"

"They're not really my thing," I say, listening closely to see which direction his voice is coming from.

"I really do like that scene from *The Return of the Vampire*. Rarely do we get an adequate vampire bursting and disintegrating from the blast of sunshine anymore. Recent vampires seem to be sparkly things or creatures exemplifying people's sexual urges or frustrations or both. Real vampires are quite miserable things. Creatures cursed by some god to live forever, bearing witness as the world shifts and changes every few years, morphing into something unrecognizable from just moments before. That's human development, constantly evolving, and sometimes not for the greatest good. We've lost so much with time. We've lost human connection, and I suppose we should just accept these changes. Because what's the point, after all, in seeking and nurturing human connection when that being will suffer and die and all you can do is watch and allow that pain to consume you again and again."

Gutierrez whispers behind me. "Should I call for backup now?"

"No," I say. We don't have what we need yet, and I feel like we're getting close. If we call for backup now, we could lose this guy forever and never know what he and Robin discussed.

I look up.

"I take that back! I've watched a few vampire movies with my wife. I sort of dug the vampires in *Near Dark*, *Let the Right One*, and that one filmed in Mexico, *Cronos*. None of those are sparkly or cute.

"Can you come down here now so we can talk about Robin? She was here a few weeks ago looking for a movie she believed could be hidden here. Do you know why that is?"

"Because Charlie Chaplin didn't think anyone else should have access to it. So, he hid it here, in Chicago somewhere."

"I'm assuming it's special because it's worth money...?

The man laughs a cold, sharp laugh. "Money? Do you really think something so rare and powerful could be sold? Would you sell the moonlight? Would you sell the howling of wolves on a winter's night? Would you sell infinity? Could you? You can't."

"My guy's a poet up there," I say to Gutierrez.

"Backup now?" Gutierrez pleads.

"No, there's nothing he's done to warrant that."

The man above in the shadows continues. "It's rare. It's the first print of Georges Méliès's *The House of the Devil*. Méliès's was a magician, not just a stage performer, but something much greater. He practiced a bit of conjuring and excelled at ritual magick. He frequented the meetings of the Hermetic Order of the Golden Dawn in Paris. He was associated with the same circles that included some of the greatest occultists in recent history— Aleister Crowley, Dion Fortune, Pamela Colman Smith, Israel Regardie. It wouldn't have been unheard of for an artist to join the Golden Dawn, as it included artists and writers like Algernon Blackwood, Sir Arthur Conan Doyle, Arthur Machen, W.B. Yeats, and Bram Stoker."

"You're losing me here, friend. You're telling me the film is rare, but there's no point in selling it. So, what's so important about it that there seems to be a steady stream of people looking for it?"

"Méliès created a film that serves as a sort of sigil, a talisman in a sense, in that it brings the viewer into direct contact with all of the seventy-two demons of the Ars Goetia. The benefit is instant, infinite, and timeless power. The negative is that sometimes death comes as a consequence when the film is viewed, for when something that strong is activated, a ripple effect of energy is to be expected. I will view it, and I will have access to everything I've ever wanted and more. Unfortunately, Robin could not tell me how to view the film when I visited her that night at the Chicago Theater. This evening, the man who lived here also unfortunately could not tell me. Just like Robin, he's now a part of the show. I suppose that only leaves one person I know who can access the film and play it for me..."

"Yeah, and who's that? Maybe we should go talk with them."

"Oh, I'd love to talk to your wife, Polly, Sebastian."

"Call it in now!" I shout to Gutierrez. I'm sprinting through the lobby. I find the stairs and keep moving.

My motions are automatic, and my weapon is in my right hand, barrel pointed upward while I try to navigate my cellphone light. My neck screams as I turn left, right, and rush forward, not knowing in which direction to focus, not knowing if there's just one person here or more.

I hear static and directions behind me as Gutierrez alerts nearby cars of our location. He's explaining the situation: "We have a suspect cornered. I repeat. We have a suspect in the killing from the Chicago Theater cornered. We're at the Uptown Theater."

The lights from our phones dance along the black-spotted and mildew-covered carpets. Clumps of once white plaster and dust and debris are caked on the steps. We reach the landing and go up another flight of steps, heading to the top level to the pro-

228

jectionist box. I feel my pulse quicken as we reach the top of the stairs. We're on the upper level now.

We no longer have to crane our necks up to look at the screen. Our eyes are level with that floating rectangle.

Laughter erupts from within the theater. The sound echoes off the crumbling walls, shattered windows, and sinking ceilings.

"Gutierrez," I call, but he's no longer behind me. "Gutierrez!"

I press down on my walkie talkie. "We're at Uptown Theater. A suspect from the Chicago Theater murder is here. We're in pursuit. We need cars now. We are in pursuit."

I step into the auditorium, and this time a new movie begins to play. There is no sound, just movement. The camera is fixed on a stone archway. The film quality is blurry, spotted by imperfections, streaks, and smears of fine lines. The film appears to breathe, the images expanding in and out from the screen. A black bat appears in the center, flapping its great wings in front of the arch. And then in an instant a man arrives in a great, large cloak. He's wearing black horns and he smiles as he straightens himself up, unfurls his jacket, and notes the position of the camera. For just a moment it's as if that man in that old film takes pause to note my presence, but it can't be.

He can't see me.

He's not real.

He's a recording.

He shouldn't be able to see me.

Something comes into view, but it's not part of the film. There's a rope dangling down the center of the movie screen. An object is being hoisted up. It's dark and round, and then it sits there fixed and floating in space. It's a human head. Its eyes are bulging from their sockets. Its mouth is open in a twisted and frozen final plea.

Before I can call for Gutierrez, the handle of something cold and metallic meets my jaw. Ringing fills my head, and before I can say anything, before I can pull the trigger, I'm struck once again. Heat spreads across my face, followed by a biting cold, and when I reach for my head, I'm already on the wet and worn carpeted floor. I try to say something, anything, but there's warm liquid running down my face, filling my eyes and clogging my ears, and all I can think about is that bat turning into a man, or was it something else?

CHAPTER 23

SATURDAY NIGHT: GRAND

After the show, I find it difficult to sleep, so I walk. The cold does not bother me, nor the slush, nor the reflection of the streetlights above glistening onto the mounds of frozen snow stretched across the city. I keep my hands in my pockets. My scarf is wrapped snuggly around my neck and my hat sits firmly atop my head, lowered over my eyes just so. I keep my head down and let my feet guide me into another block, street, or neighborhood. The architecture of houses morphs and changes as I cross different communities with varying historical and cultural influences. The names of streets tell a story of people who once made their mark here. All who come to this city are suspended on this grid, in a way. We are permanent fixtures, but still, our story, whether we want it to or not, will unfold. That is the wonder of a geographic energy center like this city. The stories we make here will ripple throughout time. A song. An echo. A story. A fable.

It's at night when it all grows the loudest, all the noises, the inhales and exhales of people asleep, nestled within dreams of comfort, or chained to nightmares. In their sleep is where I'll find them. They will dream of joy and love, of guilt and revenge, and they will wonder what should have been, and I will be there in a way, a nagging lesson.

It's when they are their most vulnerable when I can finally step out without the coats of white, black, and red paint on my skin. And so, they sleep, and so, I walk.

At night and in my real skin, no one knows me.

They don't know my missteps, and how I defied so much and fell so far for them, for all of them. Those nights were terrible, feeling my insides twist and burn. Blood would rise in my throat, and right before I would beg for it to stop, for death to wash it all away in a great storm cloud, it would all begin again. The grinding, piercing, gnawing, and ripping. I still hear the sound of skin tearing like a piece of cloth being cut with a pair of scissors.

The birds were never kind.

I'm not angry for what I endured, and what I continue to endure. I carry this burden, so they do not have to. Sometimes we must sacrifice a piece of ourselves for the larger part in the tale. I instead chose to sacrifice all I had for all of them. Of course, they'll never know what I've done. It's the weight I carry, and when infinity begins to suffocate me, I do what I can. I walk.

Often during these nighttime walks, those who are outside do not take notice of me as a man, but as a threat, and I find that curious. Some cross the street. Others look down, avoiding eye contact. No one wants to encounter a stranger during the day, let alone at night when there is no one nearby to intervene if violence were to play out. I feel sorry for them sometimes, for my very existence is a danger to them all.

I am all of the things unknown and known.

I am careful to walk in the shadows of shuttered stores and towering buildings. I find myself smiling with the fading and flickering of unstable streetlights, because they too crave to let the night sweep across the city. Slow-moving cars drive past, easing at stop signs and streetlights, so that their vehicles do not veer off in the opposite direction, carried away by the iced road.

Some nights I wish I could do this forever, walk, move, escape myself. But another morning will come, and another and another. I'm surrounded by everyone and yet no one, and I am so painfully alone.

Most nights my walks last hours. I pick a direction and move, taking in the noises that no one else can hear, of dreams that will dissipate as the sun breaks through the clouds. As they go about their day, they will forget the images that visited them in their sleep. The magic of dreamland fades so quickly, and sometimes I wish I had more gifts to grant them, to shake them out of a great state of forgetting.

Wren worries, as she does. Worry is weaved into the design of mortality. It's one of their flaws, a constant state of worrying over the inconsequential elements of today, forgetting that there may not be a tomorrow. They allow their minds to wander from one thing to the next, a frenetic playing and replaying of what-if events and of things they cannot control. All they need to do is stop. All they need to do is control their thoughts.

If you control your thoughts, you control your reality.

There is only one rule, thoughts become things, and we create our reality as we think it. But many refuse to believe in the power of themselves. Of course, there's magick, the tool we use to banish negativity, and to bring down the light, because that is what magick does. Magick brings us into harmony with the great cosmic forces, what mortals call gods and angels and demons. It's all the universe itself. That is what magick teaches us, reminds us, that we are all one, one single consciousness. Yet that idea alone is horror to many. That there is no great god. There is no fiery hell in which their enemies will suffer into eternity. All there is at the end is infinity, and complete rest. Except for me, of course. I'll never know rest.

And on these midnight walks, I reminisce. I defied the orders so long ago by stealing fire and handing it over to humanity, because I knew the possibilities it could bring them, not just destruction, but creation. With flame they created science and the tool that has given them so much life, so much to live for—art. I gave them the power to create. I gave them art. For this, I was punished by the father of all gods and humans, Zeus.

Zeus commanded I be chained to a great mountain, and it was there an eagle came to me each day to tear open my stomach and peck out my liver, clamping down on the organ and feasting on it each night. Because each morning I would be healed once again. Regenerated anew.

An immortal cannot die.

But an immortal can suffer, and suffer I did each night as I succumbed to the cold, sharp pain of skin being pierced, and the repeated stabs digging into my side. I watched as, again and again, that eagle's beak would dip into my body, producing another chunk of bloodied liver, and return again to the cavity for more. After thirty thousand nights of this torture, I was freed by Heracles, but I could never return home. Because what is greater than death is the death of all and everyone you hold familiar and dear. All of my loved ones had turned to dust.

The world had changed and all I could do was walk, take on a new form, and find a new life.

And I found a new life in Greece telling stories, as a man named Aesop.

I find myself next in this loop, not of forgetting, but in this idea of forgetting, of failing to remember, or being unable to recall. I pass closed shops and buildings. The surface of the Chicago River reflects the lights shining down from the skyscrapers above, and it looks like stars are dancing on the water's surface. What is it that I'm failing to think about, to know? I'm tired, and all of these years are a boulder I carry. Or maybe all of these years are stories, stories I collected and told and retold, and am pouring through them for meaning. Stories with great purpose, brimming with magic and wonder.

Fables.

They were my fables, another gift I granted them, and for that I was persecuted and sentenced once again to death.

I find myself standing in front of The Oriental Theater, and then I think of her.

Maila.

Now Polly.

The years are cruel reminders, and Paloma standing before me was the universe reminding me that sometimes infinity can fold in on itself, for just a blink.

Polly, the child who fell in love with monsters, and who now must face them. They know she came to visit me. I heard their claws tapping against metal, and their whispers begging to be released. Some shouted from beyond that they knew her. Of course, they know of her, she is a magician like Méliès, the others, me.

To that, the growling started and the moaning. They know that no projector, no old technology exists that can play the original film, but a magician doesn't need that technology to play this film.

Wren asks why I must task myself with this film. And it's simply because I promised to care for them, for all of humanity, and for this reason I will remain forever the caretaker of this movie unless another takes my place.

"Then destroy it," Wren demanded of me once.

"What is created by magicians cannot be destroyed," I told her.

I walk around to the Clark Street side to stand at Death Alley. I remember the crackling sound of glass and the bursting stage lights above. What year was that again? I believe it was 1903. That was long ago to them, but to me, I can still see the red velvet curtains erupt in a blast of yellow, red, and gold flames, cascading downward from the ceiling and sweeping across the stage, a tide of fire.

An afternoon matinee of *Mr. Bluebeard* was punctuated by the panicked cries of children and screams of mothers as they raced to the exit doors, many of which did not open on the main floor.

An exit door on the balcony did not open to stairs leading down to the street level. The door instead opened to death. Hundreds of mothers in their finest silk dresses and hats rushed down aisles full of black curling smoke. Some clutched their coughing and crying children to their breasts and cowered in corners. Others dragged screaming and panicked little ones to the top exit door. What all of them did not know was that outside that balcony door there was no fire escape. It was just a door that opened out over a city alleyway. A free fall to the brick below. The fire raged for thirty minutes and six hundred, mostly women and children, died of smoke and fire on a drizzly afternoon when they came to the theater to watch a fairy tale.

Inside, I had walked among the charred and ruined bodies of motionless babies, trampled children, and dead mothers cradling dead children. The cruelty of it all, I thought, that just a few inches of wood, plaster, concrete, and windows prevented so many from living. As the gold and red fire continued to beat around me, and as the meaty smell of singed flesh stung my nostrils and rose in my throat, all I could feel was the weight of this senseless death.

I spent so much time speaking of morals, writing morals, reciting these moral tales. What was the moral of that story, of mothers and babies burned to death?

Now, this alleyway in which I stand is just another route for transportation for people cutting through to State Street on their way to work or Millennium Park. This is what people do each day in the great city, walk over the locations of where people were killed, where their bones were crushed and where they took their last breath. Even a simple nondescript point can mark a moment in history of great human tragedy. And in this city, it's as if at every corner, every block, every major intersection or landmark someone at some point suffered there and died.

I refuse to ignore what has come and gone. They're all memories faded, but still there. Humanity, all of them, they are my own silent horror picture, my midnight matinee playing back ghosts long erased and forgotten, but fragments of their essence remain.

This is why I chose Chicago and why it pains me what must happen.

I haven't felt this ache in so long. The last time I felt such a pain I was chained and condemned to a lifetime of suffering. And even after I was granted freedom from that place I wandered for so long.

I was not seeking redemption.

My redemption was in knowing that my suffering allowed humans to exist with the gifts I granted them, fire, light, art. I saw cities develop and progress, rising and falling, held together by wisps of an idea whose basis was always control.

I continue to be fascinated by them and their repetition of patterns. It's always power that crushes them, leaving their cities lost in oblivion and bloodshed. What often remains is what they built with the flame I granted them. Art remains after the fall of civilizations.

I have fond memories of the past. I remember the long evenings in parlors with plush velvet seat cushions, the smell of polished mahogany stirred with smoke and absinthe on the breath of great minds. Between clouds of smoke, I listened to the

impassioned words of sculptors, painters, writers, and philosophers speak of all things beneath the umbrella of life and death.

I watched grand productions on stage in opulent theaters, and
then, one evening in Paris, I found myself in a little salon, the
murmur of poets and thinkers, the clinking of glasses, and then
silence. A man spoke. The lights were dimmed, and we gazed
upon a marvel of light and image. The gift of fire presenting its
possibilities. Our presenter, Georges Méliès, knew of smoke
and mirrors. He knew magick. He was magick. All of us in the
room that day knew we experienced something with the promise
to change everything. Real prophets do not need to evangelize.
Shortly after Méliès's presentation, I found myself in the Louvre,
speaking to marble and stone, whispering to oil on canvass, and
debating with gilded framed masterpieces, for I knew so much
was going to change. I left there that day in 1896, the echo of my
footsteps a hammer in my heart, because I knew it was time to
leave Paris. I needed to escape Méliès's marvel for as long as I
could, because I knew one day it would come to find me. And I
hear footsteps now against pavement, drawing closer to me.

I raise a hand, not needing to turn around immediately because I already see and know all.

"I suggest you do not come any closer," I say, feeling my
predator's thoughts flowing along their cerebral folds.

"Hey, do you got a lighter?"

I face him now. A man covered in layers, a dark scarf
wrapped tightly around his neck, reaching up to his nose. A cap
lowered over his eyes, offering only a small snapshot of his
cheekbones through the material.

I know that there is no such thing as coincidence. To be
standing beneath the spot where hundreds died escaping fire, to
then be asked to produce fire. Gods know that coincidence does
not exist. And for humans who have realized that they are more
than their physical form, that they are unconscious angels, they

too know that they can manipulate the events around them.

We are where we are meant to be at all times.

"I do not smoke," I say, seeing the unlit cigarette dangling between two fingers of the stranger's hand.

"If you don't have a light, maybe I can have your wallet?"

The stranger reaches into their coat pocket and produces a small pistol, the size of his palm. He pulls back the clip, a click reverberating along the brick walls of the Death Alley.

Smith & Wesson, I was familiar with the design, like I was familiar with a lot of things created by the two business partners.

I take a step forward. The man thinks, *This is unusual. They're usually afraid*, and on reflex he stumbles back a step. I remove my hands from my pockets.

"I once beat Smith at Poker." I point to his weapon. "He wasn't very good at cards, but he and his partner Wesson were very good gunsmiths."

The stranger looks down to my hands. He blinks rapidly, and then when he looks up, finding my face inches from his, I see his cheeks have grown pale.

"I don't want any trouble."

"Really? I was under the impression that's what you were seeking, which is why you've made the decision to be here with me, right now. You do understand the dilemma I find myself in?"

"Wait, I think I *know* you. Your voice…but you don't look like you look on TV. You look younger? But it can't be. What's your name?"

"I am the god of fire."

His mouth falls open.

The stranger's eyes widen with the realization that he does not know all that he thinks he knows. His thoughts are a projection of every moment he can recall, parents, school mates, lovers, and mistakes, all jumbled together in a sharp, cold pulsating flash. A blast of longing and regret surges along his synapses.

I look deep into his eyes, seeing all that was wasted. I look closer until I find that spiral of the cosmos that exists within all of us. "It's too bad you inserted the barrel of the gun into your mouth and pulled the trigger."

A gasp climbs out from his throat.

I step past him, continuing along my walk.

From behind, I hear him gag as he shoves the barrel of the gun into his mouth. I feel his neck tense and tighten. I sense his eyes begin to water, and just before he can even ask himself what it is he's doing and why, I hear a click, followed by a blast and wet burst of bullet meeting brain matter, exploding through cranium.

The body slumps to the cold, wet ground.

Just because I brought great gifts to humanity does not mean my presence is benign.

CHAPTER 24

SATURDAY NIGHT: PALOMA

My dreams aren't always plagued by memories of my mother. Sometimes my dreams are dark hallways dotted by the monsters I had seen loom and creep and crawl on screen. In this shadowy space beyond time, my monsters are all there, directing me to the end of a great hall.

I pass the Man with the Laughing Face, Quasimodo, Phantom of the Opera, Gillman, the Monster's Bride, the Monster, so many more, and finally Dracula, but it wasn't really Dracula. It was Dracula looping back to Frankenstein's monster and back. An immortal and a being brought back from death standing before me silent and serene.

Their mouths move, but I cannot hear their message. I cannot interpret the meaning of it all. Then, he, the monster that oscillates between the other, its form swinging back and forth like a pendulum between Dracula and Frankenstein's monster, raises its hand and points to a spot behind me, inhabited by dark, billowing folds, a timeless void.

From its center, a single pinprick of light appears, glowing

241

brighter, stretching itself until it takes form.

It is a shape.

It is a person.

It is a little boy.

My little boy.

I wake and feel my pulse. My heart is racing as if it wants to escape my body and exist on its own. I sit up, close my eyes and take long, deep breaths, assuring myself that it was only a dream, only a nightmare, an impossibility, but I know it's not. Because what is our hearts freed from our bodies other than our own children?

They can't have him. He is mine.

I shower. I dress. I make tea and once again I settle into my chair and plug into the screen before me. I look at the sheet of seventy-two names I wrote out for myself last night. I would read them today. I would finally issue the license to depart where it all started and finish the ritual I began so long ago but was too afraid to fully finish. But what if something changed? What if something in the atmosphere caught, snagged on my son, and swept him away into a void? What if what was protecting Bela this entire time were those seventy-two demons I had commanded to bring him into existence in the first place? What then? Demons as guardian angels? How could I ever separate them from him then?

I push the paper aside.

For now, I will go to what else is awaiting me today, the Spanish-language *Dracula*. In it, I watch as Carlos Villarías descends the same steps Bela Lugosi had just hours before. There was no film dubbing technology in 1931. Movie studios simply used the same sets they used during the day, but at night a foreign language crew would arrive to play the roles their English-speaking counterparts had played just hours before. When filming ceased for the day on Todd Browning's English production of *Dracula* staring Bela Lugosi, Carlos Villarías would arrive and don a black suit and cape alongside Lupita Tovar playing Eva, the beautiful woman menaced and plagued by evil.

"We all come to horror movies in search of something," I say into the microphone. "Isn't it funny that for some of us fear feels like comfort? Fear feels like home? Why is that? What are we trying to chase? What are we trying to solve? What are we trying to soothe that only dark shadows and screams can heal? There are those of us who challenge ourselves into an experience, searching and longing for that next extreme kill on screen, complete with wet sounds as someone succumbs to deep gashes in their neck, bite marks across their arms, or blades protruding from their sides. Some of us want to be that final person, victorious over the slow, lumbering predator who will just not stop their pursuit, until we stop them ourselves. And for others, well, maybe there's an appeal in the mechanics of the killer. No matter what, we come to horror because we want to feel something.

"I think that's why the monsters have become central to my life, because they have helped me to process my real-world horrors."

I pause the recording and stand. I clasp my hands behind my back, pulling them down as I stretch and open my shoulders. I see myself in front of the mirror, wearing a black long-sleeved faded shirt with Grand's face on the front that Bass bought me a few birthdays ago. After his show this evening, Grand wanted to talk so much about *Frankenstein* that I completely forgot to ask him about *Dracula*. I thought he'd be more interested in vampire movies considering his costume. He asked me if I knew the full title of Mary Shelley's book and I said yes, *Frankenstein; or, The Modern Prometheus*. He seemed very pleased. He said the subtitle often was omitted from the novel and most adaptations failed to mention Prometheus altogether, and that's all he said about that, which I found strange. I suppose we're all a bit overanalytical in the field of horror, constantly searching for meaning, picking apart human psychology, all while exploring violence, terror, and fear.

I sit back down in my chair and proceed with the recording, looking into the camera, serious this time.

"There's an epilogue from the original *Dracula* that's now been lost, relegated to the legends of lost films, but in the original version, Edward Van Sloan, who played Professor Van Helsing, addressed the audience directly. Van Sloan wished them all pleasant dreams and then said, 'Just pull yourself together and remember that, after all, there are such things as vampires!'

"Up until that time, a lot of horror films ended on some lighthearted note reassuring audiences that everything they had watched was a fabrication, but they didn't do this with *Dracula*. The creators chose to end the film unapologetically, owning that they presented the supernatural at face value, while leaving the audience with a belief, that vampires were real."

It wasn't difficult to see why that epilogue had gone missing. Some studio executive must have decided it was too shocking of a statement to make to audiences at the conclusion of the film that what they had witnessed could hold a dash of truth. For fear of backlash, the ending was removed, denying future audiences the experience of anxiety that earlier ones had, ones who would then believe the immortal lived among us. The suits at Universal didn't want to risk a dip in ticket sales, and so they decided that warning audiences of the existence of supernatural predators in the shadows was no longer important. And so, that infamous epilogue was removed, and now it's lost.

"Now, are vampires real?" I pause, noting here to include a few graphics, Max Schreck as Count Orlok, Tom Cruise as Lestat, Wesley Snipes as Blade, Kate Beckinsale as Selene, Aaliyah as Queen Akasha, Salma Hayek as Satanico Pandemonium, and Count von Count from *Sesame Street*, because why not? Even

Sesame Street defined our childhood with their loveable cast of monsters, signaling to children from an early age that we should turn to monsters for comfort from the outside world.

"They're real enough in that we have continued to explore them for hundreds of years. Why is that? Why do we fear the possibility of intelligent dead waking among us? Maybe because if that were true, it would just prove to us that we really don't know anything. If that were true, we would have to accept that we really can't make sense of this world, and we're really then unable to pull apart what is real and what is not."

I groan and pause yet again, knowing I'll very well have to edit out that groan later.

"Yeah, I'm totally going to lose them," I say aloud to myself, leaning back in my chair.

I could hope that someone would care and understand, but I had to relinquish that. I never did any of this for someone else. I always did this for me, my horror therapy. In thinking about vampires, sometimes I wondered if the allure wasn't in their immorality, or how they challenged the natural and supernatural design, but in the sadness of their existence, of not knowing the point of so many years stretching on before them. The wave and weight of infinity. It wasn't so different than the dilemma of the living.

An electronic bell sounds from the hallway. "Bela?" I look at the time. I peek into the hallway and find him sitting on the floor in his matching monster pajamas. His tablet on his lap and his index finger tapping the screen.

"How long have you been up?"

"Hi, Mom," he says without looking up.

Beeps and boops and whirring electronic noises fill the space.

"It's late. Tomorrow's Sunday, so you can sleep some more."

"I want Dad."

245

"Dad's at work."

"No, he's not," Bela says.

"Bela, Dad's at work."

"No-he's-not-No-he's-not-No-he's-not…" He says this in a long stream.

I raise my voice, just above his device. "Bela, your dad's at work. It's late at night. And I need you to get to bed."

"I can't sleep in there. The bird is loud today."

I feel a sharp ache in my chest. "The black bird?" I kneel, trying to get him to look away from his screen and to look in my eyes, but he doesn't.

"The black bird," he repeats.

I stand and push the door to his room open. It's warm in here, so at least I know the window is finally staying shut. I push the curtains back and look out and down. I see the snow settled on our roof, above it the bare branches of the tree in our side yard, and then I see it. The black bird. It's a large crow. Its black feathers gleam like polished obsidian.

I bang on the window with the lower part of my palm, but the bird does not stir. Its black and rainbow iridescent eyes remain fixed on me.

"It's just a crow," I say to Bela, but I'm really trying to convince myself as I close the curtains that I'm not scared. "Ignore it."

"It's too loud," he says, and I offer him to go back to sleep in my room, but he refuses, preferring to sit on the floor outside my office.

When Bela was a baby, he'd scream all through the night.

Everyone told us babies cried and fussed. They did so because they were hungry, tired, had wet their diaper, anything, really. But Bela's screams were pained. I could feel them in my jaw, shooting up my arms and resting in my shoulders. My body tensed each time I heard him wail the way he did, because he sounded as if he were being hurt in his sleep.

My mother once told me that when babies cried in their sleep it was because they were being taunted by angels who were jealous of their mortality. I wondered for a long time, *Why would an angel be jealous of a human?* and it was in reading Crowley, Regardie, Fortune, and more that it finally clicked, because humans are able to feel, able to experience touch, taste, smell, love; all of the experiences that celestial and earthbound entities cannot. Still, I found it awful that the angelic could hurt the living, but when you realize that each of the seventy-two angels has a corresponding demon, so much makes sense. You cannot access a demon without first petitioning an angel. Think of an angel as a leash and a demon as an energetic puppy. A puppy will act in accordance with its nature, running and playing, but a leash allows him to be directed along a walking path. Without a leash, well, there could be chaos as the puppy picks and chooses how it will navigate that walking path.

There are seventy-two angels of the Shem HaM'phorash. And there are seventy-two Goetic demons. When I summon demons, I do so through the aide of an angel, connecting that celestial entity with that earthbound entity. It's not that demons can't be conjured on their own. Many who work with demonic energy do not want to work with angelic energy, but I follow high magick principles as I learned them. And the most agreed upon guideline outlines first making contact with an angel in order to reach a demon. Calling on a demon without the guidance of an angel all but guarantees chaos.

As an infant, Bela continued to cry. He continued to fuss through sleep.

Most people told us that once we crossed that newborn milestone, we were going to finally enter days of normality. What was normal? When Bela was a toddler, he'd stay up past midnight, every night. We tried everything, soothing baths in the early evening, singing lullabies, anything, but his brain struggled to find a point of rest. Once he'd fall asleep, he would awaken again in just a few hours and run through the house, laughing and playing, refreshed and ready for a new day, even if it was three in the morning. It wasn't until the last few years that he finally started settling down and sleeping through the night, but now his sleep was being disrupted again, and this time due to that awful black bird.

I hold my hand out. "Tablet."

He lowers his head and hands me his device.

"I'm sorry, Bela. You have to sleep." I look to the screen. He was building in his Puzzleword game. "You made a new house?"

"Yes, I made a castle for my friend." He stands up and taps on the screen, expanding the view, and sure enough in the middle of his brilliantly multicolored, kaleidoscopic world of whimsical characters, mountains and waterfalls, and rainbow-colored houses, there was a black castle.

"I take it this is Dracula's Castle?" I smile, impressed with all of the detail that surrounded the Gothic home. There were hedges and trees, birds, and statuary.

He shakes his head no and yawns. "I'm ready for bed now." We start walking toward my bedroom when he stops and says he's forgotten something. He runs inside his room and returns with his new favorite book, *Aesop's Fables*. "Will you read me a story?"

I nod. I will always do what Bela wants me to do.

In my bedroom he crawls into my bed and raises the comforter up to his chin.

"It's not Dracula's castle, then?" I ask, not being able to let it go.

"That's not his name, Mom."

"Oh, I'm sorry, Vlad the Impaler."

"That's not his name either. You know his name, but sometimes we forget because we don't think his name is important, but he is important. He's the most important."

I laugh to myself, thinking this is some sort of joke. "It has to be Dracula…"

"I can't tell you his name. It's a secret."

"I thought you said I knew his name?" I say, setting the tablet down on my nightstand.

He shakes his head on my pillow. "It's a secret that you know."

"If it's a secret that I know, then how is it even a secret? It sounds like I just need a clue because I can't remember." I think about other famous Gothic castles. "If it's not Dracula's Castle. It's Frankenstein's Castle."

He smiles and then shrugs.

I sigh, noting we're getting nowhere. I ask him which story he would like me to read, and he tells me that he knows I will pick the best one. I flip through the pages and land on *The Crow and the Pitcher* and begin to read.

"A thirsty crow came upon a pitcher which had once been full of water; but when the crow put its beak into the mouth of the pitcher, he found that it was only half full, and that he could not reach far enough down to get at the remaining water. He tried, and he tried, but at last had to give up in despair. Then a thought came to him, and he took a pebble and dropped it into the pitcher.

"Then he took another pebble and dropped it into the pitcher.

"Then he took another pebble and dropped that into the pitcher.

"At last, after many pebbles, he saw the water mount up near him, and after casting in a few more pebbles he was able to quench his thirst."

I ask Bela, "What does this one mean?"

"It means little by little does the trick."

I close the book of fables on my lap.

"You're not going to tell me who you built the castle for, are you?"

"Little by little does the trick, Mom." He yawns and closes his eyes. Bela's chest rises and falls gently. Before he drifts off to sleep, he softly mumbles, "When Dad calls, tell him I'm sorry."

I open my mouth to say something, but he's already settled into dreamland.

At my desk now, I look down at my phone and note the time, and that's when it rings, as if I willed it.

"Hey," I say.

"I'm okay," Bass says. "I'm in the hospital, but I'm okay."

CHAPTER 25

VALENTINE'S DAY 2013: PALOMA

It's happening. I knew it would happen again. They told me it would happen again, but nothing quite prepares you for another wave of emotional suffering coupled with cramping, and somehow a wave of numbness. There's a hint of emptiness to it, because you have to dissociate from your body somehow, knowing your child is dying inside you.

The geneticist at Advocate Masonic Hospital hands me a pamphlet. Who hands you a pamphlet when you're fifteen weeks pregnant and have just been told to go home and prepare to miscarry for the sixth time?

She's talking, but I'm not listening. I can feel Bass's hand on my knee, and I think I hear him sniffling.

How? How could this happen again? I was taking my prenatal vitamins and fish oil tablets. I had eased working out to just walking. I stopped drinking coffee, caffeine, and everything, really. I was only drinking warm water with lemon in the morning and plain water throughout the day. I stopped drinking alcohol years ago. I even started eating meat again after fourteen years of being a vegetarian, because if I had to eat something dead to make something live, then I didn't care. I didn't care what I had to do. If I had to rip a hole in the galaxy to produce my child from dark matter, then I would.

In the second trimester, I had my quad screen, which screened for Down syndrome, trisomy 18, abdominal wall defects, and neural tube defects. That test confirmed Down syndrome, and I was asked if I wanted to undergo a chorionic villus sampling, another form of prenatal testing that would insert a thin needle through my abdomen. The test could reveal if the baby had any other genetic conditions and any other valuable information about their health.

I felt the pinch as the needle broke through skin. The lights were dimmed in the ultrasound room. Everything looked blue from the monitors and machines reading heart and brain waves. The screen in front of us showed a little bulging form, a small potato with buds for arms and legs. The needle was removed with a sample from the placenta. The baby's nubs for arms swayed just so as the doctor said, "Has anyone told you about this?"

"Told us about what?"

"There's a lot of fluid buildup around the heart."

More gel was spread on my stomach and the ultrasound machine kept running.

More people entered the room, looked, exited, but not in that way that exuded joy, in that way that exuded concern. Others returned, and then more fluttering of people moving in and out until it was just Bass and I left in the room, alone in that blue underwater light.

"No one told me about the liquid around his heart," I said. "No one told me."

The technician entered and asked me to get dressed and to meet the geneticist in the office. The woman was so calm and disconnected from my suffering, and I remembered that no one is required to accept your pain.

My thoughts drifted to the flurry of movement, the whispers, the little nubs swaying, and the blue glow of machines that made me feel as if I was beneath water and sinking steadily in the ocean.

"You will lose this fetus." The geneticist's voice pulled me back into the awful room painted pea green. Her voice was cold, calculated, and detached. What I was carrying wasn't some biological textbook label. It wasn't a fucking fetus. It was a baby. It was my baby.

"You'll need to prepare to miscarry this pregnancy. Do you understand? You will never carry a live baby to term," she said, and when she did, that's when I sprang from my chair and gripped her throat with both of my hands, not releasing my hold until Bass and a security guard pulled me off of her.

That's the key, *you'll* need to prepare to miscarry this pregnancy.

Not them.

Not Bass.

Me.

I would need to go home and tell all of my coworkers at the studio that there would be no cause for a baby shower and bad cake in a few months. I would then need to call Noel and tell him that he would not be an uncle, the sixth time he had heard this. I would need to pace my house as cramps shot down my spine and my legs. I would need to sit on the toilet, rocking back and forth in pain as clumps of bloody matter slipped out. I would need to do this for hours waiting for when a heartbeat within me that was not my own would cease. I waited for death to exist inside me. Then when a soft bloody mass of cells that could have been someone slipped out from between my legs, I would cradle it in my arms and pull it to my chest and cry.

Once again, my body had failed to grow life, because all my body knew how to birth was death.

Bass found me on the bathroom floor later that night.

"I'm calling 9-1-1."

"No," I cried, and rubbed my face, mixing blood and tears.

I leaned my head back against the cold tile, the warm blood continuing to flow, and I no longer cared. I wondered aloud why my children didn't love me long enough to stay. Was it that once they settled roots within me, they realized I was awful and so they returned to the heavens, where they would be born as stars within the clouds of dust in the galaxy?

"There's nothing anyone can do. My body is just tired. I'm tired."

Bass turned on the shower, and then leaned down and wiped my face with a washcloth. "Look at me. If it's only ever just you and me, that's fine. You're all I want. You're all I've ever wanted."

We wrapped the mass in sheets of toilet paper and set it on a shelf beside the door. Bass helped me out of my shirt and bra and then lifted me up and set me in the tub, and then he climbed in and just held me as warm water sprayed down on us.

In the morning we woke and went out to the backyard where we buried another star baby in our garden.

That next day, Commander McCarthy called Bass and begged him to come to work. A bullet pierced an upstairs bedroom and shot a mother through the head as she was putting her daughter to sleep.

I told Bass to go, and to try to find that little girl comfort because so much had been torn from her in a moment of pure love.

With Bass out of the house, I pulled myself away from the bed and walked over to our bookshelves. I reached down for the massive tome that sat waiting for me to return, *The Golden Dawn*. I set that aside and then pulled the two books beside it that I would need as well, *The Lesser Key Of Solomon* and *The Magick Of Demons*.

I was willing to do it all and more, to punch a hole into this reality and the next, into all of the layers of the millions of dimensions in existence, to pull my child from the blanket of infinity.

CHAPTER 26

SATURDAY NIGHT: SEBASTIAN

"I'm not letting either of you mess this up." McCarthy leans forward from the backseat. He jabs a thumb at Gutierrez and then me. "Especially you, Bass. You walking concussion. You should be at home."

We found parking right in front of the red brick bungalow. It's late. Most houses have gone dark at this hour, with only a front porch light on outside, or maybe a microwave light on in back in the kitchen. Not this house. Every single light is on, almost pulsating with an intensity, with a defiance against the night.

"Why's the media here?" Gutierrez says, removing his seatbelt.

McCarthy takes a deep breath. "They never left."

I couldn't go home now; if I did, I'd fall asleep. I needed to keep going. I needed to find out who gave me that cheap shot at the Uptown. I knew it was the same person who killed Robin, and if Gutierrez hadn't called for backup when he did, both of us would probably be dead.

"I should have your badges." McCarthy pushes the rear passenger door open and is already standing on the front lawn.

"Yeah, but it's because of us we found a body at the Uptown," I say.

"Well," McCarthy grumbles. "We've got the head. The team is still looking for the body."

"That's two murders that we know of, so far. This killer isn't going to stop until they get what they want, and they're telling us they want some film. We need patrols circling these buildings, old theaters, new. Are the patrol cars outside of my house?"

"We've got two cars in front of your house," McCarthy says. "Polly's safe, but Bass, I can't get a car stationed outside of every theater in the city of Chicago, old and new."

There are reporters and cameras positioned on the lawn in front of the small red brick bungalow. Snaps and clicks erupt as our pictures are taken as we walk across the lawn.

We push past reporters shoving microphones in our faces. McCarthy exchanges some colorful language with them, uncaring of any potential critiques by the media as his retirement nears.

"I have a lot of questions for her," I say under my breath.

"Which she's not going to answer." McCarthy walks in front of us. "Don't mess this up, Bass. Let me do the talking."

"Medina is the reason my mentor is dead. She at least owes me a little chat."

He faces me. His eyes are dark. His forehead creases. "I've known that kid since before she was born. Before you were born. I'm her godfather. Medina owes no one anything. Keep your mouth shut until I tell you to open it, or you will mess this up for all of us."

I open my mouth to fight back, but I can't counter. My head feels like it's on a tilt-a-whirl.

He smiles a smug smile, thinking he's already won. "She's

going to eat you alive in there."

"She's not going to do a damn thing," I say.

McCarthy laughs at me. "Good thing you've got bandages there on your head. Maybe she'll have some pity."

"Medina pities no one," Gutierrez says, one finger reaching for the doorbell, but McCarthy is already turning the doorknob.

"She never locks her doors," McCarthy says, pushing the door open, and then knocking on its surface to alert her we're here.

"Isn't that dangerous?" Gutierrez asks.

McCarthy is already in the living room and we're following. "She feels safe this way. Bobby? Medina? Where are you two?"

I hear footsteps above us, walking across the house, until there's a man coming down the stairs. He exhales once he sees who it is. "Hey, McCarthy. I've been locking the door, but she—"

"Oh, I know. Where is she?"

Bobby nods to the rear of the house. "In the kitchen. She's waiting for you."

McCarthy crosses his arms in front of his chest, and for the first time, I swear he's not shouting. His voice isn't condescending. "And how are you doing, Bobby?"

Bobby opens his mouth to say something and then closes it. Likely gathering his thoughts. "We're alive. The nights are hard. But we're alive. I worry about her. She's not…doing well. She misses work."

McCarthy doesn't say anything. He remains silent, nodding as he listens.

Bobby raises a hand in farewell. "I've got to get back to grading some papers upstairs, but it was good seeing you, McCarthy. All of you."

He disappears, and for the first time in a long time, when I look at McCarthy, all I see is a tired old man.

"Hey, kid," McCarthy calls as we follow down the short hallway leading into the kitchen. He throws his hands up when we find her sitting at the table, taking a sip from a white porcelain mug with a Chicago flag emblazoned across the front. McCarthy throws his hands up. "Your husband says you're not doing so good. Well, we've brought you some work to keep you busy."

Lauren Medina looks good. The same, really. Her hair is pulled back. Her face clean. She gives McCarthy a *fuck you* smile as he sits down.

"Nice to see you too, kid."

She blows over the top of the mug and takes another tip. "The hell are these two doing here?"

"Ramos and Gutierrez," I snap.

She laughs and locks eyes with me. "One, I didn't ask you. Two, I know your names."

"She's nice," I say to McCarthy, who ignores me because he's already closed his eyes and is rubbing his temples.

Medina's nostrils flare. "Don't you work narc?" she asks, sounding disgusted. She turns to McCarthy. "Can you explain to me why you got a narc and a street cop in my house right now?"

McCarthy takes a deep breath and blows the air out slowly from his mouth. "They're both homicide now." He removes his fingers from his temples and extends both arms. "Alright, kids, let's play nice." He then reaches a hand back toward Gutierrez. "Give me that folder?"

McCarthy places the folder down on the table and slides it over to Medina. "We need your help."

Medina sets the mug down, looks from Gutierrez to me to McCarthy, and then directs her attention to the folder. She removes three pictures from the Chicago Theater and lays them out on the table side by side. She inspects them for a moment, then reaches for her mug and takes another sip. "Very creative."

"Could this be your guy?"

"My guy?" She raises her eyebrows. "I've told you more than once my guy is…" She closes her eyes and shakes her head. "Forget it…" She sighs, opens her eyes, and says, "I can't help you."

Medina claimed in reports that the gunfire that erupted between Jordan Green and Elvis Van was chaotic because someone else was on the scene. Both men were startled when they heard shooting, thinking the other was shooting at them. But Medina claims the gunfire started from someone else who was at the lagoon that day.

"Kid, I think you can help us."

"It doesn't matter what I say. I'm on desk duty. Being investigated, and I'm living in this bubble…"

"What bubble? You're not under house arrest."

"I'm not?" She turns her head in the direction of the living room, where just outside media is standing by, waiting for her to leave her house. "The moment I go outside they're shoving cameras in my face. Asking me who I think the Pied Piper might be, and…" She laughs to herself. "It doesn't matter what I have to say. I just want to go back to work."

I interrupt the family reunion. "Is there anyone you know who might have done this? Do you think this is someone who may have had an interest in what happened last year? Anything?"

Medina doesn't look at me, instead she directs her attention to Gutierrez. "You're a really good cop, Gutierrez. I'm happy you got promoted to homicide." She places the photographs back in the folder and hands it back to McCarthy. "I can't help you. This isn't my problem."

I take a step forward, and my voice comes out sharper than I intended. "I thought Chicago was your problem. Isn't that what you said? That everything you do is for this city? Well, we're asking you for help to protect this city. We have a murderer on our hands who is probably going to kill again and they're using signatures I've never seen before. Movie posters, occult symbols—"

Lauren stands up. "I'm tired. I need to get some sleep."

McCarthy throws his head back. "Medina, we all know you don't sleep. All we're asking for you to do is to just think about it. Even if you think there's someone you know who may know something, that's at least a lead. We need something."

She bites the inside of her cheek and then asks me, "What happened to you?" Referring to my bandage.

"I was attacked during a search."

"You probably deserved it for being messy." She moves to the kitchen sink, where she places the coffee mug. "We're done here," she says with her back to us.

"We're not done," I plead. "Old Hollywood movies. Silent films." McCarthy's hand is on my chest now, pushing me away from getting any closer to her. I am searching through all I had encountered the last few days. "Charlie Chaplin. Georges Méliès."

The look Lauren gives me is one of pity. She pities me. She pities all of us.

"I don't know what the hell you're talking about, Bass. I'm tired. I'm sorry about Van. I really am. I think you should get some rest. I think all of you need to get some rest. So, get the hell out of my house."

A shimmering light catches my attention from the corner of my eye. I turn to see a soft golden glow emitting from beneath a door in the hallway.

"I'm sorry. Is there someone else here?"

"No." She smiles. "That's my dad's old office. Bobby probably just left the light on in there. He uses the printer in there sometimes."

When I look back, the light is gone.

"I hope you all can figure this out, but there's nothing I can do," she says, her tone firm.

McCarthy and Gutierrez are pulling me away now, but then I remembered. "Wait. Fairy tales," I say.

Medina's eyes widen. "What did you say?"

"No, not fairy tales. Fables. What about Aesop's fables?"

She's shaking her head, fighting with herself over what she has to say next, but I know I've struck something.

"Dammit, Medina," I press. "You owe us something. You're one of us. You can't keep ignoring this. You have to help us."

"The people I feel the sorriest for are all of you," she says. "The people who often think they're the most righteous are the ones doing the most harm. You all rally behind causes you know nothing about and have no full understanding on how you can solve them.

"People want to believe they're right and everyone's wrong, and that no such thing as duality exists. Most people want to believe in the inherent goodness of others, but that's not real. Stop lying to yourselves. The rehabilitation of child predators does not exist. The rehabilitation of murderers does not exist. Do you all really believe that everyone out there in the street is good? What if you had the opportunity to stop someone before they did something awful? Would you? Could you? What about those people who served and were released, and they just picked up their life again where they left off? Trafficking children and adults. We let murderers free every day, and we're okay with that because we believe in this fairy tale idea of redemption. You believe that if a person shrugs and says, 'I'm sorry,' that they should be absolved of all of their horrific crimes. Welcomed back into society with applause. You all are allowing the wolf in the hen house every day. And you're sick and you're sad, because you're allowing hurt to happen again and again, because you're weak and you believe that humans are good. We're not.

"You are the insane ones. You all believe that people are

good deep down inside, no matter how much blood they've washed off their hands. You all believe that if a person hurts or kills another, that if they just say, 'Hey, I'm sorry, that was a mistake. I'll serve my time,' then they can be forgiven. There should be no forgiving monsters."

"There is no rehabilitation of evil, and that's what makes all of you small. That's what makes all of you constant prey. You hate me because I don't accept that this world is good. I know nothing and no one is good. I know everyone out here is selfish and will slit their neighbor's throat if that means it will bring them a life of comfort."

"I feel sorry for you, Medina," I say. "That that's what you believe."

"Don't feel sorry for me," she snaps. "I sleep just fine at night because I don't lie to myself. Whatever I've done on the job was to guarantee more people were not hurt by the people I stopped, and I stopped them because they would just keep hurting people over and over again. And you know what? That's the difference between you and me, Ramos. I've saved dozens, hundreds, maybe, because I didn't eat the lie that people can be good. I rest well knowing those people I stopped can never hurt anyone again. And for whatever mistakes I made in my youth, I was just a kid! I've done things I regret, but everything I've done since I was that kid was to protect this city."

McCarthy has his hands over his ears now. "Kids, can you please just stop fighting?"

"You're the ones outside living with all of the monsters, failing to realize that each of you sitting in front of me is one themselves. We are all the monster. And so, another crime will happen. Another news and social media phenomenon will break, and it will whip the masses into a frenzied storm of typing out empty opinions that will move the dial nowhere, and I'll continue on, not even thinking about what happened last year, because there will be a new dead kid in some park somewhere. There will be a stray bullet that hits a jogger on the street. There will be a man parking in front of his house shot eighteen times because he looked like someone else. There will be a woman carjacked and will resist because she wants to free her child from their car seat, and the gunman will become so frazzled that he'll just shoot her and dump the kid off somewhere. This will never end. And whatever this is," she points to the folder, "it's just an extension of the human massacre we're all a part of."

The light down the hall returns. This time I hear a doorknob rattling.

"You sure there isn't anyone else on the first floor with us?" I ask.

"No, it's just rats." She looks up. "I have a rat problem. Don't worry, it's not the boogieman after your son, but it is a real man."

"What the hell do you know about my son, Medina?"

McCarthy raise his hands. "Please, you two. I've got a damn migraine. Lower your voice."

I'm pointing at Medina and looking to Gutierrez for help here.

Gutierrez sighs. "Medina, what do you know?"

She's looking past me and over my shoulder, to an empty space. "I don't know your son. I only know this is not a fairy tale that's after you and your boy. It's a different kind of story. Something older than fairy tales written by someone older than time. You'll find a new fable written by Aesop. "

"What?"

"I'm sorry." Medina shrugs. "That's all I got. That's all I know. I'm going to bed now. I'm not talking anymore, and you all can't make me, because I have nothing else."

McCarthy stands and gives Medina a long look. They exchange some nonverbal knowing. It's dread I see on their faces.

He nods and then walks down the hallway and Gutierrez follows.

Medina's sitting there, her arms crossed, and she presses her lips together and then says, "Take care of yourself, Bass."

And as I walk down the hallway, toward the front door, I could have sworn I heard the sound of that doorknob rattling again.

CHAPTER 27

1999: PALOMA

"You sure it's not going to be like *The Exorcist*?" I ask, seated at my desk in my small room. Noel is seated on the floor, open books scattered around him.

He laughs. "Life isn't a movie, Polly."

But wasn't it? Snippets of seconds turned into minutes, into hours or days. Scenes then features, and sometimes a sequel or series.

"Mom's going to be so mad if she finds out," I mutter. I can already picture her, clutching her Bible to her chest and calling us demons for even having these books in her house.

"Yes, she'll be so mad," Noel says, flipping through pages of a book and stopping at a spot where he removes a yellow Post-It note and pins it to the top. "If she finds out, but how is she going to find out? I'm not going to tell her and you're not going to tell her. Plus, she's going to be at church all morning."

The only time I seemed to be free of her abuse was when she was at church. Mom spent her free time in that drafty red brick building with peeling green laminate floor and pews that had been etched with the names of children who were forced to be

266

there. Mom was there during the week for morning prayer. Mom was there on Fridays for the holy adoration. Mom was there every Sunday for mass, and once a month she went on Saturdays too, for confession. She had stopped asking us if anyone wanted to accompany her, but she still made a point to tell us we were all spiraling into damnation. The more she told me I was damned, the more I knew I was blessed.

I looked around to the faded pink walls of my tiny room my dad and I had painted years ago. "Don't we have to paint one of the walls black?"

Noel laughs. "There's really no reason anyone needs all of those props, chalk, black robes, chalices, and mirrors. It's all in here." He places an index finger on his temple. "This is all you need. We are not going to do the Full Evocation. There's just no way we need that sort of power. That's beyond anything I could imagine anyone needing. We're going to start with the Ritual Opening, the Core Ritual, and the Petition for Results."

"Wait, I'm confused. I thought we had to do the three main rituals: the Petition for Results, the Connective Evocation, and the Full Evocation."

"Again," Noel rolls his eyes, like this was information we were supposed to have completely memorized, "the Petition for Results is the simplest. It allows us to transcribe what it is we want into a cipher. What we want is then communicated to the demon. By us just petitioning for whatever it is we want to the demon, it guarantees it will happen. We want results. This will get us those results."

I look around the room once again, expecting him to tell me it was going to swell with smoke and fire, and that a demon would emerge from the snapping flames to grant us wishes, our very own underworld genie. "What will happen right after the ritual?"

"Not much, really. You might feel a demonic presence, but

it's not like you're going to see anything. The second ritual, the Connective Evocation, is more about getting direct communication with the demon, where you will for sure feel their presence. You do this one in order to obtain knowledge or provide more direct communication about what it is you want. The third is so intense, because you actually *see* the demon, and I don't know." He closes the book he is holding in his hand. "It almost sounds like people just want to brag about seeing a demon, trying to get some cool occultist points like those who claim to have really spoken with their HGA."

"HGA?"

He's jotting something in his notebook now and doesn't look up when he answers. "Holy Guardian Angel."

I think of that picture framed above my bed when I was a little girl, of two small children walking across a bridge, and a glowing angel hovering above them, protecting them on their journey.

"What exactly is a Holy Guardian Angel?"

Noel rubs the back of his head. "It's your own personal angel. Everyone has one, but that's not what we're doing here, so stay focused."

Before he continues, I interrupt. "Wait, how are you just going to gloss over that? Everyone has their own personal angel? Then if we do, why are we calling on demons and not on our angels?"

He sighs. "We'll be calling an angel first. We can't command a demon without the help of an angel." He stops himself, and then says, "Well, some people go directly to the demons. That's like speeding down the expressway in your dream sports car with your eyes closed. It may feel good for a few seconds, but you'll lose control very fast. With the Full Evocation, it's not maybe a demon will appear. It's not maybe I think I feel something. It's not even like maybe that shadow or speck of dust I see floating through the air is a demon. No, you will in fact see a demon, standing in the same room with you. With us."

I tap on the heavy black book in front of me. "And you got all of that from the book Luis gave me?"

"Everything's in there, Polly." He points. "Everything we'll ever want. I don't know why he gave it to you. He's obviously into you. He visits you at the theater every Friday. You still haven't answered my question if Bass knows about him."

"Bass isn't my boyfriend, and neither is Luis."

"Pick the cool Goth guy and not the future cop."

"You do know Luis practically worships Aleister Crowley and Anton LaVey?"

"I'd rather deal with someone who worships a scandalous sex magick having socialite and the Chicago born founder of The Church of Satan than a cop. Plus," Noel stands up and picks up the book in front of me, cracking open the leather-bound cover, "what we're doing here is hundreds of years before LaVey or Crowley."

"Bass doesn't want to be a cop. He wants to be a detective and solve murders. Do you realize how many killings around here go unsolved? It's terrifying."

"Yeah," he says, thumbing through the pages. "There's no reality in which you can convince me that hooking up with a future cop is a good thing."

"We didn't hook up, you idiot."

He looks up from the book. "Okay, sure. Whatever you gotta tell yourself to make it through the day." He returns to the pages in front of him and sits down on the floor once again.

"You're annoying."

"And you love me."

"I don't know what I'm going to do without you here."

"You could always move in with your soon-to-be cop boyfriend."

"We're both still juniors in high school, you idiot."

"There's that apartment down the hall Bruce hasn't rented out yet. Maybe you can talk to him about it."

"Trust me, if I were going to move away from Mom and Dad, I'd move further away than down the hall."

"Don't worry. Before you know it, you'll be in Hollywood making horror movies, living the dream." He sets *The Golden Dawn* down and picks up *The Lesser Solomon Key*, a thin book with a glossy grey cover. "I'm sure the perfect sigil is in here for what we need."

I didn't believe in any of this, but Noel desperately wants to. Luis had been coming to the theater for months now. He'd order popcorn after the line of people had disappeared into their seats, and we'd talk for a few minutes. After his movie ended, he'd hang around, and I didn't mind. Bruce didn't mind either. I'd sweep up popcorn kernels from the theater and Luis would join in and help collect empty cups and toss them in the trash, all the while telling me about what he had read that week, and about all of the things he believed in. Luis spoke of the celestial body. Meditation. Alchemy. Extended perception. And rituals. Whatever you desired to generate on this physical plane, there was magick that could help you make that materialize. Increase fortune. Attract love or friendship. Breakthrough magick. Protection magick. Healing and health. Wisdom. Business and finance.

"What are you going to ask for?" I ask Noel, already knowing, but just needing to hear something other than the sound of sirens outside on Milwaukee Avenue.

"College. Medical school. Scholarships. To be one of the top doctors in the city. The world. Why not? I'm ready to get out of here and have a life. I just want to get away from this, Mom and Dad and the sound of emergency vehicles outside my window. It's like everyone around us is like zombies, void of happiness, of hope. Everyone is just so angry and full of hate for themselves and each other because we're all poor and have nothing to look forward to. I'm not going to fall into that hole. They loathe their lives and take it out on people who have a spark of hope. They're not going to take that away from me or you. We're breaking out of this mindset."

Noel's eyes are fixed on me. "Okay? I believe in this. I believe Luis came into your life, hell, our lives now, for a reason. I've tried some of this stuff he's taught you, Polly. It all works. But these together," he raises up *The Lesser Key of Solomon* and *The Golden Dawn*, "they will change our lives completely.

I take a deep breath and lean my head back in the chair.

"Look at this." Noel is standing over me now, touching my hand. "She could've broken your wrist. Mom is not well. No one should take their own misery out on their kids. She hates you because she's jealous of you and she sees in you what she does not have—possibility."

Noel moves back to the center of the room, dotted by books and Post-It notes, paper and pens. "We're going to get out of here, and they're never going to hurt us again. I promise you that."

As he continues talking, I stand up from my chair and pick up the book closest to me and read the full title.

The Goetia, The Lesser Solomon Key of Solomon the King: Lemegeton, Book 1 by Clavicula Salomon Regies, translated by Samuel Liddell and MacGregor Mathers, edited with an introduction by Aleister Crowley.

I flip the book around and read the back cover copy.

The Goetia, The Lesser Solomon Key of Solomon the King: Lemegeton, provides a detailed account and the preparations needed for the successful evocation of its 72 spirits.

I close the book. My bedroom feels so cramped and small, as if giving it too much attention made it only close in on me more. "We have nothing to lose."

Noel hands me a sheet of paper that has the alphabet listed out and next to each letter is another character, a swirly, looping set of symbols. Before I can ask what it is, he tells me.

"It's Theban. It's a language, an alphabet that's used in ciphers. Some people sometimes call it the witch's alphabet. We use Theban because it's not really like any other alphabet out there. If I spell something out with Theban letters, someone else will not know what it says. We're going to use this system, as a code, to write out what we want. This code allows it to really seep into our subconscious, so we can make that connection with the demon."

He hands me a blank pen and a sheet of notebook paper. "Actually, I feel like you're going to mess up, so here are two sheets just in case."

"Is there anything else I need to know before I start?"

"What matters most is that you know exactly what you are writing even though no one else can read it. Also, I'd write out the intent first on some notebook paper in English, and then start the coding on the parchment."

I roll my eyes. "I figured."

"You're the one asking all of the questions."

"Never thought I'd have an occultist for a brother, but here we are," I murmur.

He looks up from his writing. "You were the one who taught me magick. So. This is all on you, magician."

I carefully think about what it is I want. What are my deepest desires?

"And, Polly, I'm serious, be careful what you ask for, because it will happen."

"Stop reading my mind," I say.

We both go silent, consumed in our own thoughts, thinking of what wishes we want granted. I hear Noel writing furiously, stop, tear up a sheet of paper, and continue again. We all think we know what we want, but when asked to state your deepest intention, it's difficult to express it in a single present tense statement.

I am happy. I am healthy. I am wealthy. I am successful. I am loved.

What does that all mean? How do you specify and quantify happiness? What does healthy look like? What is wealth? Money in a bank account? Material objects? What does success look like? "Be specific," I hear Luis's words in my head. I can see him now, sitting in theater five, a wondrous smile on his face, because he believes in all possibilities. He handed me *The Golden Dawn* with instructions to work through it. To do the rituals, and to allow my dreams to be limitless, but "Be specific in your request," he said. Meaning, don't allow the universe to choose for me, because I am the creator.

Noel tears up another sheet of paper and I hear it fall into the trash can with a whoosh.

"Who messed up their intent now?"

"I'm ignoring you." He returns to his sheet of paper, and I continue to stare at mine, those horizontal blue lines begging me to give a command.

I press pen to page and carefully code, looking from the Theban alphabet over to what I have written out in English. When I finish, I have two incomprehensible lines of characters.

I wheel my chair around and find that Noel is smiling. "You ready?"

"Are you going to tell me what yours says?" I ask.

He presses his paper close to his chest. "Are you going to tell me yours?"

"No."

"I'm okay with that. Let's start."

Noel pulls out a pink cauldron no larger than a coffee mug from a Tony's Finer Foods plastic bag.

"Where did you get that?"

"I bought it The Occult Bookstore. They didn't have any black ones left, but this pink one is pretty cool."

"What are we supposed to do with that?"

He produces a box of matches and sets them next to the cauldron. "Burn our petitions."

"Burn them?"

"It's called alchemy, Polly. Get with it. First, we're going to add the demon's name to the back of the paper. Then we fold it up, looking at the demon's seal while we're doing this. Then we touch the folded paper to the seal and then we place the paper into the cauldron and burn it to ashes. By doing so, we accept that the results are inevitable."

I look at my cipher. "Which demon name do we use?"

"One that corresponds to the desire and intent of your petition."

"You're not going to pick any of the obvious ones, like Bael or Belial or Paimon?" I ask him.

"They are each associated with powers. Like Bael's powers are to remain unseen, make someone lose interest in your affairs, bring confusion or torment to anyone who asks about something you don't want them to know. Also, to compel others to keep secrets for you. Then they have a corresponding key."

"Key? Like a literal key?"

He rubs the back of his head. "No, I guess they're like senses. Like sights, sounds, tastes, and smells that are associated and specific to each one of the demons." He places a finger on a page. "Like, Bael is associated with shifting dark colors and textures, earthy smells like bark or soil, and even the smell of blood. Bael's also associated with the rumbling of thunder and strong wind gusts, and a bitter taste in your mouth."

Noel waves me over to sit on the floor next to him. I grab my cipher, comfortable knowing that my brother cannot quickly read what I am petitioning given it is written in Theban.

"Why don't you go first?" He hands me the book.

I begin slowly turning the pages, scanning their names, their specific keys and associations. I can hear the tinkling of bells, my eyes began to water, and then I came upon a sigil I know I have never seen before, but that is somehow familiar.

"Bime," I say, and as soon as I do, I wonder if uttering its name gives it immediate power. What is that saying again? Speak of the devil and he'll appear, but what if you speak of one of his princes, dukes, or generals? Will they too come? What if I call all of them?

Noel gets up and closes the curtains.

"What are you doing?"

"It's called ambiance, Polly."

He digs into the plastic bag and produces a candle holder and white candle.

"I thought you said no props."

He shrugs. "Yeah, we don't need it, but it's sorta cool. This is just to help us get focused."

He turns off the bedroom light.

My room is cast in a supernatural red glow from the florescent LOGAN sign beside my window. It is as if we are living in a Giallo film, swimming in red and waiting for harsh musical chords to strike.

"Now, you say, 'I call on thee, Bime.'"

I repeat his words.

"Alright, now the Conjuration of Bime." Noel slides the book over to me and points to where I should begin.

"Next, scan your encoded sentence. Look at the letters, allowing your eyes to take in each word, and know that your subconscious and the demon know what you petitioned. You don't have to think about what it is you actually want. Just look at the characters you wrote out in Theban."

Noel then sets the page with the seal between us.

"Do not say anything. Just look at the seal. Allow yourself to now think about the result you want. Feel like you've already gotten what it is that you have requested. When you are ready, and you believe that you have the right feeling—as if what it is that you have requested is here with you now—then speak the sentence aloud exactly as it's written.

"Start with the Shem angel, followed by the angelic emissaries." He points down on the page and I read.

"In the names of El, Elohim, Adonai, Ehyeh asher Ehyeh, El Shaddai, Elyon and YHWH-Shammah, and by the Power of Hahahell, Haamiel, Ademiel, and Abael, I call on thee, Bime."

"Now take your folded paper and cover the demon's seal with it, so that the seal is completely covered. This is the moment where you make your offering. In your imagination, show the demon what it is that you will give. Having imagined the offering, return to the feeling that the demon has provided you with the results. Now, remove the paper and reveal the demon's name again.

"Know that the demon is with you, Polly, but do not give it any more attention than that. Know that the power of its seal is now entwined with the coded sentence in your paper. All that remains is for you to transform the paper to ash."

I then place my petition paper in the cauldron and Noel hands me the Bic lighter.

"Right." I hold the paper in my left hand and the lighter in my right hand.

"Look at the seal once more and know, believe that it is done."

I flip the lighter and place the folded paper in the cauldron, red and yellow flames shooting up before gently falling as the paper curls in on itself black. "Now what?"

"Now, we perform the License to Depart."

"What's that?"

"This is the most important part. I guess think of it like saying goodbye while using a Ouija Board. Or closing the circle in witchcraft. You have to close the portal you opened to make sure…"

"Make sure what?"

"Umm…well, I mean, just to make sure the demon goes back to wherever they belong."

"You're telling me now there's risk in what we've done?"

"Polly, there's risk in everything." He holds the book up to his face and clears his throat. "Just repeat after me."

"Oh, spirit Bime," Noel begins and I repeat his words. "I hereby license you to depart to your proper place quietly and with the peace of yah-weh between you and me. Amen."

"And if we had forgotten this part?"

"Oh, well, I'd image that'd be very bad."

CHAPTER 28

SATURDAY NIGHT, CONGRESS THEATER: SEBASTIAN

What did you see? What did you hear? McCarthy's words meld into a stream of questions, one running right into the other. As soon as we left Medina's house, the call came that there was another body. This time at the Congress Theater.

"The Congress has been closed for years," I say, hitting the gas, going east on Fullerton. The Ford Explorer hits forty-five in a twenty and bulbs blast as a speed camera snaps my license plate. I hit the lights because cars need to start moving out of my way now. We're not going to slow down until we arrive. I accelerate, turning right onto Milwaukee Avenue. The wheels screech. McCarthy's holding on to the armrest and Gutierrez is leaning as far forward as he can in back, even though he has his seatbelt on.

"It's not connected." I'm thinking out loud, remembering Medina's words. "But this is still layered. This isn't just a person who's going around killing people. The intention here is greater."

McCarthy waves his hand forward. "Your job is to drive, Ramos, not give us a philosophy lesson."

As soon as we pass Armitage Avenue, we see the explosion of red and blue. A firetruck, an ambulance, and patrol cars blocking the street and redirecting traffic, which there isn't much of given the time of day.

Detective Rutkowski waves us through, and we park in front of the theater.

The only thing I can think of in this moment I say aloud. "This is a Balaban and Katz movie palace."

McCarthy steps out of the car, his hands on his hips as he looks up at that neglected marquee.

The perimeter is being secured with police caution tape behind them and before them.

"What's your partner talking about, Gutierrez?"

Rutkowski pats him on the shoulder, looks to me and says, "This is all you, Ramos."

"Have you been in there yet?" I ask.

"Yes," she sucks some air between her teeth, "and I wish I hadn't. I'm going to remember that for the rest of my life."

We walk through the opened doors of the Congress Theater. The black-and-white tiled floor lit only by the streetlights and our flashlights is covered in a layer of grime. It is once again the decayed decadence we experienced at the Uptown Theater, but the air here feels different, a lingering heaviness and unease. Our flashlights are disconnected beams, floating along the surfaces.

We follow Detective Rutkowski past the imperial staircase, to our right, where dark, heavy drapes hang, leading to the opening of the auditorium. Rutkowski enters first, followed by McCarthy, and that's when we all stop. Inside, they had set up some stationary lighting. McCarthy sways a bit, but reaches forward, catching his balance on the back of a broken seat. He turns to me, eyes wide, and all I can see is fear. We are dealing with a brutal serial killer here.

Gutierrez hangs back for a moment, taking in the grisly display.

"I don't understand the point. Shock? Disgust? Why are they doing this?"

I think of the reasons any serial killer enacts the brutality that they do. "Anger, ideology, thrill. It really doesn't matter what their motive is. A serial killer kills because they want to."

"Officer French got some lights up for us," Detective Rutkowski says. "CSI is on their way. We'll get more lighting in here, but for now this should be enough for you to see."

The seats around us are covered in thick layers of dirt and debris. It is cold inside, and I can hear the wind howling outside. Flurries catch in the light beams pointing toward the stage, shining on this evening's main show.

"Does this place have a regular maintenance person, anyone other than the city or maybe owner who visits regularly?"

"I live in the neighborhood," Officer French says. "No one's worked here in years."

I look up to the human remains dangling from the ceiling over the stage. "Who's this, then?"

"Once we cut her down, we'll see."

The silence is a timpani, or is it my heart beating against my rib cage? I want to ask where the skin is, what could they have possibly done with the skin, when Detective Rutkowski says, "It's in the front row."

"Our killer skinned this person, peeled their skin right off, walked it down to the front row, and positioned it in a front row seat so that they could watch their flesh as they died," Commander McCarthy says to no one in particular, and then rolls his head back. "I've got my wife, grandkids, and a boat waiting for me just outside my house in Tampa. I'm not extending my post here. I need this figured out now, Ramos."

He's looking at me. I'm standing here, barely able to stand still without swaying, a concussion blooming beneath my skull.

"McCarthy...I..." I hesitate, because I don't know what to say, when Gutierrez steps in.

"We're getting prints from Uptown Theater. We'll start prints here. We haven't been able to lift anything from Chicago Theater. We'll go back and look at Robin's history again. We'll dig into the backgrounds of her co-workers and we'll get an ID of...whoever this is."

My eyes follow his focus. Our death on display. My head stops spinning long enough for me to ask the most obvious question. "If this place isn't operational, how did we even know there was a victim here? Who called it in?"

"Someone called 9-1-1. Officer French checked it out and here we are."

The body is floating in space, suspended ten feet above the stage floor. Their arms are outstretched, as well as their legs. A series of wires connected to their wrists and ankles, extending outward toward the balcony, keeping the deceased hanging in air. Their intestines hung from the open cavity, fleshy tubes like party streamers dangling below them. Meaty organs were placed in the center of the symbol drawn on the wood. Another sigil.

"Do you smell that?" Gutierrez asks.

"It smells like shit," McCarthy says. "The intestines were likely punctured, so there's excrement leaking all over the place."

"Yes, that, but do you smell cleaning products?" Gutierrez inspects the stage from afar. "It's been cleaned. Look at the rest of this space. It's falling in on itself, covered in debris, but the killer took care here, to sweep, mop. and polish this stage. He knew he wouldn't be disturbed."

"Of course, the place is abandoned. Who'd come in here?" McCarthy says, his voice too loud, and I can feel a stabbing behind my eyes now. He curses under his breath as his phone starts ringing. "The mayor," he mumbles to himself, and steps away to take the call.

"It's important to him," I say. "That the symbol is written on a clean surface, that the offering is presented exactly as they need.

They know that these theaters are dilapidated, fading and crumbling in neighborhoods where they once stood as central locations to these communities. These buildings are decaying as life moves on around them, but they're really dead things. Husks, even empty of memory, but whatever the killer's trying to do, they're trying to take us back to something."

Before anyone can say anything, I turn to Rutkowski.

"What did you dig up about those sigils?" I ask as I start moving toward the stage. Rutkowski moves ahead of us.

"Occult, obviously. A quick Google image search turns up similar ones. The one from Chicago Theater can be found in a number of occult books, all dealing with demonology. It was associated with the demon Vassago, who aides the summoner in helping to find an object or document that has been lost."

"What about that one right there?"

"I checked it before you got here. That's the sigil for Purson. Purson's associated with bringing fortune to a project that is close to one's heart."

I pinch the bridge of my nose. "I don't understand what any of this has to do with this scene from *Hellraiser* in front of us."

"Your killer is someone with a working knowledge of the occult, demonology, film history, particularly the history of film in Chicago, and high magick."

"High what?"

"High magick. It's ceremonial magic. These are people who practice rituals with the aim of creating shifts in the real world. This killer is looking for something and their results are directly tied to some type of project and fortune."

"That's it?" I press.

"Really? Do you have anything? Because it seems like you haven't done anything other than let your guard down." She nods at my head.

"Damn, Rutkowski, thanks for stating the obvious."

I look back to the gruesome show and release a stiff and stran-
gled breath. Occult. Demonology. Film history. High magick. A nice,
convoluted combination. I reach for my phone and message Polly.
I want to be sure the patrol car is right there, parked in front of our
house. It's some reassurance, knowing someone is with her, taking
care of her.

Bass: *Is the car out front?*

Paloma: *Yes, I see them.*

Bass: *I'm glad. I'll be home as soon as I can. If you need anything, please call me.*

We listen to the steady *splat splat splat* as the corpse continues to
drip fluids onto an object beneath it.

"What's our clue this time?" I ask. "We've seen a movie poster
before. We've had a film played for us. What did they leave behind
this time?"

"Your clue is right on stage," Gutierrez says, and points to the
large round metal film canister.

"That's just half of it," Officer French shouts across from the
stage. "She's holding the other half."

We turn to the perfectly positioned sheet of human skin in the
front row. The other half of the film canister is on its lap.

I move around to the other side of the stage where Officer French
is standing. I hoist myself up and move closer to the film reel. There
is a white index card taped to the cover. Written in clean, simple
black script are the numbers 1-8-9-6.

"It's a year," I say. "Eighteen ninety-six."

"The year *The House of the Devil* came out," Gutierrez says.

"This is feeling a lot like Humboldt Park last year," Gutierrez
says.

I don't want to agree with him, because whatever Detective Medina insinuated happened last year sounded like complete madness,
but here we were, in strange, tangled loop of the occult, demonology,
high magick and fables.

I rub my forehead and then start moving toward the exit. "I'm fine," I say before they all start asking if I am feeling dizzy, which I still am. "I need to make a quick phone call."

As I step outside on the sidewalk, a man approaches in a black wool coat.

"I'm Luis. The owner." He motions to the doors behind me with his cell phone in his hand. "I got a call there was an accident here." He is looking over my shoulder, trying to get a glance at what is happening inside.

"I'm Detective Ramos. We received an anonymous call about an incident involving an individual in the property."

"What? I keep this place locked." Luis tucks his phone in his coat pocket "I want to press charges."

I couldn't release any information about the condition the person inside was in, but what I could say was that we had no idea who it was. "Actually, we called you because we're trying to ID the individual. We want to start with the apartment building adjoining the theater…"

"That's my property too," Luis says.

"Great. Do you have a list of numbers for your tenants so we can make sure everyone who is supposed to be in the building is here?"

Luis reaches into his pocket and produces a set of keys. "Why don't we go knocking on some doors?"

We walk together down the side street to the entrance at 2133 Rockwell.

"How many units are in this building?"

Luis looks up as he turns the key. "There are about forty-six units in the building now, but I might change that. Many of them are single units and I might combine a few."

We walk past mailboxes, some of them with mailers protruding from their slots, and up a single flight of stairs to a narrow hallway. Luis knocks on the first door to our right.

"What do the tenants think about that?"

"Less than half of the building is occupied right now. I imagine I'll lose half of that in coming weeks and months. People don't like to live in a construction zone."

He knocks again but there is no movement within.

"Sounds like they're not home."

I point down the hallway. "There's no one else who lives down that way?"

"No, all down that way are unlivable units and the backrooms to the storefronts along the side."

We walk in silence up the second-floor steps. The hallway here is dimly lit by light fixtures covered in decades' worth of dust.

"How do you think they got into the theater?" Luis asks, breaking the silence.

"Not sure. If you have cameras or an alarm system, we can review those."

"No," he says quietly. "There are no cameras or alarm system yet. Like I said, I just acquired the property, but I'll change that. I'll make sure there's lots of security in the building."

"Wait," I say, only just now realizing the connection. "Luis Villalobos, right? The real estate guy. It seems like you own most of Logan Square now."

He laughs. "I grew up in the neighborhood. It's home, and I made a promise to myself a long time ago I'd stay here."

"You just purchased the Logan Theater from Bruce?"

"We just signed the paperwork."

"You know my wife, Polly. I think you both used to—"

"We never dated. We were just friends. I liked movies. I'd go to the Logan on Friday nights and she'd be there and we'd talk movies. Sometimes books. Sometimes I'd stay back and help her clean up. We lost touch after her parents died. I hope she's doing well."

"She's doing great. She makes more money than I do as a social media influencer, well, horror host. I'll tell her I saw you."

"Actually, since you mentioned security. I'd like your opinion about something. I just realized there is a way someone can access both the theater and the apartment building. It's through this unit."

We reach the middle of the hallway and Luis opens the door. The lights are off, but the room is illuminated from the streetlights just outside the interior window that look out toward the theater. The floor crunches beneath my foot, sheets of plaster and broken glass. Just outside the window I can see a fire escape.

Luis moves toward the window, and I don't believe that is where we are heading until he says, "Right this way."

The window opens with ease. The wind bursts in, and there is the crackle of the whirl of detritus.

Luis disappears out the window and up the fire escape that shakes as he ascends to where, I am unsure.

My pounding skull tells me to stay here, but I follow.

Outside, I hear Luis's voice above the wind. "Polly's always liked scary movies. Maybe once I get this place rehabbed you'll come visit us. I'd love to show movies here. Old movies. Movies with heart. Passion. Cursed movies."

When I get to the top, I find him standing on the rooftop of the building, looking over the massive exterior of the Congress Theater's auditorium.

My phone begins to ring. It's Gutierrez. "Yeah…"

"Where'd you go? We've been trying to reach the owner of the building, but we haven't heard back yet. McCarthy said don't go snooping around like we did over at Uptown."

"I'll be there in a sec." I end our call and pull the phone away from my ear and look to Luis. "My partner says they've been unable to contact you. How'd you know there were police here?"

"It was a beautiful theater once," Luis says without acknowledging my question. "Even with the retail storefronts all boarded up, and the scaffolding that hasn't moved in years, and non-existent workers. There's securing permits and going back and forth with the city, state, and national officials, and it's all me defending how important this place is, all of these old theaters. These buildings are special. They're magick. They're storing history within their very fibers, and if we demolish them, then we lose all of the magick. But you know what?" Luis points toward the building. "Nobody cares about these places anymore and the power they hold, but I do. They're not just architectural gems. They're something more. They're cathedrals to art. It doesn't matter if these places don't matter to them. I will make sure they matter."

I look down and then regret I did. The building beneath me feels like it's swaying. We are corks bobbing in the great ocean. I move my focus to Luis. "Who told you there was an accident at the theater, Luis?"

He continues talking, like he hadn't even heard me. "That's why I need Polly. The cards told me long ago she would be the one to finally show me that movie. When I would help her close up at night, I'd look, in the storage room, and in the projectionist booth and office. I looked in every single place I could, but I couldn't find it. I then doubted myself thinking it was in another theater. Thinking that these others could show me to the movie, but I was wrong. Polly's the only magician with the power to make that movie play."

I start moving my fingers slowly to my waistband. "Why'd you kill Robin? The person at the Uptown? The person downstairs?"

"They had pieced together too much of this silent film puzzle and it was better to get them out of the way."

"Luis." I approach cautiously. "Why don't we go inside? We can talk more there. You can tell me all you want about this movie."

Luis does not stir, but just a few feet away from him, something else does. It is like a spark. A crackle. An ember that jumps out from a great bonfire and is suspended in air for just one moment. I am unable to move, my entire focus is drawn into that silver light, a drop of mercury that glows, spilling downward and filling in the contours and spaces of a man.

It is a walking photograph, frozen in time but existing here and in this moment. The quick flashing images of a film reel cast on the night sky.

"This isn't real," I say, unable to move, and staring on as the form approaches.

"You're right, Sebastian," Luis says. "Just tell yourself that, that magick isn't real. Tell yourself that real magicians with the power to manipulate reality aren't real. Tell yourself whatever you need to. Tell yourself that this is only a movie. It's not real."

The pulsating impossible light rushes forward. My head continues to throb, my world now begins to spin, and as it brings its flashing eyes inches from my own, I take a step back. There is no time to move. To reposition myself. There is no time for questions and there is no time for words, and as I fall, all I can see above me are silver stars.

CHAPTER 29

SATURDAY LATE NIGHT: PALOMA

"Bruce, are you ready to turn off the lights?" I ask.

He nods, and for the last time I flip the switch that will dim those beaming fluorescent bulbs.

"Are you okay?"

"I'm nervous. I'm sad, but Luis said he will take care of this place and I believe him." He turns to me. "You know, it's not too late. I can call my lawyer and say I made a mistake, that I was confused. This is your home."

I don't know why I said no the first time. Regret boiled inside me, but I knew the money Luis paid to purchase this property would care for Bruce through retirement. "You made the right choice, Bruce."

"The right choice was leaving this place to you, but I'm going to respect what you want, Polly. You and Bela." He chokes back tears. "You. Bela. Noel. You're all my kids." He wipes his eyes and nods toward the window. "That's him. Let me go get the keys so I can walk him through everything."

I wave at the man who was now walking toward the entrance, a man I remember talking to very often and very long ago. A man who I loved for a small time in my life, Luis.

"You're still here? After all of these years. Bruce didn't mention you."

I don't know what to say, and I don't know what to feel. There are those people who once meant the world to you, whom you spoke with near daily, who you couldn't wait to see again. Luis was that person, but he left me after my parents died. There were no more calls and no more visits. There was the aching pain from his departing my life, and then there was emptiness, and all I felt for him now was nothing. I loved him a very long time ago, but that time was gone, and I was no longer that person. I realized with the years that even though Luis and I were friends, he didn't love me enough to be there to support me when I was transitioning to a new part of my life.

"And why would he?" I said. "I don't work here anymore."

"Right. I heard you've got a pretty big following online. That's exciting."

Luis already knows the public spaces of the theater. He had been here often to watch horror movies in his youth. He shows me the area where he is going to install a bar and a casual lounge for people to gather and talk.

"I remember saying how one day you wanted to have your own show like Grand," he says as we walk past the concession stand.

"Do you still have those books I gave you a long time ago? Not that I want them or anything. Just being here with you reminds me of them."

I want to tell him yes, but I lie.

"I honestly can't remember what happened to them."

"That's too bad."

"Bruce said you were also looking at other theaters?"

"Yes, I just purchased the Congress and I'm going to rehab that, but I'm going to focus on Logan first. There's a lot within these buildings that can be built upon and restored," he said.

He laughs to himself. "I don't know if you remember, but there was a story you told me a long time ago, about theater number five, that one of the reasons it was haunted was because the ghosts knew there was something special hiding in it. You said all Catholic churches have some type of relic inlaid within the altar. You said that Logan was special because of that, that there was something special hidden within this theater, and that's why people felt it was haunted and believed they saw ghosts here. You said there was a movie hidden in here. A very old movie that the average person could not watch because the technology needed to watch it did not exist, so even if someone found it, well, they couldn't watch it. Unless the movie wanted them to see it, then it would play on its own. It was a strange story and stuck with me for so long."

"It is a strange story, isn't it?" I said, not adding anything more, gathering Bela who was in theater five watching *The Witches* with Angelica Huston. When he looks up at me, as the credits roll, he smiles and says "Magick isn't bad or good. The bad or good depends on the people. There are bad people, and there are good people. Magick just is."

After the theater, Bela and I drive straight home. I park the car in the garage, but I see them as we exit and walk through the backyard. The lights. Beaming. Flashing. Red and blue.

"Mom, what's that?" Bela asks.

I can't answer. I fumble for my house keys. They fall on the sidewalk, and I gather them up, open the door, and close and lock it behind Bela. I run up the stairs, through to the front of the house, and my chest is already hurting, my breath back at the garage. I open the front door and there are lights flashing everywhere. Blue and red blinking, pulsating all down the street. The entire street is full of squad cars. Our neighborhood street is blocked on either end by them, allowing no one in.

Gutierrez and McCarthy are standing on my porch. Their faces. Their eyes. They're pink.

"G…"

He takes a small step forward. "Polly…" His voice cracks, and then so does he, collapsing in a wave of tears. Sound muffles and everything sounds so far.

McCarthy stumbles back on the porch, holds on to the railing, and he sighs heavily, and a man I didn't even know knew how to cry does so, in a torrent of tears. "Polly…" he says, a hand reaching up to his chest. He sways, and before he falls, Rutkowksi runs to his side and holds him up. Rutkowski looks to me, her lip quivering, and then she hangs her head. I know this is not her news to share. This falls on a partner, a relationship very much closer than best friend or sibling or spouse. A partner in homicide is someone you walk life and death with.

"No," I say, as if those two small letters can stop all of this from unfolding.

"Polly." Gutierrez's arms are already around me, and I keep repeating the word. That magic little word I hope can make time stop, reverse, and play out in the timeline differently.

"No. No. No. No."

I push against Gutierrez, but he's just whispering in my ear now, his voice all anguish.

"He loved you so much, Polly."

"Where's Sebastian? Where is he? I need to see him. Please. Let me just see him." I know this is a mistake. I know Bass is okay. "Where is Bass?"

I'm on the ground now, and G is still holding me. His words come through a sheet of sobs. "We all love you, Polly. We love Bela too and we're so, so sorry."

I hear Bela's voice behind me and it's so tiny and so distant, and how am I supposed to tell him we're alone?

We're alone.

I don't want to be alone. I don't want to be alone. I just don't want to be alone.

I'm scared to do this by myself. I'm scared to live this life by myself. I don't know how to live a life without Bass. Without my best friend. The only person who has ever kept me safe.

"Where's Dad? Mom? Where's Dad?"

"Rutkowski." I hear McCarthy's voice and it's muffled. "Take the baby inside."

"Polly." I hear Rutkowski. "I'm taking Bela inside. We'll be in the living room." I feel her hands on my back. Her hands are now on my shoulder and she's whispering in my ear. "Polly, we love you. We're going to take care of you and Bela. I'm going to be right inside with him."

Rutkowski's voice fades. "Bela, why don't you bring some of your toys to the living room? Mom will be inside soon."

G is whispering still, and I feel like I can continue collapsing, disintegrating into a million pieces, into dust that will settle into the crevices of all that is this city. I hear him now, in my ear. I'm being rocked on his lap and he's brushing my hair out of my face, and my face is wet, and I'm crying, and I don't think I will ever stop crying. I don't think I will ever be able to breathe right again or think right or look at this city with comfort again, because this city, the organism I love so much, stole away the person who loved me the most.

I just want my husband. I just want my friend. I just don't want to be alone again.

G's whispering in my ear over and over and over.

"He loved you and Bela very, very much."

CHAPTER 30

SUNDAY MORNING, LOGAN THEATER: POLLY

I wake. I hear wind, but maybe that's the sound of the heater running. I'm on the sofa in my office. The lights are on. I sit up. My eyes are puffy. My throat is raw. I fall back down onto the cushions as I play it through my mind, as I try to make reason why. A fall from the roof of a four-story building. Why did he go there without Gutierrez?

I stumble over to my desk, searching for my phone, when I accidentally push the mouse. The computer screen comes alive, and there I see the notification indicating there are hundreds of new emails in my inbox, waiting.

I click on my email and see the subject line repeated for rows.

A SILENT PICTURE SHOW AT THE LOGAN THEATER NOW
A SILENT PICTURE SHOW AT THE LOGAN THEATER NOW
A SILENT PICTURE SHOW AT THE LOGAN THEATER NOW
A SILENT PICTURE SHOW AT THE LOGAN THEATER NOW
A SILENT PICTURE SHOW AT THE LOGAN THEATER NOW

I click to open one of the messages but it's blank, as is the next and the next. The messages were sent an hour ago by Quasimodo.

Bela.

Where's Bela?

I step into the hallway where it's dark, except for the soft glow of the television screen in the living room. There I find Rutkowski asleep on the floor and Gutierrez and Hector asleep on the sofa.

They should sleep, I think, so I step out of the room and move to Bela's bedroom. I turn the doorknob and don't need any more light than what is streaming in from the streetlight. The window is pushed fully open. The child safety lock Bass had installed has been ripped away. Outside is now inside, a flurry and wonder of glowing midnight snow that accumulated on the floor. I open my mouth to scream, but then I remember the email.

Bela.

I know Gutierrez can't help me, or Rutkowski, or even Hector, and none of them deserve to confront what I've stored away for so long. It's cost me Noel. It cost me Bass. I should have ended this when I started it.

Bela's yellow jacket is missing from the hook. I search for Romero, but Romero is gone too. I open the backdoor, and there are Romero and Bela's footprints, dotted down the sidewalk leading toward the gate. As I looked closer, there are two sets of crosshatch shapes beside Romero's prints. Was it the markings of a bird? At this time? The snow continues to fall, and I follow the outline of Bela's sneakers, Romero's paws, and this animal I know to be the black bird.

I walk for blocks, following their path, until, as I expected, the impressions turn toward Milwaukee Avenue. I stop at the corner. Here these little hatch marks that indicated a bird's feet end and there begin the impressions of a pair of shoes. The markings are smooth. They aren't gym shoes or work shoes. These are dress shoes. A grown adult's dress shoes.

The red fluorescent lights of Logan Theater are on, even though it is late, and I had helped Bruce lock up hours ago. I reach the entrance and inside all of the lights are on, including the ticket booth and the concession stand.

This place was my home for so long because I didn't have a choice living upstairs in that cramped apartment with an abusive mother and disconnected father. I had nowhere else I could hide away, just in that small television screen in my room, and then here, this place, the only place she let me go unsupervised.

Movie theaters are cathedrals. The movie screen hangs before us in the sanctuary and there we come to gather and sit in silence as we watch the essence of people play before us. They are frozen in time, a reproduction, a simulacrum, but there's something holy, divine, about the experience, all of us seated, row after row, our eyes gazing upon a great screen, our physiology synching, and for just a few minutes in time we experience the same heartache and thrill together. We are in heart and mind coherence. We are bounded in those moments, as if in prayer. Watching a horror movie together, the emotions are heightened. We feel sorrow, disgust, ecstasy, dread, and terror. Horror reminds us, allows us, demands us to feel, and all I've ever wanted was to feel something, really and truly, because everything within me was already so cold. I needed to see faces frozen in terror, to be surrounded by the looming soundtrack, and to hear those screams, over and over again, in order to connect to a feeling, any feeling, all feeling that my mother had stripped away.

The worn, red carpet leading toward the screens is wet. Or is that stained? I follow the large smear beginning at the ticket booth stretching to the entrance doors at theater one, and there's no reason to enter, because there he is stationed, forever an usher and a guardian. Bruce. His eyes were torn from his skull and one placed in either open palm on his lap, each individual finger has been sliced off. Shoved down his throat and spilling out from his mouth are his fingers. Tossed onto his lap is a roll of red ticket stubs.

ADMIT ONE.

The sound of an organ plays, but an organ hasn't played here in a very, very long time. I don't need to search because I know the music is coming from theater number five. It was always in that room, in that temple. Of course, I knew it was there, carefully stored by an actor who came to America long ago with hopes of being a star, with dreams of commanding that silvery screen made of vinyl and coated with magnesium carbonate.

When I step into theater five, there it is, that reflective material that looks chalk white. I know within moments of my entering it will scatter light across its surface, and we will watch what Méliès's intended for so few to access, because he understood the all-consuming terror of his design.

He created a window into another dimension, where intelligent entities lurk with the original print of *The House of the Devil*. Somehow this film played for me when I was a teenager, when I was here late one night cleaning. That bat and that demon appeared on that screen, and I screamed. Then, when I wanted to become pregnant, I knew I wanted to conduct the ritual in the most powerful place I knew, and so, I summoned all of the demons here, but just as I was about to close the ritual, and conduct the license to depart, the film began to play again, and I grew so afraid I left. Weeks later I was pregnant, and then months passed and years, and I tried to ignore what I very well knew, that Bela didn't have a guardian angel, he had seventy-two guardian demons. Not finishing the license to depart made Bela a beacon, a glowing light, strengthened and protected by demons, but detectable to other magicians.

I approach the two figures seated in the center of the theater, and there is Bela seated beside Grand.

"Stay away from my son!" I demand as I reach into the seats and pull Bela into the aisle, and it's then that I notice he's struggling under my hold.

"No! Mom! It hasn't started yet. It has to begin so that it can end," Bela says, and then repeats himself, "It has to begin so that it can end! It has to begin so that it can end!"

"Bela!" I grab his shoulders. "We have to go now."

Grand stands, and I stagger back. My eyes are deceiving me, perhaps in the dim light, or…

"Grand is the bird, Mom! I wanted to tell you, but we had to keep it a secret, but it's okay, Mom! We're going to fight the wolf! Just like in my story."

"How…? I don't understand," I say, taking in his face, which is no longer that of a man in his seventies, but decades younger.

Grand faces me. "I never sleep. I don't eat. I don't age…" His obsession with Frankenstein. Dracula. He was an eternal monster.

"You're a vampire?" I say.

He laughs and shakes his head. "No. I am one of the former gods. I stole fire to gift it to humanity. I gifted you with technology, science, and art, and as my punishment, I continue to exist. I am what has given you genius and tragedy. In one life I was Aesop, but I am now and forever Prometheus."

I push Bela behind me, shoving him further back, hoping he starts running, because I can't run. I can't move. I can't think, because Bela is now screaming for me to understand what it is that's happening, and I can't comprehend it.

"He's trying to save us, Mom. He's trying to help us finish this story. Please understand, Mom! The wolf is coming. The wolf is coming!"

"Grand Vespertilio…" I say.

"It means the great bat," Grand answers.

I'm the bird, Paloma. A dove.

Bela is my baby. A baby bird.

Sebastian, Bass, was the fish.

And Luis Villalobos…Villalobos means the town of wolves,

298

and so, he's the wolf.

We are the animals in this fable, in Bela's fable. The moral of this story, this fable, is that a loving mother will fight life and death itself to protect her child.

The theater door swings open and there he is, as I knew he would be, because why would it be anyone else? It was always going to be him.

"I knew you'd come, Polly."

I walk up the aisle, dragging Bela by the arm. He's tugging, trying to break free from my hold.

"No! Mom, Grand's our friend!"

"Luis, get the hell away from me and my son. I don't want any part of this."

"But this is already you, Polly. This has always been you. *The Golden Dawn*. Beyond. You knew it was here this entire time. I was here every week, practically, for over a year, but no matter what I did, or how hard I searched, I couldn't find it. How'd you figure it out?"

"I don't know what you're talking about."

Luis reaches behind me and grabs Bela, pulling my son towards him. It's then that I see the knife dig into Bela's fat little cheek.

"Tell me where the movie is!"

He presses deeper, the knife puncturing and then penetrating through that gummy flesh of Bela's cheeks.

"Master Bela..." I hear Grand say, so calm and steady.

I lunge for the knife, but instead it finds me, digging deep into my forearm, snapping through tendons. The knife grinds against bone as he twists. I'm on the floor now, staring at the dark ceiling, blinking back tears, knowing that somehow, I was always going to die in this theater, because that's what I deserved for what I did to my mother and father. My mother hated me, and I hated her so much, my rage blinding as I stood outside her bedroom door many nights holding the kitchen knife in my hand, because in those moments I would rather have spent the rest of my life in jail than go another day suffering her abuse, but Luis changed that.

Luis, who I loved for such a short time, but loved so fiercely. I knew then he would be the end of me. No one can or should love like that, a love based on magick.

"Play the film, Polly?"

The knife is torn out of my arm and my body scrambles to find some relief in knowing the blade is no longer inside me, but then Luis straddles me. He raises the knife and plunges it into the top of my thigh. I hear the crunch of bone once again, and the knife cuts down my leg, colliding with my kneecap. I am choking on my own vomit when Bela reaches behind me, and he turns my face so I don't choke. I feel moisture on my forehead and hear whimpering. Romero, licks my cheek, begging me to get up, but I can't. I no longer want to feel this way.

I hear Bela's cries. His pleas for the man to leave his mom alone. I hear Luis demanding to know where the film is over and over again, but even though I know it is in this theater, I don't really know *where* inside it that cursed thing is located.

And so I begin, with the only breath I have left:

"Oh, spirit Baal, I hereby license you to depart to your proper place quietly and with the peace of yah-weh between you and me. Amen. Oh, spirit Paimon, I hereby license you to depart to your proper place quietly and with the peace of yah-weh between you and me. Amen. Oh, spirit Beleth, I hereby license you to depart to your proper place quietly and with the peace of yah-weh between you and me. Amen. Oh, spirit Purson, I hereby license you to depart to your proper place quietly and with the peace of yah-weh between you and me. Amen…"

"Master Bela…" I hear Grand speak through the dark theater. "Why don't you show Mr. Villalobos the film?"

I try reaching up and grabbing Bela's hand, but it is too late. He is already standing, as is Luis.

"Yes, Bela." Luis steps over me, holding the bloody blade in his hand, his hand stained red up to his wrist. "Show me where I can find the film."

I continue issuing the license to depart, to Asmodeus, Vine, Balam, Zagan, and Belial. I can see Bela, turning away from Luis, looking toward Grand for, I don't know what. Luis takes another step forward and I scream under the weight of the pain because once again my body is not my body and because of my physical failure another child of mine will die.

And then, there's a beam of light above us, a bright white, ethereal cylindrical beam of magick that kisses the screen and *The House of the Devil* begins to play.

"Is this…?" Luis nearly collapses into a seat, his eyes focusing on the images I have seen thousands of times before, but these images are not those blurred forms I've seen in the past on my computer screen. These characters and shapes are crisp. The whites are an angel's halo. The blacks are devil's teeth. The shimmering silver is an undulating sea of mercury. This is Méliès' perfection.

"I don't understand. Is there someone in the projectionist booth?" Luis asks.

"No," Grand says. "There's no one in the booth."

"Then how is this playing?"

"Our Bela is making it play. Georges Méliès was a high magician, as is Polly, and now, as is Bela, and only a masterful real high magician can play the film or watch it."

A streak of crimson appears at the far edge of the screen, slowly sweeping across until the entire image is covered in red.

Luis is screaming now.

He stands up, and reaches for his face, his palms now covering his eyes. As he removes his hands, we see that there are no eyes, just a bubbly, foamy, milky stream of material running down his face that is now beginning to collapse in on itself.

"You may know magick, Luis, but you're not a masterful high magician. And only a masterful high magician can view this film," Grand says. "You see, demons are very powerful, and what they have to offer, not all humanity can access."

A thumb falls to the floor, and then a hand as Luis's body begins to detach itself from him. He tries to move, to lunge toward anything, anyone, but each leg slips out from under him as chunks of bloody flesh continue to melt into pink and red pools, soaking into the carpet.

And as Luis opens what's left of his mouth to scream, the devil and his imp appear on screen, followed by those shrouded figures, and by the time the screen goes dark, all of Luis is dissolved into the fibers of the carpet, and this building.

"Mom!" Bela is next to me now. "The wolf is dead! He's dead now, Mom. He can't hurt us anymore."

And in that moment, I know that whatever tragedy I had taken part of, had conducted, it gave me my son. As I close my eyes, I finally realize what Grand really is, who he has always been. And it is so simple, as simple as a fable, or something older.

EPILOGUE

POLLY: 78 YEARS LATER

"I'm tired."

Prometheus places his hand on my left shoulder. We are both facing the movie screen in this empty theater. It's been a long time, too long, and I don't think I want to do this anymore. I look just like I did nearly eight decades ago, in this very theater where I almost died. And right now, all I feel is a great suffocating weight, and the yearning to end this all.

"How many times have you watched the movie, Polly?"

"Thousands."

We sit in silence and watch *The House of the Devil* on a loop.

If anyone were to walk in and see us sitting here, they'd take us for young lovers or friends, not two people damned to exist for eternity.

"He lived a good life, Polly," Prometheus says facing the screen.

I don't care if he lived a good life. He is no longer here with me, and I can no longer go on. "I don't want to be alone."

"How old was he?"

I take a deep breath, relaxing into the seat. Remembering those decades that Bela and I ran the Logan Theater together, the most wonderful years of my life.

"Eighty-six." My son, Bela, died at eighty-six years old yesterday morning. He lived, and I remain here, unchanged, the guardian of this cursed film, unable to age or move forward.

"He lived a good, long human life, my Paloma."

"Then why does it hurt so much?" I turn to Prometheus. "I want it to end. I can't live like this. I can't do what you did, exist without the person you loved and that loved you back. You fell in love with Maila, and you said yourself she was the only person you ever truly loved. I lost Bass years ago and now Bela. I can't continue without both of them. There is no living without both of them. I can't even breathe. I don't want to breathe. Please, I just want it to end. I'm begging you to please let me end."

This mourning, it wasn't mourning. It was all-consuming brilliant physical and emotional pain, and I refused to imagine infinity like this, let alone another minute.

Prometheus takes my hand in his. "This is your burden…"

I lived for all of these years, beyond the normal range of a human life, because Bela lived, the sweetest part of my existence. Bela was all love, pure love. In turn, I protected the film, keeping it from evil, but through the years I saw evil continue to hurt and harm. Without the only light that kept me going, I could not remain alive to be this film's caretaker anymore. I could not stop evil, because humans are evil, and as long as they exist, people will hurt people, and I no longer wanted to hurt. I just wanted to be with my Bela.

"I just want to die. I cannot live without Bela…"

We turn back to the screen and watch a film made hundreds of years ago, simple chemical reactions bursting against a screen of white, light dancing across the fabric.

"Are you sure?"

"It's all I want."

And before I can even think of the answer, he leans forward and kisses me gently on the cheek in this dark movie theater that has stood so long, and that I hope will continue to stand for years to come, but without me. Prometheus finally gifts me rest.

"Sleep now, Polly."

-FIN-

ACKNOWLEDGMENTS

Thank you to Jason Pinter at Polis Books.

Thank you also to Gerardo Pelayo and my children, Lane Heymont, Chantelle Aimée Osman, Michael J. Seidlinger, Hailey Piper, Karmen Wells, Kealan Patrick Burke, and Todd Keisling.

Thank you especially to TC Parker and Jonathan Lees for your expertise in the field of film and television. Thank you for answering all of my questions about film and the history of cinema. Your time and your kindness were invaluable to this project.

Finally, thank you to my mother Alida Rodriguez. And most importantly, thank you to my father Roberto Rodriguez who got me my first video rental card, VCR, and a little television for my bedroom. I wish you could read this book, Dad, and I wish you understood really and truly how those monsters on that television screen saved me.

ABOUT THE AUTHOR

Cynthia "Cina" Pelayo is an International Latino Book Award winning and three-time Bram Stoker Awards® nominated poet and author of CHILDREN OF CHICAGO, LOTERIA, SANTA MUERTE, THE MISSING, and POEMS OF MY NIGHT, which was also nominated for an Elgin Award. She holds a Bachelor of Arts in Journalism from Columbia College, a Master of Science in Marketing from Roosevelt University, a Master of Fine Arts in Writing from The School of the Art Institute of Chicago, and is a Doctoral Candidate in Business Psychology at The Chicago School of Professional Psychology. Cina was raised in inner city Chicago, where she lives with her husband and children. Find her online at www.cinapelayo.com and on Twitter @cinapelayo.